TED ALLBEURY

The Twentieth Day of January

**MULHOLLAND
BOOKS**

HODDER

First published in Great Britain in 1980 by Granada Publishing

1

This edition published in 2018 by Mulholland Books

A CIP catalogue record for this title is available from the British Library

Paperback ISBN 978 1 473 67937 5

Typeset in Plantin Light by
Palimpsest Book Production Ltd, Falkirk, Stirlingshire

Printed and bound in Great Britain by Clays Ltd, St Ives plc

Hodder & Stoughton policy is to use papers that are natural, renewable and recyclable products and made from wood grown in sustainable forests. The logging and manufacturing processes are expected to conform to the environmental regulations of the country of origin.

Hodder & Stoughton Ltd
Carmelite House
50 Victoria Embankment
London EC4Y 0DZ

www.hodder.co.uk

*This one is for
Terry Kitson and John Sexton,
with love.*

THE UNITED STATES CONSTITUTION

ARTICLE XX
(Proposed March 1932; Adopted February 1933)

SECTION I

The terms of the President and Vice-President shall end at noon on the twentieth day of January, and the terms of Senators and Representatives at noon on the third day of January, of the years in which such terms would have ended if this article had not been ratified; and the terms of their successors shall then begin.

I

James Bruce MacKay sat with his feet up on the low coffee table, an open copy of *Time* magazine spread across his lap as he lit a cigarette. He waved out the match, tossed it into the ashtray and picked up the magazine again. He turned through the pages to the double spread entitled 'People'. There was the usual picture of Shirley Maclaine, a piece about a defector from the Bolshoi, and a long paragraph about the author of another biography of Hemingway. As he turned to the book reviews the duty signals officer slid a typed sheet over the magazine pages. He read it slowly and carefully. Kowalski had been pulled off the plane at Warsaw airport and taken back into town. The four men who had taken him had been in plain clothes and had spoken Russian not Polish. He looked up at the signals captain.

'Where's Anders?'

'Off duty, sir.'

MacKay reached in his pocket for a Biro and initialled the report. As he handed it back he said, 'Get him in.'

He looked back at the magazine but the print was just a blur as he thought about Kowalski. It had happened two hours and forty minutes ago and by now he'd be unconscious. The interrogation team would have a drink and then there'd be an injection to bring him round for the next session. But that was going to be Anders's worry, not his. He shook his head like a dog coming out of water and focused his eyes on the magazine pages.

Ten minutes later he tossed the magazine on to the coffee table and stood up, glancing at his watch as he stretched his arms. It was 01.30 hours on the first of November.

He walked over to the duty director's bunk and started to undress. He heard the noise of a car door closing from down in the street. It was probably Anders arriving to sort out his problems in Warsaw. From the nearby Thames came the impatient blast of a boat's siren. As he pulled the khaki blanket over his shoulder he could smell the ozone from the radio room and hear the agitated chatter of a Telex down the corridor.

James MacKay was an Edinburgh Scot with one of those neat, small-featured faces that never seem to grow old. Medium height, and slimly built, with a liking for bits and pieces of clothes rather than suits. But there was a flair to the clothes that he wore. The kind of flair that Parisiennes are said to have. Not that he was in any way effeminate; but in a calling where diplomats and civil-servants abounded, a shirt or shoes worn a little ahead of the general fashion could make a man noticed. Not with disapproval by any means, and perhaps it was more that he was remembered than noticed.

He had joined SIS straight from university at a time when univer-sities were providing more problems for Special Branch than recruits. Like a graduate police constable, an eye was kept on him. With a father who was a banker and a mother who was a professional musi-cian, his masters were never quite sure which set of genes was going to prove prepotent. And there were not all that many members of SIS who could mingle with undergraduates without changing their appearance.

It had been remarked, not necessarily with disapproval, that MacKay seemed to be seen with a whole series of pretty girls and it was put down to his charm. Even his male contemporaries agreed that MacKay had charm. And what they liked even more was that he seemed totally unaware of this attribute. He was as charming to men as he was to women. In a trade where cynicism and ruthlessness predominated, MacKay had proved exceptionally successful. A crit-ical senior had once commented that a MacKay interrogation was more like old friends comparing notes than Her Majesty's Secret Intelligence Service pursuing the Queen's enemies. But MacKay got results, and that was what counted.

* * *

It was nearly an hour later when he woke, and as he stood up he slid his arms into his jacket and shuffled through to the next room. It was empty, reeking of cigarette smoke and with the bare bulb still alight as it hung from the ceiling. The copy of *Time* was still there and he leafed through the first few pages to find the photograph. It was on here, under the headline 'Gallup and Harris say it's Powell'.

He sat down in the chair, shivering slightly from the cold. There were eight people in the photograph, all smiling into the camera, and the caption read: 'With a 19 per cent lead in the polls, candidate Logan Powell and campaign manager Andrew Dempsey return to Hartford for the final days of the campaign.'

He bent forward and switched on the electric fire. If you saw a face in a magazine you assumed you recognized it because it was well known and familiar, a film star or some public figure. But that wasn't why the photograph had stayed in his mind. He remembered Dempsey now.

It had been in Paris. May 1968. And the song had said it was the Dawning of the Age of Aquarius. But China had exploded her first atom bomb, France her first hydrogen bomb and the North Koreans had captured the first US Navy ship to be taken since 1807. And on the streets of Paris the students were demonstrating against the Government. That was where he had last seen Andy Dempsey, with bright red blood soaking his white shirt from a broken nose as they slung him into the black van.

After the taunting shouts, they had thrown cobbles from the streets at the police before the SDECE, with the black crosses on their white helmets, came in. It was they who had beaten up Dempsey, and his girl, as the barriers came down. Her mouth had been wide open as she screamed as the thug twisted her breast and kneed her groin. Then he had lost sight of her as she fell to the ground in the forest of feet and legs.

Dempsey was an American and his girl was a Russian or a Pole. He couldn't remember which. That was the last time he had seen them. He had been withdrawn to London just afterwards. It had been one of his first jobs for SIS, a low-profile penetration of student

3

groups in Paris. And Dempsey had been on his list as a member of the Communist Party and intimately involved with a Soviet citizen. His reports would still be on file.

He switched off the fire and went back to bed.

It was midday before he had time to go to Central Records. He sat in front of the micro-film reader for over an hour. There was more than he remembered. Apart from the typed reports there had been a handful of photographs and several pages of notes in his own handwriting. The round careful script looked naïve and juvenile now. He had forgotten about Kleppe.

He walked back to the house in Bessborough Street. It was one of those rambling turn-of-the-century houses that wealthy merchants built for themselves when cotton was still king but Manchester was beginning to lose the fight to London as the centre of trade. Now it was the operational base of one of those special units that were spawned from time to time by SIS. Highest security, but liable to be disbanded at any time. The present incumbents were designated as SF14. Special Force 14 were responsible for planning and mounting deep penetration operations into the intelligence services of the Soviet bloc. MacKay was one of its two operational directors.

He slid his card into the slot and the door chunked open. The Field Security sergeant at the small desk had known him for three years but, as always, they went through all the routine of passwords and identity checks. Some day somebody was going to renege and four feet from the door was where they aimed to stop him.

Magnusson was obviously not too pleased at being disturbed on a Sunday morning for speculative discussion. He was too civilized a man to say so outright, but too hard pressed in his job not to make clear that if the appointment was not urgent and about a current operation, it could wait its turn after the weather, the problems of protecting chrysanthemums from the first frost, and the possibility that Cooper's Oxford marmalade might not be maintaining its quality.

Magnusson sat with one slippered foot on a sleeping Labrador that quivered after rabbits in its sleep. As he refilled MacKay's glass and handed it to him he finally said, 'So what was it, James?' And MacKay gave him a report on what he had checked out. He held out the envelope of photocopies but Magnusson waved it aside.

'And what are you suggesting that this all adds up to?'

'That the campaign manager of what looks like the probable next US President was a Communist in 1968. That his girl was a Russian and bound to be a Party member, or she would not have been allowed to go to Paris. That a man named Kleppe, a rich man with some sort of Soviet influence, got them both out of jail when the US Embassy wouldn't lift a finger.'

'Go on.'

'There isn't any more.'

Magnusson raised his eyebrows. 'So what do you see—another Philby?'

'Could be.'

'And what d'you you think we should do, my boy?'

'Mention it to CIA liaison at Grosvenor Square.'

'Why?'

'They ought to know.'

'Why d'you think they don't know?'

'Maybe they do, but we had all the information on file about Philby and his Communist wife, and nobody checked it out.'

Magnusson nodded. 'I'll speak to the Minister and let you know. Has there been any news about Kowalski?'

'Nothing since the first report, except a confirmation that the Poles haven't got him. It's KGB for certain.'

'What's Anders doing about it?'

'I don't know, sir, but he's already on his way to Berlin.'

'There's a nice little pub in the village if you want a bite on your way back.'

And MacKay took the hint and left Magnusson to the *Sunday Times* and the *Observer*.

May 1968 had been one of the times that he knew he would always remember. It was the first solo assignment that he had done for SIS. It looked like a piece of low-key routine, and he had wondered what

5

interest SIS could have in the students at the Sorbonne. He had decided that they were merely testing out the fluency of his French or maybe his ability to maintain a cover. But they obviously knew more than they had told him at his briefing meetings. He had only been there three months when the demonstrations started, and he had been recalled in the second week of August.

It had seemed a spring and summer of ceaseless sunshine, the kind of weather that always seems to herald declarations of war. And it hadn't just been the war in the streets of Paris for him.

He had come back to the empty flat, knowing it would be empty but not expecting all those reminders. Torn up letters that he pieced together and then wished he hadn't. Two or three unsigned contracts for shows in Birmingham and Leeds. The remnants of two boxes of milk chocolates. Panties and a bra on the tatty washing-line in the bathroom. Unwashed dishes and glasses in the sink. A membership card for a Soho Club. A pile of *Melody Maker*s and an old copy of *Stage*. The bullfight poster, hung slantwise on the wall from a single pin. Make-up and cosmetics on the bedside table and a pad with two scrawled telephone numbers. And everywhere the stench of men and lust.

He had picked up the mail and gone out for breakfast at the Coffee Shop in King's Road. He opened the envelopes one by one as he sipped his coffee. The electricity bill, a come-on for *Time-Life* books, a statement from the bank showing a credit balance of £341.73 to the account of J. B. and T. M. MacKay. A note from his mother pointing out that she had warned him even before the marriage, etc., etc. There were two letters for Tammy and a card calling her for audition at a theatre in Portsmouth. And there was a letter from their solicitor asking him to make an appointment to see him as soon as possible.

Back at the flat he phoned John Davies, who could see him at noon.

There were Audubon rose prints instead of the usual hunting scenes in the solicitor's waiting-room. They had picked John Davies when they were first married because he had showbiz experience. But showbiz clients were often divorce clients later and John Davies helped clear up the mess.

He'd only had to wait a few minutes before the door opened and John Davies waved him into his office. When they were both settled on their respective sides of the teak desk, it was John Davies who led off.

'You know, Jimmy, that it's one of my duties as an officer of the Court to do my best to effect a reconciliation of the parties to a divorce. Some solicitors don't even go through the motions, but I do. Especially when I know both of them, and am fond of them. So let me say now that I *have* tried. And I've failed.'

'What did Tammy say?'

'Well, I wasn't even sure that she was listening, but I made one mild criticism of you and she jumped right down my throat. Normally by the time it's got to me it's cat and dog stuff and all I can do is stop them from actual violence. With you and Tammy that doesn't apply. All I can do is help cut out as much pain as possible.'

'I guess the pain's all mine, John.

'I don't think so. You pay for this sort of thing one way or another. Most people say that it must be six of one and half a dozen of the other. It seldom is. But the problem is that the one who takes it most seriously is the one who gets hurt first.'

'Why?'

'Why? Well, the one who goes off with somebody else has got their little prize already wrapped and delivered. If the other one hasn't done a damn thing, he or she feels that it's all mighty unfair, which it is. And if that one happens to be a man he fights all along the line about money, children, blame, the whole bag of tricks that the law allows. So I need to find out if I can carry on for you both or not. It's positively frowned on by the law. But sometimes it can help.'

'There are no children, John, and Tammy's the one with the money.'

Davies looked at MacKay's face for long moments before he spoke again.

'If you cared to make a fight of it, Jimmy, you could probably put her career back to square one.'

'Why should I?'

7

Davies shrugged. 'Hurt feelings, anger, pride, revenge. We could give it all a high moral tone, of course. It wouldn't have to look so crude.'

'I love Tammy, John. I don't love what she does, but I wouldn't do her harm.'

'Would you do her good?'

'In what way?'

'You haven't lived apart for two years, so there has to be a matrimonial offence thrown in.'

'So?'

'They've all been hers and the showbiz press and the nationals would make a meal of it.'

'You mean you want me to sleep with someone?'

'Paula Manning volunteered.'

'Jesus. What bastards they all are. Surely it must have been possible to make it in show business without screwing with everyone in sight.'

'You can if the talent's big enough right from the start.'

'Wasn't Tammy's?'

John Davies' eyes were watching his face.

'I guess not, Jimmy. Not if you're in a hurry, anyway.'

'How much does Tammy make now?'

Davies pursed his lips. 'It ought to be confidential. She makes five hundred a week on her present contract. In five weeks' time her new contract doubles that. What made you ask?'

'I wondered if it was worth it for her.'

'Is it?'

'No.'

John Davies leaned back in his chair, moving aside a pile of papers. Then he looked up at MacKay.

'Have you got a girl, Jimmy?'

'No. Tammy was my girl.'

'Can I say something? Something you might find offensive?'

'Go ahead.'

'When I first met you and Tammy, about a year before you were married, I could have forecast that this would happen. If it hadn't been for one thing.'

8

'What was that?'

'Tammy was every man's dream girl. The golden girl we all fanta-size about. But even then you could see the ambition, the determination to make it in showbiz. I thought it might survive because you were a good-looking man. An attractive man with charm. But I didn't know one vital thing.'

'What was that?'

'I took it for granted that when Tammy gave what we call "management privileges" to agents, impresarios and the rest of the gang, you'd be taking your pick of Tammy's pretty friends. There's many a showbiz marriage survived on that basis when they were making their way. But you weren't in showbiz and you were a bit of a puritan. So it didn't work. And I was wrong.'

'Would you have told me then if you had known?'

'No way.'

'Why am I a puritan?'

John Davies smiled. 'You have to love them, or like them a lot, before you screw them. Other men are satisfied with a pretty face and a willing body.'

MacKay thought of the girl in Paris and realized that Davies was right.

'How long will it take?'

'The way I suggested, two months. The other way . . . how long since she told you?'

'Seven months.'

'The other way about eighteen months.'

'She'll be at the top by then.'

The solicitor shrugged. 'Maybe not.'

'I'll think about it.'

'OK.'

John Davies smiled, relaxed and less formal. 'How are you doing in the job?'

'No complaints so far.'

'They made a good buy when they chose you, my friend.'

'How're Sally and the kids?'

'Sally's fine. Sends you her love and a standing invitation. The kids both have measles, so they're pretty tame at the moment. Have you got a lunch date?'

'No.'

'Let's go over to the Law Society. No, sod it, let's go to the Wig and Pen.'

James MacKay had spent his statutory night with Paula Manning and for the first time in his life had discovered that, with no love and only marginal like, and despite a cloud of misery, if the girl was very pretty, with long legs and nice boobs, then James Bruce MacKay was as other men were. Lustful and happy with it. There had been other nights with Paula Manning until he wondered if she told Tammy. He still wanted to be the white knight with that particular human being.

The divorce had made a three line paragraph in the two London evenings and there was no mention of other parties. Just 'irretrievable breakdown of the marriage.'

Tammy had always sung under her own name and most of the public had seen Tammy Lane as a single swinger. SIS had liked it that way, too. It wasn't really their image.

He had seen gossip-column pieces about her in the nationals and her face looking out from record sleeves in shop windows. The big grey eyes pensive and pleading, the big soft mouth slightly open. He had seen the first of her own shows on BBC2 and had got drunk for the first time in his life. And there had been one ghastly evening in his flat when he had made love to a girl and then gone to make them coffee and she had called to him. She had switched on the TV and was watching it avidly. 'Isn't she fantastic, Jimmy. Just listen.' It was the Royal Command Performance and Tammy Lane was singing her fans' favourite song— 'Smoke gets in your eyes'. The camera was close-in, full-face, and her eyes swam with tears as she sang the words. 'They said someday I'd find, all who love are blind . . .' And when the girl had turned to look at him she had seen his white face, his eyes closed and the tears on his cheeks. But it was never like that again. He didn't forget her. But he didn't remember her either.

And as the years went by there were other things to occupy his mind. Maybe time doesn't heal all wounds, but it brings the perspective of a longer lens and puts healthier tissue where the wounds have been.

Magnusson phoned him the following afternoon.

'The Minister's not at all keen, James. Thinks it might be construed as some sort of sour grapes. He pointed out, by the way, that all Powell's statements about the Soviets have been more anti than pro.'

'Right, sir. I'll forget it.'

'I didn't say that, my boy. I said that that's what the Foreign Minister thinks. How's your own operation going at the moment?'

'We've got some daytime radio problems but we're OK at night when we've got an all-dark signal path. It's early days yet, sir.'

'Quite. I thought you might like to take a few days of your leave, and take a trip to Washington. Have you got any friendly contacts at Langley?'

'Only Peter Nolan.'

'Yes. What's he doing now?'

'I don't know, sir. He's still in the Soviet bloc division. The last time we met he was in New York, controlling the operations against the KGB at the United Nations and the Soviet Consulate-General.'

'I'll send a personal message to Morton Harper. Non-committal, of course. When do you think you could go?'

'Can I use Movement Control facilities?'

'Certainly.'

'I could hand over this evening and use the early Concorde flight to Dulles tomorrow morning.'

'Do that.'

Concorde drooped into Dulles at 09.00 hours and the sun was trying to get through the thin cloud from the east. The forty or so passengers were near enough to the terminal buildings to walk and MacKay, with only his cabin bag, had gone straight to immigration.

Nolan was waiting for him there and after the immigration officer had given a brief glance at his visa he was passed straight through. Nolan drove him downtown for breakfast at the Sheraton. There was only small talk until the coffee and then Nolan lit a cigarette and leaned forward across the table.

'I don't know what the hell this is all about but Harper had some sort of signal from your guy that said you were coming over on leave and would I stand by for courtesies, whatever that means.'

'It means I'm bringing bad news and please don't crap on the messenger.'

Nolan half smiled. 'What's the bad news? We already picked up the rumours about Kowalski.'

'It's nothing to do with any current operation, it's from way back. About one of your citizens named Dempsey. Andrew Dempsey.'

'Who's he?'

'Logan Powell's campaign manager.'

'Yeah. I remember the name now. What's he been doing?'

'In 1968 he was a Party member. So was his girlfriend. She was also a Soviet citizen. They were both beaten up by the French police during the student protests in Paris in May 1968. An American named Kleppe got them out of jail after your embassy had refused to help. We were suspicious of Kleppe at the time but we never proved anything, and after I went back to London it was left to the Sûreté and the Dutch police to follow up. I don't know if they ever did.'

Nolan looked over the top of his coffee cup before he drank.

'Why hasn't this come through official channels?'

'Like what channels?'

'Foreign Office to Secretary of State, for instance.'

'The Minister was asked. He said your people would either ignore it, or think that the British were crying wolf to square things off for when you froze out Philby.'

'So why tell us anyway?'

'I suggested to Magnusson that you may not know. It's over ten years ago. It happened in Europe, not here. We made the same mistake with Philby. He was married to a Party member in Vienna. It kind of got lost in the wash when he was being investigated, even after Burgess and Maclean lit out to Moscow and he was suspect.'

Nolan leaned back in his chair, his eyes avoiding MacKay as he sucked a hollow tooth reflectively. Then he turned back and looked at the Scot.

'How long are you staying for?'

'Until you tell me you don't want me to hang around any more.'

'Let's go back to Langley.' He turned and waved to a waiter.

Morton Harper had come to the CIA from teaching law at Yale, and in the early days there were those in CIA and the Washington jungle who thought the professor was going to be an easy ride. His moon face and plump body had added their weight to the theory.

In less than two months they had learned how wrong they were. There had been new brooms and axemen before, and the CIA knew how to absorb them; but this time it had been more like a scalpel. There had been almost no pain, and Old China Hands and the inefficient had gone first; and there was a feeling among the survivors that Morton Harper had some sort of bullshit detector. A lie, a cover-up, a snow-job was fatal. Somehow he knew, and you never got a second chance. No record, no medals would protect you. There were no explanations, no taking you apart. You just went. That was not to say that the CIA had suddenly changed its style. Just that the Director had to know—everything. If he was to carry the can he wanted to see the rough edges.

Harper sat at his desk as Nolan told him the brief facts. When he had finished Harper was silent for what seemed an eternity, then he reached forward and touched the long curving ash of his cigar to the crystal ashtray, watching it bend, fracture and fall in one piece. Then he looked up and across at Nolan.

'Have you checked our files on Dempsey?'

'Yes, sir.'

'What have we got?'

'Nothing, sir. It's just press clippings. But I've checked with our Paris embassy and they do have a record of a request from Dempsey for help for himself and the girl. There's a handwritten minute on it—a negative.'

Harper leaned back in the big leather chair and sighed.

'What was the girl's name?'

'Halenka Tcharkova.'

'Anything on file about her?'

'No, sir. Nothing.'

Harper swivelled his chair to look at MacKay.

'Why wasn't this information given to the FBI? It's more their area than ours.'

'I think there are several reasons for that, sir. The first one is that it's not official. As Mr Nolan said, the Minister thought it would be tactless, and he wasn't all that impressed with the facts. Our analysis was that the events concerned took place in Europe and that that made it a CIA responsibility. Magnusson felt it should be kept on a very low level with nothing official and nothing in writing.'

Harper's face showed no response, and something compelled MacKay to continue.

'And we don't have a good relationship with the FBI at the moment.'

'How long are you here for?'

'I've got a week's leave, sir. But I shall stay until you tell me to go.'

Harper leaned forward, his arms folded on the desk as he looked from one to another of the two men.

'Let me tell you what we shall do. Between now and election day I should like more information on Mr Dempsey, the girl, and Mr Kleppe. And let me emphasize something. These are routine inquiries of no special significance. They have no political significance. They are not connected with the election campaign. They concern private citizens in their private capacity. Despite what I have just said you will not reveal to anyone the purpose of your inquiries. If Logan Powell is not elected President I shall pass this information to the FBI. If he is elected then I shall need to consider the situation and possibly seek the advice of others.'

He stood up and walked round his desk to open the door. As they made to leave Harper said, 'The Agency will pick up Mr MacKay's tabs, Mr Nolan, you see to that.'

2

The empty plates had been pushed to one side, and Nolan and MacKay sat facing each other at the long table in Nolan's office.

'How about you cover Dempsey's girlfriend and I cover Dempsey and Kleppe?'

'I'd need to go to Paris.'

'How long would you need?'

'A day each way and probably two days there. Maybe three.'

'Can you spare the time?'

'I'll have to fix things with Magnusson first.'

'D'you want to get Harper to do that?'

'That could help.'

Nolan walked across the room and into the small hallway. MacKay could hear Nolan's voice as he spoke on the phone, but he couldn't hear the words. He realized that Nolan had been very cautious in dividing up the responsibilities. They didn't want a foreigner investigating American citizens so he got the girl. On the other hand it was better that way. They didn't have his contacts in Paris, and he didn't know his way around the United States for that matter.

Nolan walked back and nodded as he sat down.

'That's OK. He's contacting your guy himself. Unless we hear in the next half hour, it's OK. D'you want to travel overnight or have a night in a hotel?'

'What flights are there?'

'There's an Air France flight in two hours' time.'

'Book me on that, then.'

Nolan came back. He'd booked a first-class seat so that there was a chance for MacKay to sleep. MacKay yawned at the thought before he spoke.

'What do you think Harper thinks of all this?'

Nolan shrugged. 'I'd say interested but cool at the moment.'

'Maybe I'm wasting your time?'

'You don't believe that, do you?'

'No. What about you?'

'The same as you. Instinct, training, experience tell me there's something odd. Maybe it's something that doesn't matter. But we'd better find out.'

Nolan drove him to Dulles and waited with him until the flight was called.

The Air-France overnight flight landed at de Gaulle in the morning darkness and it was 8.30 before MacKay had cleared customs and immigration.

He booked in at a small hotel on the Boulevard des Capucines and bathed and shaved. As he waited for a taxi there was a gleam of sun piercing the November grey but by the time he arrived at the rue Soufflot there was a thin drizzle of rain. He looked at his watch. There was just about time for a coffee.

He wondered what her reaction would be. He had not kept in touch with her but unless she had changed that wouldn't matter. When he had checked in the telephone directory he had felt that it was typical of her that she still lived in the same studio. She was beautiful and warm-hearted, and in the old days she would have these great passions that barely lasted a week. Nobody would see her in that week and then she would return to her circle, not sad or grief-stricken, but calm and serene. He knew that she relied on him in those days not to sink into the whirlpool with her. He had slept with her sometimes but he refused to join her in the torrent. And she was grateful, he knew, that he stayed on dry land and could reach out his hand to save her from the next emotional flood. He paid for the coffee and left.

It was almost eleven o'clock when he walked up the rue Mouffetard. They were putting fresh trays in the windows of the *pâtisserie*. Eclairs, *mille-feuilles*, meringues, and strawberry tarts with smooth, glazed surfaces.

As he crossed the road he glanced up at the house. It still looked much the same. Even the shutters were the same blue. He pressed the bell and stood waiting, with one foot on the bottom step, looking down the hill. It was a stinking, sleazy street but he hadn't noticed that in the old days, and even now it had a raffish, attractive air in the pale winter light.

Then the door opened and the same brown eyes looked at him, one fragile hand pushing the dark hair from the side of her face. A moment's perplexity, and then she recognized him.

'Jimmy. My God, what's the matter?'

'Adèle. Nothing. Why should there be?' He smiled.

Her long slender fingers touched her cheek as she laughed.

'It's so long ago. I must have been back in those times.' She stood aside. 'Come in, *chéri*. Have you eaten?'

He closed the door behind him and followed her up the stairs. At the landing he could see the room beyond the open door. Still clinically white and antiseptic. Canvases leaning against the wall and the smell of turpentine and linseed. The massive mahogany easel still dominating the light from the big window. She was wearing an orange towelling bath-robe and she stood smiling in the centre of the room, shaking her head in disbelief.

'I can't believe it. Why didn't you let me know you were coming?'

'I didn't know until late last night and I've been flying through the night.'

'Coffee?'

'That'd be great.'

He walked with her into the small kitchen and pulled out one of the tall stools. She looked much the same. There were some wrinkles, but only at her eyes and mouth, where she smiled. When the coffee had percolated she poured out two cups and sat looking at him. 'How long ago was it, Jimmy? Ten years?'

'About that. And how are things with you?'

'I heard that you were a policeman or some such thing now.'

'Not me, my love.'

She sipped her coffee, her brown eyes studying his face.

'You look more of a loner than you used to.'

17

'Older, maybe.'

'Yes. But surer . . .' She put down her cup and sat with her hands on her knees. 'Tell me why you came, *chéri*.'

'I wanted to talk to you about two people we knew in the old days.'

'Who?'

'Andrew Dempsey is one.'

She laughed. 'He was just like you, Jimmy. Handsome, charming, some talent, kind, and amused at us foreigners with our funny ways.'

'What else?'

'Rich daddy, money no problem, girl-struck. What else can there be for a young man?'

'Do you remember when he was arrested?'

'Oh, God, yes. I was standing quite near him. They'd smashed his nose, and his clothes were covered with blood. He was unconscious when they threw him in the van. You were there. You were *with* me. Have you seen him again?'

'No. How long was he inside?'

'He was in Fresnes. It was a long time for something so little. Two months maybe. They let them both out at the same time. Him and Halenka.'

'Who got them out?'

'An American. I don't remember his name.'

'What happened to Halenka?'

'She went back to Moscow. She's done terribly well, you know.'

'At what?'

'Painting. She had shows in Leningrad, Moscow, Prague, Warsaw. All over. She's very good.'

'I can remember that she was very pretty. What was she like?'

'A sweetie. Very gentle and sensitive. I think she and Andy would have married if they hadn't sent her back to Moscow.'

'Was Andy a Party member?'

She looked at him carefully and then averted her eyes.

'You *are* a policeman, aren't you?'

'Kind of.' He half smiled and shrugged.

She stood up, folding her arms in that defensive move that all interrogators recognize.

'What happened to Andy?'

'He's a politician. A leading man in Powell's election team.'

'Powell's the man they say is going to win, isn't he?'

'They say so.'

'And somebody wants to stab Andy in the back with his membership card. I thought that had all finished with McCarthy.'

'It did.'

'So why the questions now?'

'So why no answer?'

She smiled and shrugged. 'I expect you know the answer anyway. Yes, he was a member. So was I. So was Halenka, and she was the only reason he joined. He loved her desperately.'

'Did she love him?'

'Oh yes, she adored him. They were like lovers from a book.'

'I can't remember, did they live together?'

'Yes. They had a place by the Musée de Cluny.'

'Now tell me about you.'

She shrugged amiably. 'I do quite well. Two one-man shows. One here in Paris and one in Düsseldorf. I've got a cottage near Honfleur. I get by nicely.'

'No grand passion?'

'Why so sure?'

'Because you look contented and level.'

'*Touché.*' She laughed. 'And you?'

'Much the same as I used to be.'

'You haven't lost your French, anyway.'

'How about we have lunch together?'

'OK. I'll get dressed. Help yourself to a drink while you're waiting.'

He sorted through the pile of old 78s and it was still there. He put it on the player and sat in the wicker chair listening. It was Charles Trenet singing '*Il pleut dans ma chambre*'. He wondered if she might come back into the room when she heard it. She didn't.

They held hands as they walked down the hill to find a taxi, and lunched at le Petit Bedou in the rue Pergolese. There had been a tension at first, but slowly she relaxed so that he was encouraged to ask her to dinner that evening. When she left she blew him a kiss from the taxi as it turned to cross the bridge.

He phoned the embassy and waited in the Ritz bar for his SIS contact. He came in twenty minutes later.

'Hayles. What can I do for you?'

'MacKay. I need a check on the records of Fresnes, May, June, July 1968.'

'What's the prisoner's name?'

'There's two. One's an American named Andrew Dempsey, the other's a girl; Halenka Tcharkova.'

'What were they in for?'

'The student demonstrations.'

'What do you want to know?'

'Most students were released after a couple of days. These two were held for nearly two months. I'd like to know why. And I'd like to know if anyone used influence to keep them in or get them out.'

'Was the girl Russian?'

'Yes.'

'How long have I got?'

'As soon as you can. Two days at most.'

'Where can I contact you?'

'Hotel du Nord. Boulevard des Capucines.'

'See you.'

'Thanks.'

MacKay was impressed. He liked men who didn't need the social flim-flam but just got on with the job.

The hotel lobby called him in his room to announce that a Mr Hayles was in attendance. He asked them to send him up.

Hayles was opening his notebook as he sat down. He glanced quickly at MacKay and then started reading from his notes.

'Andrew Joseph Dempsey. American citizen, born 1947. Arrested 9 May 1968 on charge of causing affray. Charge later altered to conspiracy with others to incite public violence. Released 14 July

1968 with surety from Viktor Kleppe, United States passport number 917432, point of issue New York.

'Halenka Alexandrova Tcharkova, Soviet citizen, born 1949, passport issued Smolensk. Two-year French visa starting date August 1967. Arrested 9 May 1968 for conspiring with others to incite public violence. Released 14 July 1968 on medical grounds. Three months' pregnant. Handed over to Soviet embassy officials 14 July and taken direct to Orly where she was put on Aeroflot flight 409 to Moscow at 18.30 hours local time.'

MacKay smiled. It was a real policeman's report but he guessed that there would be more to come. Those were the facts but there would be *some* chit-chat.

'First-class, Mr Hayles. Did you get any background stuff at all?'

'Two items that might be of use. A warder from the prison was sent to check at Orly that the girl was actually put on the plane. There was a scene. The girl and Dempsey were very distressed and the girl had to be forcibly removed by Soviet embassy officials. Dempsey was restrained by the man Kleppe. The warder's not certain but he had the impression that the Russians knew Kleppe well, and also that when Kleppe got angry at the scene he shouted at them in Russian.

'The other thing is that Kleppe was having an affair with a Dutch girl, also at art school here in Paris. It was generally known that he was very wealthy and a dealer in diamonds in New York. That's all, I'm afraid.'

'Would you like a drink now, Mr Hayles?'

'No thanks. I've got things to do. By the way, I'd guess that they changed the charge against Dempsey to keep him inside longer.'

They dined at Châtaigner and he took advantage of being her host to ask a few more questions, and she replied without discernible resentment.

'Yes, I remember several people saying that Halenka was pregnant, but I think it was just putting two and two together because she lived with Andy.'

'Did you ever meet a man named Kleppe?'

'Not that I can recall. What was he taking?'

'He wasn't a student. But he had a student girlfriend. A Dutch girl.'

'Was his name Viktor?'

'Yes. D'you remember him?'

'No. I never met him. Just heard about him. Rich American. Some people said he was a crook or a gangster.'

'What was his girlfriend's name?'

'Marijke something or other—van Aker or some name like that. A good painter. I've seen notices of her stuff in *Figaro*. I think she lives in Amsterdam. She paints the kind of stuff you used to like. Realistic.' She grinned. 'Drops of water on rose petals and highlights on pewter jugs.'

'Maybe she'll grow out of it.'

She reached across and touched his hand.

'I said something this morning that sounded all wrong. I want to apologize.'

'What was it?'

'I said for you to have a drink while you were waiting for me to dress. It sounded as if I were saying keep out of my bedroom. I didn't mean that. It wasn't warning you off. It was just what I said. Nothing more.'

'My love, you only think that it could sound like that because you're an artist. You notice what other people never see, you hear what other people never hear.'

'But you played that Charles Trenet song, and I thought maybe I had made you sad.'

'No. Just me and Proust "*A la recherche du temps perdu*".'

'Are you sure?'

'It was ten years ago, my love. Kindness, happiness, some loving and a lot of talking are not a permanent credit card for bed. You are the only person I could ask these questions.'

'Will you walk me back?'

'I'd love to.'

* * *

22

He had used his SIS identity card to make contact with CIA at the embassy, and the tall Texan had made him welcome in one of the reception rooms.

'What can I do for you, Mr MacKay?'

'I'm checking on a Russian girl who was here about ten years ago. She was an art student, and was put in prison during the student demonstrations. I've heard that an American student who was also jailed tried to help her, and asked for help from the embassy. I wondered if you have any record of that.'

'What were the names?'

'Halenka Tcharkova was the girl, and I believe the boy's name was Dempsey. Andrew Dempsey.'

'I can check the records. Would you care to wait or shall I contact you later?'

'I'll wait if that's OK.'

'Sure. There's magazines on the table.'

A secretary brought him coffee and cream, and he browsed through a small pile of *New Yorkers*. It was fifteen minutes before the CIA man came back. He was holding a thin file.

He sat down, looking speculatively at MacKay.

'Are you working with Langley?'

'What makes you think that?'

'I didn't say that I think it. I'm just asking.'

'Let's say I'm not.'

'Then let's say I can't help you. There's nothing on the records.'

'You wouldn't say that in Building 13.'

The Texan laughed. 'OK, but there's not very much.'

Building 13 was where CIA employees took their lie-detector tests.

He opened the file and turned back a couple of pages. He looked up.

'This guy Dempsey wrote a letter to the embassy asking the ambassador to get him and the Tcharkova girl out of jail. Seems he was in for conspiring with others, etcetera, etcetera. There's a minute from our guy saying no, and there's a reference to our local index. Dempsey was a member of the Communist Party. The branch that caters for students in Saint-Germain-des-Prés. The girl was a member too, and she was on a Party grant as a student.'

'Is that enough to warrant no assistance?'

The Texan shrugged. 'I guess it was, in those days.'

'Anything else?'

'Are you working with Nolan?'

'He's a friend of mine.'

'Is that so? *He* queried this record a couple of days ago.'

'About the girl?'

'No, about the guy. I did some cross-checking with the French. It seems they were got out of jail by an American named Kleppe. The Soviet embassy came into it. Seems like they leaned on the French for both of them to be released into Kleppe's custody. The girl to go straight back to Moscow. No restrictions on Dempsey, but Kleppe had to bail him for about a thousand bucks. The French have put a permanent visa block on Kleppe. I asked them why, but I didn't get a satisfactory answer. Referred me to the Quai d'Orsay. They referred me to SDECE. And they gave me a vague story about suspect diamond deals. Kleppe's a diamond dealer.'

'Nothing more about the girl?'

'No. Nothing.'

'Any known associates on the index for Dempsey?'

He opened the file again and turned over a buff card with a green diagonal stripe. He turned his head on one side to read the text.

'Two. D'you want to note them?'

'Thanks.'

'Pierre Benoit, 15 bis rue Jean de Beauvais and Jean-Paul Prouvost, 14 rue Lagrange. Both of them Party members in 1968.'

He ordered a meal in his hotel bedroom, and when he had finished eating he read again through his notes. He wondered what Morton Harper and Nolan were discovering, and he wondered, too, what their attitude was to him. There had been no congratulations on his revelation, and no hint of thanks. They must find it embarrassing and annoying that an outsider had spotted the flaw. On the other hand there had been no attempt to whitewash, no haste to send him packing, and none of the bland disclaimers they would have got in London if the positions had been reversed. By the time he got back to Washington they would probably have decided to close ranks and send him back to London, so that they could deal with the problem in their own sweet way, and without the inhibitions that came from being observed by an outsider. But Americans were an odd kind of people. If a similar problem had come up in London, Magnusson would have had a discreet word with the Foreign Secretary and all the efforts would have gone into sweeping it all under the carpet. But Americans never reacted that way. They ferreted away until they got at the truth and to hell with who got exposed. And they generally did it in public with the TV cameras letting you watch it happening. There would never be a Watergate in Britain. The axes would grind and there would be nods and winks among the knowing, a couple of D-notices and much waving of the Official Secrets Act. It would be interesting to see how the Americans dealt with this little can of worms.

MacKay took a taxi to the Place Maubert and then walked slowly down to find 14 rue Lagrange. It was a narrow building above an archway that led to a row of garages. There were six names against the bell-pushes and Prouvost was number 4. The front door was ajar and he walked inside. There was no elevator and the stairs were ill-lit, but everywhere was clean, and the heavy wooden doors gave an air of mild prosperity. Apartment 4 had a door with a stained-glass window and, after pressing the bell, MacKay heard footsteps inside.

When the door opened, a man in his middle thirties stood there smiling.

'I'm sorry but it's already gone.'

'M'sieur Prouvost?'

'Yes. You came about the cello, yes?'

'I came to speak to you. My name is MacKay.'

The eyes behind the thick lenses were friendly but puzzled. But after a moment's hesitation the man opened the door and waved MacKay inside. The narrow hallway led to a big room. It was more a workshop than a room. A heavy bench littered with woodworking tools ran along one wall, and on various tables lay stringed instruments and parts of instruments. Three old-fashioned armchairs were placed round a low table and the man waved MacKay to one of these and sat down himself. He looked expectantly at MacKay.

'If it's insurance I'm afraid that's out of the question.'

MacKay smiled and shook his head. 'No, m'sieur, I wanted to ask if you could remember two men who were students when you were a student.'

'Ah yes. It seems a long time ago but it was, how long—ten years perhaps. Who were these students?'

'One was Pierre Benoit.'

'And what did you want to know?'

'What kind of man was he?'

Prouvost leaned back smiling. 'Hardly a man in those days, but certainly with talent. He could paint, no doubt about that. But not an artist. Too narrow, too derivative.' He shrugged. 'He lacked originality, and inspiration. Mind you, he might have developed if he had been given time.'

'Given time? What happened?'

'He's dead. Long ago. Five years, six it could be.'

'What was the cause of death?'

'Killed himself. Gas. Money troubles and that ridiculous woman.'

'He was a member of the Communist Party, wasn't he?'

Prouvost grinned. 'Of course. We all were. Paid our dues. Even went to meetings if there was nothing better to do.'

'Are you still a Communist?'

'Well, I never resigned. You forget about these things when you've got work to do. Are you a policeman, my friend?'

'No. I just want to get the feel of those times. Research. The other man who interested me was a fellow named Dempsey. D'you remember him?'

'Oh yes. A lovely fellow. Had the painter's eye but not a painter's hand. Hopeless. Hopeless. But charming, delightful.'

'He joined the Party too?'

'I believe he did. He wasn't really interested, of course. Too lazy, too happy. But his girl was Russian and I think he just joined to identify with her.'

'Did he ever discuss Communism?'

'Dempsey?' Prouvost laughed aloud. 'He just laughed at them. Thought they were crazy.'

'Why did *you* join?'

Prouvost smiled and waved his arm at the violins and 'cellos scattered round the room.

'I joined because of Tchaikovsky, Rachmaninov, Prokofiev, even Glazunov. I suppose even then I knew I couldn't paint. Poor artist. Poor musician. But lots of feeling, lots of love.' He shrugged and smiled. 'But they say I am good at all this.'

'Does it pay?'

'I eat. I drink. And I'm happy and respected. What more could a man want in these grim days?'

3

Nolan and MacKay sat in silence as they waited for Morton Harper. The message had said that he would be ten minutes late. There was no reason to talk. They had gone over every aspect of the information they had gathered and it was for Harper to decide.

MacKay's eyes wandered round the room. The walls were all painted white. There were no paintings, no photographs or decoration. The desk was typically Scandinavian in plain teak, the chairs were comfortable but not luxurious. There were no book cases or shelves. Indeed, there were no books. No silver-framed photographs of wife and family on the desk, no clue to the character or mind of the man whose office it was. And, MacKay thought, perhaps that was the clue to the man's character. He felt no need to persuade or influence. The room was a room for listening rather than talking, so far as its occupant was concerned. Harper came in, quietly for so large a man. He smiled and nodded to both of them as he walked around and settled at his desk. He reached for the ashtray and lit his cigar.

'I've seen both your reports, gentlemen, but I find no logic in them. You state the facts, both of you, and then draw conclusions that appear to be based on instincts rather than facts. Explain. You first, Nolan.'

'Kleppe is a long term immigrant. Came from Norway via Canada. Has been a citizen for about twenty years. He deals in precious stones, mainly diamonds, and has shareholdings and interests in a wide range of businesses. He operates out of a luxury apartment in Sutton Place that is packed full of electronics. Security devices. He has no servants, not even a daily help. He has contacts at top level in most government departments and with influential politicians in the Republican Party. Dempsey has been a frequent visitor over the last ten years. There's

28

nothing on our files, the FBI files or the NYPD. Not even a traffic offence.'

Harper waited to see if there was any more and then nodded to MacKay.

'I found your report intriguing. Tell me more.'

'I must emphasize, sir, that these are my views, not my service's views. They may share them, I just don't know. I believe we assume too readily that people join the Communist Party from considered conviction. That they have weighed up capitalism and found it wanting. In my experience there are very few of these, and in my view Dempsey is typical of most people. He joined the Party when he was a student; a more carefree student than most because he had no worries about money or career. His father was, is, a millionaire. And he joined the Party because he was in love with a girl who was not only a Party member but a Soviet citizen. It was a gesture to her. And because of her he did not see Russians as monsters. His own Russian was beautiful, she didn't dig the streets of Moscow, she painted. And I've no doubt he got a picture of a society that had a human face. When he and his girl were beaten up and jailed he turned to his own government's representative for help. It was refused. He would guess why. With their usual long-sightedness the Soviet authorities stepped in. Not directly, but through an American. A man who can draw on Dempsey's goodwill for years to come. The girl goes off to Moscow—a perfect hostage. Dempsey will hate his own government and feel grateful to the Russians. And you couldn't have a more malleable puppet than that. It's not difficult to love a regime that exists thousands of miles away, that you never see.'

Harper leaned back in his chair, looking at some distant spot on the white ceiling.

'Are you married, Mr MacKay?'

'No, sir.'

'How old are you?'

'Thirty-seven next birthday.'

There was a long silence and then Harper slowly sat up in his chair and faced the desk. He seemed to be watching the ash on his cigar. Then his head came up slowly.

'You needn't give reasons; and I'll ask no questions. But I want you both to say what *you* would do as of now. You first, Nolan.'

'The election is tomorrow. I should wait for the result. If Powell wins I should go ahead with a full investigation.'

'And you, Mr MacKay?'

'I should wait for the election results but I should go ahead with the investigation whether Powell wins or loses.'

Harper half-smiled. 'You force me to cheat. I *will* ask a question. Nolan, why does it depend on Powell winning?'

'The influence that Dempsey could wield on a President could have devastating results. But only on a President.'

Harper nodded. 'And you, Mr MacKay?'

'To me what matters is that if Dempsey is being used to influence Powell it's because the Soviets intended that. Whether Powell knows or not is of vital importance, too. But most important of all is, have the Soviets tried to do this?'

Harper shook his head and said softly, 'I go ahead with everything you've said except that. The most important thing at the moment is, if it has happened, can we prove it?' He closed his eyes as if to exclude everything except what he was saying. 'I want you to imagine what happens if the worst turns out to be true. From tomorrow night we should have until the twentieth of January to establish hard evidence. Evidence that high officials would find credible, and sufficient to impeach a President-Elect; or, if not that, so destroy his credibility that his position would be hopeless. And who do I tell, gentlemen? The incumbent President who represents the opposing Party? The Chief Justice who has no power to act? This would have to be for Congress if it went that far; and you can imagine the damage it would do to this country—to the world, perhaps. The trauma of Watergate would seem like light relief compared with this.' He turned to them both.

'Nolan, wait until tomorrow night after the result is declared. If something went wrong I could be accused, perhaps rightly, of influencing the election. Then, whatever the result, you go ahead. Let me know what resources you need and I will arrange them. And Mr MacKay, would you object if I asked my friend Magnusson if you could be attached to Langley for a period?'

'No, sir.'

'I think you should cover anything that concerns Europe. That should be your official position, anyway.'

He stood up. 'You must keep this between the three of us, Nolan. And I should like you to read again the Fourth Amendment. You, too, Mr MacKay.'

MacKay slept until midday, shaved and bathed, and leisurely breakfasted watching TV.

He read through the Fourth Amendment in a copy of the Constitution that Nolan had found for him. And, because he was British, he turned back to the first page where it said, 'We the People of the United States, in order to form a more perfect union, establish justice . . .' And he read on and on through all the Articles and Amendments. He felt a great warmth for those men two centuries ago who had argued and fought to ensure that the abuses and privileges of Europe's monarchs and despots could never happen in their new country. Even two hundred years later it was still of its time. The old-fashioned words still applied. It was often abused, and frequently difficult to practise, but it was there. A bench mark, a rock in a sea of troubles. He thought of Morton Harper and Nolan. They hadn't dodged the issue, and when Harper had said that they should read again the Fourth Amendment he had meant it. Not as a cover for himself but as a reminder of the other side of the coin.

Magnusson telephoned and gave him the OK and, despite being on an insecure line, told him to watch his step. He was treading on very thin ice, Magnusson said, and the bouquets could easily turn into brickbats.

In the late afternoon Nolan telephoned to say he would be along about eleven. His mother was going to have three weeks with them in Washington and he was meeting her at the airport, at nine.

MacKay had met Nolan's wife. She was an admiral's daughter who had met Nolan when he was a Navy flier in the Korean war. A pretty girl with a sense of humour and well used to the vagaries of service life that kept men at long stretches from their families. The five-year-old daughter was some consolation. Nolan was a frequent visitor to London, generally on his way to Berlin, and there was clearance between CIA and SIS for an exchange of a wide range of intelligence between SF14 and Nolan's Russian section. MacKay envied Nolan his vast resources and the American valued the British organization's uncanny, instinctive analysis of the KGB operations that covered them both.

It was well after eleven when Nolan arrived, and they sat watching the network election programme. Powell's lead had been cut but there was little doubt that he was going to win. The blue-coloured Powell States were beginning to dominate the election map, and the commentators were slowly coming down off the fence.

Just before two o'clock Grover conceded, and the cameras moved over to Hartford where Powell and his helpers stood in a milling mass in front of the State Capitol. On his right was his wife, and on his left was Dempsey. Nolan identified a few of the other local worthies for him. Then, as the microphones were thrust towards him, Powell spoke. He was sweating under the TV lights.

'I want to say thank you to all those who have worked so long and so hard to get me elected. I shall be leaving shortly for Washington but I shall be back here in a few days' time and then we'll really celebrate. God bless.'

Nolan reached forward and switched off the set, then opened his black leather briefcase and tossed a thick brown envelope on to the bed.

'There's money, open air-tickets and CIA documents in your name. You might need them. You can draw on CIA funds at any of our embassies or consulates.'

'I thought maybe Amsterdam first to see if I can find Kleppe's old girlfriend?'

'OK. Wherever you go, will you liaise with the local US embassy or consulate so that I can contact you quickly? We'll use the diamond business as our cover on this. And we've given it a codename. Operation 66. We've got sixty-six days before the inauguration.'

'When are you starting?'

'Tonight. I'm putting in for surveillance teams, signals units and researchers. I'll have them by tomorrow.'

'Who are you checking first?'

'Dempsey, but I'll have enough people for Kleppe if you come up with anything.'

'How does Harper feel about me being involved in this?'

Nolan frowned. 'I don't understand.'

'Well, a Britisher helping to investigate an American citizen, the President-Elect.'

'When Harper spoke to your guy the deal was that you were liaising with us and that, apart from the question of routine, you would not inform your own people about what we are investigating or what we uncover.' Nolan looked at MacKay. 'We trust you, and we trust Magnusson.'

4

Powell sat in silence in the white MG as Dempsey drove him to the airport, and as the car swung into the VIP parking area and stopped, Dempsey turned to look at Powell's face. It was drawn and tired.

'I've fixed a temporary suite for you at the Sheraton and Rod's arranging office accommodation on the same floor, as from tomorrow.'

Powell turned to look at him.

'Can you fix for Jenny to come over from New York?'

'You mean now, tonight?'

'Yes.'

'That'd be crazy, man. Just asking for trouble. You'll have the press and security and the whole circus round your neck. Let the dust settle, for God's sake.'

When Powell didn't speak Dempsey went on, 'Remember, it's taken weeks to get Laura to co-operate. We need all that; at least until the inauguration. Why rock the boat? An out-of-town girl will be noticed. Look, I'll be across in Washington tomorrow. I can fix you the prettiest gals in town. At my place. No problems. If anything leaks they're mine then, not yours. OK?'

'OK. Give her my love.'

'Sure I will. If I see her.'

There was a crowd of reporters waiting in the main hall but the airline staff escorted Powell through to the manager's office. They were holding the Washington flight, and after a drink he walked across to the plane, accompanied by four security men. Dempsey walked across to the campaign helicopter carrying his own bag.

It was four weeks to Christmas, but the snow was Christmas snow. Drifting slowly past the windows on the thirtieth floor, it lay in big soft cotton wool folds along the window ledges, and was piled up on the balcony, reflecting in pale gold patches the lights inside the apartment. It was so thick that you couldn't see the Island. You couldn't even see the East River.

Dempsey sat in his green corduroy jacket, perched on the edge of the polished table, with one long, jeans-clad leg stretched out to keep his balance. As he looked out at the falling snow he slowly sipped a drink and listened to the music. It was Oistrakh playing Khachaturian's violin concerto off an old Moscow film-track. When the music stopped abruptly he slowly turned and looked at the man who stood alongside the tape-recorder.

'They'll have to give you the Order of Lenin at least, Viktor.'

Kleppe turned, his face impassive as he walked across to the table. He waved to another chair as he sat down.

'There'll be no medals, my friend. Remember I told them it wasn't possible. That was your opinion too.'

Dempsey laughed and shrugged. 'It *wouldn't* have been possible with any other man but Powell, I swear it.'

'He thinks he did it himself?'

'I wouldn't say that. He acknowledges helping hands here and there. And when he doesn't like what he sees he turns a blind eye. You've got to remember that he doesn't know most of what has been done.'

'Is he fully under control?'

'By no means. I can pressure him but I can't just snap my fingers and make him jump.'

'Moscow assumes that he *is* under control.'

'Then Moscow should be disabused of that idea. At once.'

'You mean you can't make him deliver?'

'Sure I can make him deliver; and when I've told him the facts of life there'll be even fewer problems. But it's not a press-button service. He feels his power, and I don't want to destroy that. Just programme it.'

'Is there any chance he could renege?'

'No. He's been sour with ambition from the moment he became State Governor. Every little aspect of presidential privilege and protocol he knows by heart. He can't wait to get the emperor's clothes on. Like all the rest of them he's promised to slash taxes, cut unemployment, and achieve peace on earth. He doesn't know how he's going to do it but, by Jesus, he's gonna do it.' He paused, smiling. 'And we'll show him how.'

Kleppe nodded. 'I'm leaving for Moscow tomorrow. I'll be back next Wednesday. Can you see me that evening?'

'God knows. It's going to be chaos. Maybe you'll have to come over to me in Washington or Hartford. And don't forget we'll be surrounded by FBI men, White House security, and all the rest of them.'

'D'you want to stay here tonight?'

'No. I promised I'd see Jenny.'

'She's still got the photographs.'

'I know she has. But I won't need them, Viktor. I've got enough without them.' He laughed softly. 'It's really gonna shake him.'

'Does he still see her?'

'Sometimes. He wanted her to go over tonight. He's crazy. He uses her like a hooker, but thinks of her place as a sanctuary. I guess he's fond of her.' He grinned. 'Provided he can take her pants off.'

Kleppe shrugged. 'It's a wicked capitalist city, my friend. And I love it.'

Andrew Joseph Dempsey was twenty-nine, slim, about 5 feet 6, and attractive to women who fancied poets with a Byronic air. He wasn't a poet but he looked like poets are supposed to look. Pale, hollow-cheeked and with fair wavy hair. His aesthetic aura was helped in the eyes of some ladies by his being heir to the Dempsey insurance fortune. But it would be only fair to the younger generation to make the point that with girls up to twenty-five his fortune had small significance. His looks and charm were enough.

Dempsey senior was the son of an Irishman from Skibbereen, who had earned a living gutting fish in New Haven. It had taken him five years of mean living before he had his own business buying and selling fish. And another five before his was the biggest outfit on the coast. People say you can't go wrong in food because whatever happens people have got to eat. Joe Dempsey and the 1930s proved them wrong. As Joe himself said, 'There just weren't enough Fridays.' The 1930s didn't bankrupt him, but it had been tough, and so was getting his boy through high school and university.

Joseph Junior had taken the first job he could get and that was as a clerk to an accountant. By the time he was twenty-seven he had his own small insurance business, and by the time he was thirty he was able to look after his old man. People still called him Joe Junior long after his father had died, and not even his friends could say that they really knew him. He was a real businessman, that was for sure, but he dabbled in things that his business circle found odd. He read a lot. History and politics, books about Europe, and different religions. And, as if this part of his life was nothing to do with them, he never talked about these interests. Except to his son, of course. He had talked to him for hours, from the point when the boy's mother had died, when he was almost eight and a half. And there had been no financial problems in putting his boy through school and university. Nor had there been any pressure on the young man to join the business. In fact there was no pressure for Andrew Joseph Dempsey to work at all. His father was a happy victim of his charm; and even others said that when the boy smiled he looked very like his mother. After a few years painting in Paris he had ended up as part-time art critic on one of New York's more esoteric magazines, with an occasional contribution to arts shows on TV.

In the New York streets the snow was a grey slush, and as there were no cabs free he walked. A biting wind came off the river as he turned into 42nd Street and it followed him down South Park to 38th.

The porter recognized him and walked over to the elevator to press the button for the penthouse floor. There were eight penthouse flats, and Jenny's was the one facing the elevator. She paid a little less because of the barely audible noise of the gates opening and shutting. She would have paid extra had it been necessary because her visitors could leave her apartment so easily without being seen.

Dempsey pressed the door-bell of P4 and stood waiting. A couple of minutes later he pressed the bell again and the door opened immediately. Whoever opened it was behind the door and he walked in slowly as the door closed behind him. The girl who stood there, smiling, could have come straight off the cover of *Vogue* except that she wasn't flat-chested and she was naked. And her eyes weren't the eyes of a woman in love, but they were big and blue and friendly.

'Why so long?' he said.

She shrugged. 'There was a john on the phone.'

'Business good?'

'Never better. Two conventions in town.'

The telephone rang and he watched her as she walked over to answer it.

'Hello . . . yes it is . . . which Joe Taverner is that . . . from New Haven . . . yes, sure. What did you want, Frank . . . well, not tonight I'm afraid, my daddy's in town . . . that'd be OK, Frank . . . that's right . . . yes, two hundred bucks . . . sure you can, anything you want, I'd like that . . . tomorrow at three then, Frank . . . you bet. Bye.' She hung up and then took the receiver off the cradle. She stood looking at Dempsey and he looked at her. And finally she said. 'Are you gonna stay, Andy?'

'Sure I am, if it's OK.'

'It's OK,' she said softly.

Viktor Kleppe had been born Viktor Aleksandrovich Fomin in Yerevan in the Soviet Republic of Armenia. He was seven years old when the war ended, and an orphan. But a bright orphan who went straight from school to university, and from there to the KGB training school just outside Moscow. After two years at the old building in Dzerzhinsky Square he had been filtered into Norway with genuine papers and an identity taken from a headstone in a small churchyard in Stavanger. Two years later he had emigrated to Canada and worked at a boat-yard in Hamilton, Ontario, until he'd got a work permit for the United States.

Despite the parsimony of Moscow he had converted the KGB's 5,000 dollar fund into a small jewellery business that he operated from his apartment in Brooklyn. He was used as a cut-out for one of the KGB men at the United Nations, and then he was given a low-grade solo mission to penetrate the US Navy yard at Brooklyn. Although most of the information he got there was classified, none of it was news to Moscow. But they sent him down to Mexico for a coding and radio course, and when he came back to New York he was told to set up an espionage network to cover computer technology and electronics. By 1968 he was Director of all illegals covering New York and Washington. He dealt only in precious stones now, and his success and reputation were cover enough for the apartment in Sutton Place. His valuable stock was cover enough, too, for the extraordinary security precautions that he installed. He had perfect cover for his journeys inside the USA and overseas, and his business provided an almost check-proof channel for illegal funds which came in as the diamonds and rubies in which he specialized. He had acquaintances and contacts, in business and politics, at every level. And no friends.

He did favours large and small, and never asked anything in return from either individuals or organizations. He wasn't a soft touch, he listened to the stories, and asked pointed questions; and when he paid out he knew whether it was for the expansion of a business, influence in a political party, a demanding mistress or an impending audit. He made no judgements and gave no advice, but it all went down in the little black books which, when they were full, were sealed in plastic bags and taped inside the cold water tank in the roof space. Not that there were all that many people in New York who could read shorthand in Armenian.

After Dempsey left, Kleppe walked over to the control panel alongside the row of hi-fi equipment. There were twenty-four heat-sensing buttons, a few of them marked with symbols, the majority coloured but blank. Kleppe's forefinger lightly touched eight of the sensors and alerted the elaborate security controls that protected the apartment.

He walked slowly up Sutton Place, and used a public telephone to speak to his contact at the UN. He turned left at 57th, and two blocks later he took out a bunch of keys from his coat pocket and opened the door of a small jewellery shop. Inside he switched on the showroom lights and walked through to a small back office. On the glass table were piles of invoices and receipts, and he leaned over, looking at a typed list of figures on a sheet of paper as he took off his coat. Still reading, he pulled up the chair and sat down. He reached inside his jacket and took out a small calculator, and one by one he totalled the receipts and invoices. He sat for a moment looking at the totals and then scribbled a note on the pad by the telephone. When the door-bell rang he stood up and walked unhurriedly through the showroom, and nodded to the man who stood there brushing snow-flakes from his hair.

'Come in, Yuri, you can do that inside.'

The other man stamped his feet on the mat inside the door, and leaned with one arm against the wall as he slid off his galoshes.

Kleppe closed and locked the shop door, and walked back to the office. He was sitting on the edge of the desk when the other man came in. The man had an unsmiling face, and he lowered his big frame awkwardly into the chair, pulling his wet coat loosely together, as if to exclude himself from the luxurious setting. His hands were enormous, with finger and knuckle joints so large that they looked swollen. One eye didn't move, and he squinted up at Kleppe with the other.

'Is this place safe, comrade?'

'It has been for the last five years, Yuri. But you don't have to stay long.'

The man's big hand lay flat on the glass table and unconsciously smoothed its surface as he spoke.

'Colonel Rhyzkov was not impressed. He assessed him as a neurotic, and arrogant with it.'

Kleppe half-smiled. 'Dempsey is an American, well educated, intellectual and independent. He would be bound to react aggressively against a man like Rhyzkov. Dempsey wasn't impressed by Rhyzkov, for that matter.'

The big face jerked up quickly. 'What were his comments about him?'

Kleppe swung a leg as he sat on the table, apparently looking with interest at his black shoe and its silver buckle.

'He just asked if we couldn't afford to pension off old soldiers.'

'But Rhyzkov isn't old. He's barely fifty.'

Kleppe sighed, and turned to look at his companion. He spoke very quietly.

'I suggest you keep him out of sight in this country, Yuri. He gives a bad impression. He's a political dinosaur and he looks it.'

The big man's eyes blazed with anger. 'That is a scandalous thing to say, Viktor.'

Kleppe smiled with cold, hard eyes. 'You must accept my judgement, comrade. I have survived for years among these people, Rhyzkov would not survive for a day. I don't want him near my operation. Is that understood?'

'Are you threatening me, comrade?'

'Threatening, no. Warning, yes. Moscow have instructed me to do something. Leave me alone to get on with it.'

The one blue eye moved to look at Kleppe's face.

'Have you no sort of real hold on this man?'

'It's not necessary, Yuri. The man is committed to us. Has been since he was in Paris. Always will be.'

The big man stood up, his one sound eye still on Kleppe's face. Then he turned and walked slowly to the shop door and let himself out. It was still snowing, but his mind was too occupied to think of his galoshes. He carried them in his hand. It was a strange, wild country, America. He was glad that he could keep to the Soviet enclave in the UN building, and the apartment on East End Avenue.

5

Nolan's team covering Kleppe followed him to Kennedy and waited to check that he actually boarded the plane and that the plane took off. They checked his booking with SAS. It was a direct flight, non-stop to London, leaving London an hour later for Copenhagen and Stockholm. Kleppe was booked through to Copenhagen under the name of Greenbaum.

Just before ten o'clock they went up the fire-escape stairs at the back of the block and the team put the big rubber suction pads on one of the windows, holding the glass in place while the glazier cut the glass at the edges of the frame.

As the team leader moved the long, thin, electronic lance across the floor of the apartment Nolan looked around the room from the window area. The walls were all panelled in a reddish-coloured wood and the floor was of oak parquet blocks. On a long shelf on the right-hand wall was an array of hi-fi equipment, and some sort of control panel. Across the space in front of the window was a long polished table with eight chairs spaced round it. There were no pictures, and no books. The team leader's voice broke into his thoughts.

'It's OK, Mr Nolan, but you'll have to keep to the white tapes, there are weight switches under the parquet blocks.'

'Can you check the walls for me?'

'You betcha.'

Nolan looked at the hi-fi without touching. There were two Sony 7055As. Two Sony cassette recorders, two big Revox tape-recorders and the control panel. He counted the square heat-switches. There were too many just to control the hi-fi. Some of them probably controlled the elaborate electronic security devices. But even with that there were too many. He leaned over to look at the connections on the backs of the receivers. Plugs and wires linked the recorders and there were four sets of leads from the speaker sockets into the control panel. Both receivers had leads from the antenna sockets to the panel. Nolan straightened up and beckoned the radio expert.

'Can you trace where the antenna wire goes to without touching the equipment?'

'Sure we can. I can use the cable tracer.'

The antenna lead went under the shelf panel, behind the wall panelling, and was lost at ceiling level.

They found the access to the roof void in the ceiling of a broom cupboard. They checked for electronics and found an elaborate circuit that would trip if the cover was lifted. One of the team took instrument readings and another pressed buttons on a pocket calculator. A long wire was fastened to a pipe with a crocodile clip, and the other end of the wire was taped to a corner of the access cover.

Nolan lifted the cover gingerly as he stood on the middle rung of an aluminium ladder. It was dark, and he peered over the edge of the flooring as he slowly swung the torch. It was a big area, and empty except for three standard water tanks. And it was clean. Far too clean. He went up on his elbows, swung up a knee and stood up. He called down for the radio man, who came up the ladder with his black leather case.

'Show me where the antennae are, and tell me about them.'

He shone his torch on the far wall as they walked over carefully. The man clamped a fork-like instrument on the first cable and then the second.

'They're both normal 75 ohms jobs.'

'What about the third one?'

'That doesn't go down into the room, it ends at the floor here.'

'What is it?'

The man took Nolan's torch and followed the wire upwards and across and then round the timbers on the loft.

'It's a short-wave aerial, Mr Nolan.'

'Receiving or transmitting?'

'It's OK for both. It's got remote controlled cut-offs for various wave-lengths. The first one's about twenty metres operation. Round about fourteen megahertz.'

'Was there anything downstairs that could use it?'

'No they're FM and AM. No short-wave stuff.'

Nolan knelt down and shouted through the opening.

'Rod, are there any electronics in the ceiling area of the flat?'

'No. We checked before you went up. Just the access panel, that's all.'

Nolan walked across the whole of the floor area running the torch light along each plank of the flooring. It took ten minutes but there was nothing.

He took the plyboard covers off the water tanks and shone his torch into the water. In the second tank he saw the black plastic bags. He took off his jacket and rolled up his shirt sleeves. When the bags came out of the water he let them drain off. He untied one bag and lifted out the book. As he turned the pages he saw that it was all handwritten.

He lowered them down to the team below.

'Photograph them now, both sides of each page, and let me have them back.'

As he was straightening up he saw the socket on the wall by the antenna wires. He shone his torch upwards. It was in a wooden, bracket-like box right in the corner, and as the radio man unscrewed the front panel he guessed what it would be.

They lowered it carefully to the floor. It was in a dark green metal housing and the radio man whistled softly as they looked at it.

'It's the latest they've got. I've never seen one before but we've got photographs and an operation manual for it.'

'What's it do?'

'It's a top-grade receiver-transmitter. It puts out very high-speed morse. You could transmit four thousand characters at least in half a second. That's probably why he's got two Revoxes. Uses them to gear up the speeds. The boys will go crazy when they see this.'

Nolan laughed. 'Afraid not. It's staying right here.'

'Can I have some photographs, Mr Nolan?'

'Sure. Tell Rod you want them.'

It was another two hours before everything was back in place and the glazier was waiting to put in a new window. When he had finished, they washed all the windows, cleaned the snow from the balcony, folded the plastic floor coverings, and left.

Logan Powell spent the whole day taking briefings and situation papers from the present Administration. President Grover was philosophical about his defeat. His four years in office had seen no great issues resolved. If anything, issues had been ignored, and it looked as if the American public liked it that way. They wanted peace and prosperity and a chance to play with their toys.

For two days Dempsey had examined position papers and reports and made those routine decisions that allowed his temporary team to function while Powell's major appointments were being considered. It was a time to convert euphoria to usable energy. He picked up Powell from his temporary office and drove him to the hotel. Dempsey had arranged for them to have adjoining suites with the flanking suites taken as offices.

They sat in shirt-sleeves in comfortable armchairs and Powell gave him instructions about various people he wanted to see in the next two days. Dempsey poured them another drink before he started what he expected to be the first of a series of tense dialogues.

'There's something I need to talk with you about, Logan.'

'I've told Cheevers to put out a press release tonight that I've appointed you Presidential Chief of Staff.'

'It wasn't that. It's about you.'

'Oh? What about me?'

'You know that we've had a lot of help from way back to get you into the White House?'

'Sure I know. They'll all get their pieces of cake in due course.'

'Most of the help came from the same quarter, Logan. I'm sure you recognize that.'

'What are you trying to tell me?'

'There are things that they want.'

'Like what?'

'A peace pact, troops withdrawn from Europe, trade both ways.'

'Those are issues for governments, not individuals.'

Dempsey looked steadily back at Logan Powell. 'That's what I'm trying to tell you, Logan.' For a moment he was almost convinced that the surprise on Powell's face was genuine.

'Are you saying that the Soviet Government were on my side during the election?'

'They were on your side long before that, Logan. They got you into the State Capitol.'

'What the hell are you talking about?' Powell's face was reddening with anger.

'What do you think made you Governor?'

Powell shrugged. 'They liked my programme. They wanted change.'

Dempsey shook his head. 'There were a dozen contenders who would have been equally suitable. It was the strike got you nominated and it was the strike got you in the State Capitol.'

'And I arbitrated and settled the strike, for God's sake.'

'How do you think the strike started, Logan? Why do you think it just happened when your nomination was a totally outside chance?'

Powell was silent for long moments, and then he said quietly, 'Are you saying that those bastards fixed a strike so that I could arbitrate and look good?'

'You knew that at the time, Logan. You and I don't need to pretend. But you knew when you were negotiating with Siwecki that the strike had been fixed.'

'Did Siwecki tell you this?'

'Logan, Siwecki was doing what he was told to do.'

'What else have they fixed?' Powell's voice was edged with anger.

'It's cost about thirty million dollars and cashing in on twenty years of organization.'

Powell shook his head. 'That's their view, not mine. The people voted and they voted for me. They're too late, my friend. I'm President-Elect and if they play games with me they'll be exposed and sent packing.'

'Your programme promised peace and prosperity. You can deliver it—with help.'

'What we do to get peace and prosperity will be negotiated between governments, no other way.'

'Nobody's suggesting any other way. To get prosperity we need peace. They want that, too. To get peace we need disarmament. They want that, too. With a peace pact you've got tens of billions of dollars to direct and provide the prosperity. Half a dozen Administrations have tried to deliver it. Yours can be the one that succeeds.'

Powell leaned back in his chair.

'You've been with them all the time, Andy. You've known.'

'You wanted to win, Logan. I helped you do it. Others helped me.'

'And what happens if I refuse?'

'Refuse to cut down arms? Refuse billions of dollars of Soviet trade? Refuse decades of peace? You'd have to be very stupid or very stubborn to do that.'

'Answer me, Andy. What happens if I refuse?'

'You'd cease to be President. When the scandal died down I guess you could earn a modest living somewhere in Europe.'

'And how would they fix that?'

Dempsey shrugged. 'A leak to a journalist would be enough.'

'The leak would expose them, not me.'

'The Communist Party of the United States would take the blame, not the Soviets.'

'Nobody would believe the Soviets didn't know and support it.'

Dempsey said quietly, 'And nobody would believe that *you* didn't know and support it. You've been back-marker all the way, Logan. For the Governorship itself. And four years later you're given the Party's nomination as presidential candidate. An unknown. And on January twenty you will be President. How do *you* think that was possible? I'll tell you. Millions of dollars, and collecting old debts and obligations. Theirs, not yours.'

Dempsey leaned back in his chair. He had gone as far as was necessary. He had watched Logan Powell turn a blind eye to a hundred situations that stank of conspiracy and contrivance. But turning a blind eye was not the same as not knowing. Powell was bitten by the power bug the same as all the others. From the moment there was a chance that he could be Governor of Connecticut he would have done anything to make it certain. And all the initial diffidence, when it was put to him that he might be the Party's candidate for President, was gone the moment it looked a real possibility. Logan Powell had left the dirty washing to him and hadn't given a damn how it was done. Now he had the prize, the power, he'd cling to it as all the others did.

Dempsey leaned forward and poured them both another drink. He raised his glass.

'To Jan twenty, Mr President.'

Powell shook his head as if to break his thoughts and lifted his own glass.

'To both of us, Andy. May God help us.'

Dempsey knew that already Powell's mind was back in the White House. And at the back of his mind he would be working out how to cash in on the political prizes that the Soviets were laying out in front of him. Powell would rationalize them as being what he intended all along.

Long after Dempsey had gone, Powell sat hunched up in his chair, his mind recalling incidents from way back. Grainger, the frontrunner for the party's gubernatorial nomination, stepping down in his favour and buying a half-interest in the Johnson real-estate business a couple of weeks later. Siwecki's half-smile as they finalized the strike arbitration. Campaign funds that never seemed to run dry. Wards, cities, counties, States, delivered against the odds, where newspaper analysts had shown that to get his turnout he must have picked up votes from militant left-wing areas. Visitors in Dempsey's apartment who were never introduced. Times when the talk stopped as he walked in, and never started again. Strong Democratic cities who had given him their vote. State-level politicians who came out in his support with whom he had never exchanged a word. Militant Trades Union leaders who had carried 'Powell for President' placards. The TV lighting that had made Grover's face look old and haggard, and the Gay Libbers who cheered so vociferously at Grover's meetings. He could swear he hadn't known. He *hadn't* known. Guessed maybe, for a split second here and there, but guessing wasn't knowing. But his signature would be on documents and instructions. They would have made sure of that.

He thought about Dempsey. Andy Dempsey, the smiling character in the green corduroy jacket. Tireless and energetic. Heir to a packet of millions, dilettante art-critic, every girl's favourite escort. The charmer who screwed but didn't tell. Even with Jenny he never knew if Dempsey slept with her. She had been introduced as Andy's girl at the party, but there had been no come-back when he took her for himself. Just the usual happy Dempsey smile and no comment.

Thinking of Jenny made him think of Laura. She had agreed not to make any move for a divorce until after the inauguration. From the moment he had been a gubernatorial candidate she had closed the bedroom door and all the other doors. Quiet, unassuming Laura had views of her own. She had said he'd never make it, and even after he was Governor she would have no politicians in the house. He would miss young Sam, but Sam was part of a package, and the price of the package was for him to get out of politics. Her father had tried to talk her out of it way back, but she had been adamant and scathing. She had said he was a stooge, the monkey who took the chestnuts out of the fire for the professionals, the wheeler-dealers. She wanted him back teaching at Yale but would settle for him staying in the consultancy. She had been jealous of his every success. Nothing convinced her. She'd probably even voted for Grover, the bitch. But he would miss them, they had been the only security he had. But if Dempsey and his friends thought he was a stooge . . . He stood up and switched on the TV.

Nolan swore softly under his breath, stopped the car and got out. He'd told them a hundred times not to leave their cycles lying in the drive. As he lifted up the cycle and leaned it against the hedge the six-year-old blonde came running towards him. He mentally toned down what he had intended saying. She was so pleased to see him, and anyway he loved her.

Walking behind the child was his wife, smiling, because both his women were well aware that they could disarm him in seconds.

As he swung up the small girl he bent to kiss his wife.

'Both lots of slides have come back. I've had a sneaky look at them and they're great.'

'Are those the Disney World ones?'

'Yes. D'you want to read Sal the Riot Act about her bike?'

He grinned. 'I guess not. But it is a damn nuisance. I have to leave the car across the path half in, half out.'

'It's getting too cold for her to play outside. And too dark.'

The small girl was stroking his face. 'Will you fix my bike for me, Dad?'

'What's wrong with it?'

'It's the chain again.'

Nolan drove the car into the driveway and carried the cycle into the garage. He switched on the light and put the cycle up on the bench. He cleaned and oiled the chain and fed it slowly on to the wheel. He tested both brakes and they were hopelessly slack. Like most CIA men, Nolan did not find it incongruous to come from dealing with the seamier side of the country's life to fixing a bicycle chain on a child's bike. Their training and their experience had taught them the value of routine and perspective. A routine that automatically checked brakes on kids' bikes meant that you never carried a .45 Browning that wasn't reliable. And a perspective that made the vigilance worthwhile, because your family was your stake in the country you were protecting. And you then valued other men's families, too. Without a stake you were just playing games.

6

At Copenhagen Kleppe paid cash to continue to Stockholm, and when the plane landed at Brumma he took the airport bus into the city. At a bookshop in Kungsgatan he picked up a Dutch passport in the name of Van Gelder and took a taxi back to the airport.

The Russian at the Aeroflot desk saw the KU in front of the passport number and looked up for a moment as he reached for the boarding card. As he handed it over he smiled faintly.

'Have a good trip, Mijnheer. They'll be calling you in a few minutes. Gate seven.'

'Dank U heel.' And Kleppe smiled back. He liked KGB men with a touch of humour.

At Sheremetyevo it had stopped snowing, but even the few yards across the tarmac to the big black Zil were breathtakingly cold.

There was nobody to meet him except the driver, but that was normal. Why give any watchers a clue, however insignificant?

It was eight o'clock local time, and there were lights in all the apartment blocks that lined the road to Moscow. There were gaunt skeletal frames silhouetted in the moonlight where new blocks were under construction.

He looked out again as the car turned into Kalinin Prospekt. He sighed. No matter how you looked at it, Moscow was a dreary city. Pittsburgh on a Sunday night. And all over the Soviet Union men sold their souls and women their chastity for the privilege of a Resident's Permit in this grey city. The place in the Soviet Union where it all was at. He smiled to himself, and wondered idly what he would do if they ever recalled him.

The car stopped, and the driver stood holding open his door. He picked up his bag and stepped out into the snow. He looked up at the front of the house. They never put him up twice in the same place but it was always luxurious. The driver gave him two keys and he walked up the stone steps and unlocked the big door. An old *babcha* stood smiling in the open doorway on his right.

It was like a stage set for Turgenyev. Heavy curtains, rose-wood panelling, large pieces of furniture and the smell of steam heating. He loved it. It was nice to be back. It was Russia. The prodigal son must have felt like this. His Russian was sometimes clumsy now, but the old lady smiled and nodded as he talked to her.

There was a small pile of envelopes on the brown chenille table-cloth. They were propped up against a shining brass vase that held half a dozen large chrysanthemums. He picked up the envelopes and opened them one by one.

There was a KGB identity card in his name, complete with an up-to-date photograph. They were probably showing him that some of the boys in New York still kept an eye on him as well as taking his orders. Two permanent passes for ten days at the Bolshoi, with a printed list of performances. A card with a list of official telephone numbers and another with girls' names and their numbers. The big envelope had two thick wads of ten rouble notes. There was a short note of welcome to him from the Secretary to the Presidium, hand-written. As he picked up the last envelope the telephone rang. He picked it up.

'Yes.'

'Comrade, they ask if you could attend for a very short meeting this evening. Ten o'clock at Dzerzhinsky Square. A car will come.'

'Is that Ivgenia?'

'Yes.'

'Tell them for you alone I come.'

He heard her laugh softly before she hung up.

It had started six years before. He had been in Moscow on a routine visit and he had given a talk at the training school in Leningrad for senior KGB agents. The subject was the two American political parties, and he covered their structure, finances, method of operation and the election processes.

He had been called back a month later, and for two days a team of four had questioned him about the way in which a State Governor was elected in the United States. Everything was noted and analysed down to the most routine details. They had spent four hours on the powers of a ward-heeler. They had raised points that he couldn't answer, that most Americans wouldn't be able to answer, either. They had gone over the Constitution word by word, and State election laws. Back in New York it had taken him three weeks of hard work finding out the details that they wanted. Copies of official forms, photocopies of old forms that had been completed. There were requests for novels and films which dealt with American politics. There was so much material that he had had to take it to Washington for onward transmission in the diplomatic bag.

There had been nothing on the subject for the next four months. Then he had been recalled again. The meeting had been in the main operations room. There had only been four others beside himself. One of them was Andropov, the Director of the KGB, and the other three were all members of the Presidium. When they had told him what they proposed it was impossible to hide his incredulity. He had been aware of Gromyko's grim face and the piercing grey eyes watching his face as he argued against their plan. They had listened without comment or argument to what he had said and then they had broken off for lunch.

When they had reassembled they were joined by a KGB colonel. He had recognized him right away. It was Rudolf Abel, his predecessor in the US. The man the Americans traded back to the Russians for the release of U-2 pilot Gary Powers. Abel looked old and ill, his white hair sparse and lank. His hands trembled as he sorted through a pile of papers, but his eyes were alert as if all his vitality were concentrated there.

Andropov had started the meeting.

'Comrade Kleppe, maybe we should have put this to you before this meeting so that you'd had time to absorb our proposals. In your training talk you planted the seeds of this operation. Our friend the comrade colonel will explain.'

He nodded to Abel who looked at all the faces round the table, and finally at Kleppe's.

'Comrade Kleppe, when you were last here you went over the details of the United States election process and an analysis was made of the conclusions, to see if they would allow my proposals to be considered.' He paused and pressed his chest as if he were in pain. Then he continued.

'Let us deal with basic simplicities. It is clear that in the United States a man is elected because of a combination of money and influence. You stated this many times in different ways. Agreed?'

'Agreed.'

'All I am saying is that we have the money, *and* the influence to get a man elected. That is a fact, yes?'

'Maybe. I'm not sure.'

'Which do you doubt, comrade? The money or the influence?'

'It depends what level of election we are talking about.'

'State Governor.'

'That would cost a lot of dollars.'

Abel's eyebrows went up, and his thin lips were scornful.

'The cost of a small patrol boat?'

'I guess so.'

'So you doubt the influence, yes?'

'Yes.'

'How many politicians do you know, comrade?'

'Several hundred.'

'Important businessmen?'

'The same.'

'Trades Union leaders?'

'A dozen.'

'Fine. And you are only *one* of our people in the United States. We have three or four more of your calibre, hundreds who are efficient and tens of thousands who can carry out simple instructions. Is that influence enough?'

'Sure. But there's the question of finding a man. The timing. There are specific qualifications.'

'Time—we have decades, comrade. Qualifications are age, residence, citizenship and no criminal record, yes?'

'And willingness to co-operate.'

Abel smiled coldly, and looked at Andropov who nodded.

'I think we have such a man.' Abel leaned forward towards Kleppe. 'One of the people reporting to me from the United States has the possibility of such a man. He wishes to be in politics for business reasons. He is young, a typical American, little money, no influence, likeable but almost no chance of political success. He lacks the two ingredients you identified—money and influence. We could supply those.'

'How could we approach him?'

Abel nodded and smiled. 'We have no need to do that. The person who reports to me is this man's friend from schooldays, from university.'

'And how should we control the control?'

'That would be your responsibility, comrade. The control is already known to you. He is obligated to us, and obligated to you. He has co-operated for five years without reward. Not extensively, because we have not asked for much. But he will do as we ask without pressure.'

Kleppe smiled. 'I'd prefer with pressure.'

'Ah well, comrade. There are some points of pressure.'

'Who is the man? Your contact?'

'Dempsey. Andrew Dempsey.'

'I don't know him.'

'You do, actually. We instructed you to get him out of Fresnes in 1968. And his lover Tcharkova.'

'My God, yes. A young fellow. The scene at the airport. Those fools from our embassy. Yes. That has possibilities. Who is his friend?'

'A man named Powell. Logan Powell. We thought we would try to make him State Governor of Connecticut.'

'And then?'

Abel shrugged. 'And then maybe nothing. Or maybe we do the

55

same exercise elsewhere. It is an experiment, a tactical exercise. What our friends in the US would call practical democracy.'

Kleppe laughed. 'It could be very interesting.'

'It will be, comrade. It will be.'

He had spent a week with Abel and his team planning the details, and being given a picture of the Soviet resources in Connecticut and New York that were not already known to him.

They had given him a letter and some photographs from Halenka Tcharkova. The photographs were of the girl and her daughter.

But that had all been years ago. They had done what they set out to do. And more. They had made their man the Governor of Connecticut. And now he was President-Elect of the United States. They had put up a complex of heavily guarded buildings thirty kilometres outside the Moscow Ring Road. And over two hundred specialists had planned the operation, analysed the reports and given advice to their people on the ground in the USA. People who had worked day after day to help Powell's campaign had no idea that they were serving some Soviet end. And others had worked with single-minded dedication, knowing that they were working for the Soviet Union but without any idea of what the Soviet plan might be.

He had been reluctant at first, despite the planning, to risk his KGB record on the back of this audacious operation. But as the months went by the impossible became possible and the possible a fact.

What was so amazing was that it had not, in fact, been difficult. It had been hard work. But no harder than the two American political parties normally experienced in State and Federal elections. It was just that there were no balloons, no smoke-filled back rooms. There were no discussions, no wheeler-dealing; people were given orders and they carried them out. Even the cheating, conniving, and pressures were little more than politicians normally employed. But there was no need for fund-raising except as a show, and the secret workers were not motivated for a few months. They had been motivated for years. What was more, they knew that their candidate could actually deliver what he promised. There would be genuine benefits for all. For just under thirty million dollars in cash the Soviet Union would have the Americans out of Europe. The end of NATO and the end of Europe as an independent entity. Not a shot fired, and the United States would be limited to its own territory. Slowly being squeezed, decade by decade. Even the Soviet's most hawk-like plans had only envisaged its destruction, not its occupation. And as Krushchev once said, 'The wolf does not fear the dog, but his bark.'

The Kremlin were amazed and euphoric about their success and his own position was established for all time. There would be pressures and arguments about how Powell would be controlled, but he could cope with all that. And when the crunch came he would bow out gracefully and let them take over.

The car came for him at twenty to ten and when he went up to the meeting there were smiling faces waiting for him. The congratulations were genuine and, although bordering on the fulsome, very welcome.

A little later they sat at a small table and Gelov brought out his check file. He re-read the first page quickly and then looked up at Kleppe.

'Are you satisfied about Dempsey?'

'In what way?'

'We have no current pressure on him except the girl.'

'We have. When we got him and the girl out of jail it was a turning point for him. That and the girl will be enough. He helps us with conviction.'

'Conviction?'

'Well, maybe not conviction, but let us say with enthusiasm and goodwill. He has the hope that in time the girl can come to the United States with the child but I have given no firm promise.'

'He was pleased with the proxy marriage?'

'Very pleased.'

'And his pressure on Powell, is that enough?'

'I expect to hear statements from Powell in the next few weeks that will confirm he is responding. He has no choice, of course. And what we require of him fits the American mood.'

Gelov nodded. 'It fits our mood too, comrade. We need consumer goods and food to keep the people quiet. They have seen the success of the dissidents in Warsaw and Prague. There are some who would like to try that here.'

'Where's the colonel?'

'Abel, you mean?'

Kleppe nodded.

'In hospital. Dying. A week maybe, not more.'

Gelov stood up, gathering his papers.

'Tomorrow then, Viktor. Say ten o'clock.'

Kleppe was shaken awake from his deep sleep at four in the morning by a KGB major and a man in plain clothes. He sat up in bed, looked at his watch and looked with disbelief at the two men.

'What the hell is going on?'

'A problem in New York, comrade.'

'What problem?'

'They have been inside your apartment in New York.'

'Who has?'

'There is no information on that.'

'How do we know this?'

'The listening post at the Consulate-General reported that the activator in your telephone registered.'

'Oh for God's sake. Those bloody electronics are never reliable. Activator switches are always jamming on or off.'

'They think the telephone was lifted and put back. There are two registrations with a gap of several seconds.'

'Any recorded noise or speech?'

'No, comrade. But they want you to go back immediately. They are holding the London plane for you. Major Gelov is on his way to the airport to meet you.'

Kleppe sighed and stood up. He was at Sheremetyevo an hour later. Gelov was tense and agitated.

'They have booked you on a flight to Canada, comrade, and suggest you go on by car to New York. Contact Washington immediately with your situation.'

7

MacKay contacted the CIA man at the US Consulate at Museumsplein. There was a long message from Nolan giving an estimate of Kleppe's trade in diamonds and urging him to check for positive evidence of smuggling. It was also requested that he identified himself as CIA, not SIS.

He walked slowly from the Consulate to the Amsterdam police headquarters at Elandsgracht, and asked for Inspector van Rijk.

The Dutch and their police have a civilized tolerance about the facts of life. They do not find it incredible that men want to sleep with pretty girls, or that pretty girls might be willing to allow all sorts of exciting privileges in return for guilders, dollars, marks and yen. Or that there may be those in the community who prefer their sex in books and films. As long as everything is kept neat and tidy, and on the administrative railway-lines, the vagaries of the human libido are accepted as realities.

But in two areas their fuses are shorter. One of the areas is hard drugs, and the other is diamonds. The special diamond squad in Amsterdam is constantly aware that a market's reputation, which has taken a dozen decades to build, can be destroyed in a week. There's not much goes on in the Amsterdam diamond market that the squad is not aware of. It doesn't always do something about what it knows, because informers and sources might be identified that way; and there are more ways than one of skinning these particular cats. So when MacKay pushed his piece of paper across the Inspector's desk he guessed that something very near honesty would be the best policy. A question or two would decide how near.

Inspector van Rijk pushed the paper back across the desk.

'Yes. They're both big dealers. Both have international dealings.'

'If you particularly wanted Russian diamonds, which one would you go to?'

Van Rijk half-smiled and patted the ball back.

'You could get them from either.'

'At short notice?'

Van Rijk smiled openly.

'Mr MacKay, these men deal in millions of dollars' worth of stones every year. They can supply or buy anything, just so long as it exists.'

MacKay realized that it was going to have to be something very close to the truth that cracked this nut.

'Do you understand what I mean, Inspector, if I talk about "laundering" money?'

'Yes. And to save you the question, yes, people do "launder" diamonds from Russia.'

'Which of these two would be most likely to "launder" diamonds from Russia?'

'Mijnheer van Elst.'

'Why him?'

'Because the other one is a Communist and he knows he would be suspect.'

'Is it illegal?'

'Indeed not. A man brings you Russian diamonds, you exchange them for South African diamonds to a slightly less value. There is no crime there.'

'So you have no objection to this sort of trade?'

'On the contrary, we have every objection. Particularly when they come from the Soviet Union. The official Soviet diamond dealing keeps absolutely to the rules. There is no need to "launder". But Soviet diamonds do come in unofficially and we object strongly. They can be used to depress the market, and we also have security objections.'

It was going to be almost the whole truth, so MacKay plunged in.

'We suspect a New York diamond dealer of working for the Soviets. We think he could be exchanging illicit Soviet diamonds for others. He has imported no Soviet diamonds so far as we know in the last ten years.'

Van Rijk shrugged.

'You mean Kleppe?'

MacKay sighed and leaned back in his chair.

'You know about him, then?'

Van Rijk stood up and walked over to a row of metal filing cabinets. He sorted through one of the drawers and pulled out two files. One thick one, and one which was almost empty. He sat down at the table and opened the thin file. There were three typewritten sheets and van Rijk read them through silently and slowly. Then he looked up at MacKay.

'I can't show you these but I can tell you the parts that will interest you. But I shall need a request from Washington.'

'I'll get CIA Langley to speak to you immediately.'

Van Rijk shook his head slowly.

'It would have to be a request from the State Department to Foreign Affairs in the Hague.'

MacKay squinted sideways at van Rijk.

'I guess I'll have to pass, Inspector. It would take days and I haven't got days.'

He knew from the look on van Rijk's face that the Dutchman didn't believe his story. The Inspector sat there silently, waiting for him to continue. When he saw that the CIA man had nothing to add, van Rijk said, 'Of course I could show you Kleppe's file. He's an American national.'

MacKay waited silently as the policeman opened the thick file and leafed through the pages. Van Rijk turned down the corners of several sheets and then looked up at him.

'It's in Dutch so I'll read it out for you. OK?'

'Fine.'

'Kleppe comes over here twice a year. He books in for two days at the Hilton. Pays the bill but he doesn't stay there. He shacks up with a girl, Marijke van Aker. Very pretty, about twenty-eight, paints pot-boilers to be sold in Düsseldorf and Essen. He stays a week, usually. The first full day he buys a few stones at a number of merchant houses. Totals about ten thousand dollars. The second or sometimes the third day the girl goes to the Hague to a house on Groot Hertoginnelelaan.'

Van Rijk looked up smiling.

'You've heard of it?'

'No.'

'It's the best whore-house in the Hague. Embassy people, politicians and film-stars. And very expensive. You don't come out for less than a hundred and sixty guilders.'

MacKay tried to work it out in dollars but stopped calculating because he knew he would never remember the street. And van Rijk was going on.

'The girl goes to one of the private rooms and is visited by a man from the Soviet Embassy. Generally the same man. I can give you his name. He's known KGB. He stays for an hour usually and he hands over a package which she brings back to Kleppe in Amsterdam.'

Van Rijk stopped. His eyebrows raised in query.

'So ask me.'

'Does he screw her?'

Van Rijk laughed. 'Americans. Yes, he screws her, but that wasn't the question I had in mind. I thought you might wonder how we know about the handover.'

'I'd guess you filmed it.'

'Right. Back to our mutual friend Kleppe. He exchanges the Russian stones for South Africans and Venezuelans. Van Elst filters the Russian stones through the market to other dealers and some as direct house-sales. Wholesale value of average purchase by Kleppe each trip about half a million dollars. Retail value about double, unmade-up. Five times that value as jewellery. Four months ago Kleppe made an extra trip. Using an Egyptian passport under the name Ali Sharaf he left Schipol on the Aeroflot flight to Moscow. He came back eight days later. Came back here to Amsterdam and took a flight the following day to New York via London. He neither bought nor sold diamonds.' He pursed his lips. 'That's about it, my friend.'

'Thanks. Can you give me the departure and return dates of the trip to Moscow and the flight numbers?'

'Sure.'

Van Rijk picked up a ball-point and, checking the file, wrote out the details on his pad, tore off the page and slid it across his desk to MacKay, who folded it twice and put it in his pocket.

'Can I invite you to a meal, Inspector?'

'Afraid not. We've got the English here tonight playing Ajax and I've got a ticket. Maybe next time, eh?'

They had fixed him an office-bedroom at the Consulate, and he sat down at the small desk and wrote out his report to Nolan. He ate while it was being encoded and transmitted, and then checked out the girl's address in the telephone book.

It was an hour later when Nolan came through on the telephone.

'This report, Jimmy. Would your contact make a notarized state-ment?'

'They'd want a request from State.'

'Why isn't Langley enough?'

'I don't know. I think it's their rules and regulations.'

'Right. You're staying at the Consulate?'

'Yes.'

'Get them to transmit me photostats of those passenger lists. Both outward and return flights. OK?'

'OK.'

In Washington, the Netherlands ambassador was at the British embassy, so was Morton Harper. And medals were being worn to celebrate the anniversary of the declaration of independence by some part of the former empire. Harper and His Excellency van Laan had been allowed to retreat to the privacy of a spare bedroom. They sat like uneasy children on the spring beds, Harper with his hands in his pockets, and the ambassador with his head on one side expectantly.

'You remember, Your Excellency, that your people approached me a few months ago regarding one of your nationals in Lansing. It was thought that he might be concerned with a drug line?'

'Let's not be too formal, Morton. I remember very well you gave me some unlikely story about needing the permission of the Secretary of State.'

Harper barely smiled. 'I need some information most urgently from your police in Amsterdam. Can we trade?'

'What's the information about?'

'A United States citizen named Kleppe who deals in diamonds. We think he's been "laundering" stones for the Russians.'

'I'll be flying to the Hague at the week-end. I'll bring anything we have back for you.'

Harper shifted his huge bulk uneasily.

'I need it in hours. There's more to it than it sounds.'

Van Laan's tongue explored a hollow tooth as he looked at Harper.

'I'll go back to the embassy now. Just let me say my farewells to H.E.'

'The Dutchman in Lansing is working for us. He's part of a Federal Bureau of Narcotics team. I can arrange for you to interview him, if you want.'

His Excellency stood up. 'Thank you. We'll talk about it some time. Meantime let me say "au revoir" to Joe.'

Even with total co-operation it was seven o'clock next morning before Nolan was opening the brown envelope. It contained a single sheet of 6" × 4" microfiche and he walked over to the reader in the coding annexe and sat reading page after page of the translations of the files on Kleppe and van Elst. He had made a list of the pages that he wanted in hard copy and walked back to his office.

He phoned through to Harper and told him that he was moving his group, except the two surveillance teams, down to the house at Hartford. They had evidence now of criminal activity by Kleppe and they had established Kleppe's contact with Dempsey. Both in New York and way back in the Paris days.

A US Navy helicopter took Nolan and his team from Floyd Bennett Field to Hartford. The Brainard Airport buildings were just visible from the house and there was an entry to the southbound carriageway of Highway 95 a mile from the main gates. The house had been built at the turn of the century for the retiring partner of one of Boston's leading law firms, and stood in its own five acres of woods and landscaped gardens. It was secluded and ideal for the operation.

Nolan checked the Hartford files that covered Powell and his associates. There was very little useful material but there was one lead, Gary Baker, who worked as an investigator in the Hartford District Attorney's office. He had been a CIA contact for a number of years and Langley had helped him from time to time in return. Nolan had met him a couple of times in the days when he had run the CIA's New York office. Nolan telephoned him and fixed to see him after lunch at the DA's office.

Gary Baker had the crew-cut look of a man who spent most of his time outdoors, and he gave Nolan an amiable welcome.

'What can I do for you?'

'I'm doing a bit of background checking on Andrew Dempsey. I wondered if you'd got anything on file.'

'Nothing that would interest you. He's clean as far as we're concerned. Anyway, he's a Washington responsibility now. It was in this morning's papers. He's been appointed Powell's Chief of Staff.'

'Anything on Powell?'

Baker looked up quickly. 'Like what?'

'Like anything you've got.'

'Local boy. Lived here all his life. His old man teaches at Yale. He was a lecturer there himself for a time, then he set up shop in town here as a business consultant.'

'Successful?'

Baker pursed his lips and shrugged.

'In a small way. He was barely established before he went into politics.'

'How did he get started?'

'He just came out of nowhere. He was one of six or seven possible runners. A complete outsider, then—boom—he was the Republican candidate.'

'How did he make it?'

'Nobody knows. There was the strike. That put him on the map locally, and a week after that he was the candidate. The GOP has had the State governorship in its pocket since Adam and Eve, so like all the others, the candidate became the Governor.'

'What was the strike?'

'It was about five years ago at Haig Electronics, a big plant on the other side of the river. Six thousand workers laid off. Most of their stuff goes to Detroit for the car plants. There were contingency delivery penalties, and Haig's was very near to going down the pike. Powell was made arbitrator. Settled it in three days and that was it, I reckon. Fame and fortune.'

'Who appointed him?'

'Old man Haig agreed and the union local agreed.'

'Who was the union negotiator?'

'Siwecki, Tadeusz Siwecki. He was plant negotiator.'

'How come you remember so much, Gary? It's a long time ago.'

Baker looked across at the window, silent for several minutes. Then he turned back to look at Nolan.

'For the same reason you asked the question, I guess.'

'Tell me.'

'It stank. It was so convenient.'

'Did you do any checking.'

'I started. Then I stopped.'

'What stopped you?'

'I got the message from on high.'

'How high?'

'From the State Attorney's office.'

'Did you find anything before you stopped?'

'There had been some stock dealing a week before the strike. Some more afterwards. That's about all.'

'Was it significant?'

'God knows. I didn't have time to check.'

'Can I see your files on it?'

Baker smiled grimly. 'There ain't no files, old friend.' He reached for his cigarettes. 'If you want to know more I can introduce you to a girl who might know.'

'Who is she?'

'Her name's Angelo. She works in this office as the DA's secretary. She gets screwed by a guy named Oakes.'

'Who's he?'

'Senior partner in a successful downtown law firm. Got to be successful about the same time as Powell. Specializes in trust administration and tax. He's a stockholder in Haig's. Since the strike.'

'What's the girl like?'

'Gorgeous, but don't be fooled by the big, melting brown eyes. She's a tough baby. I know she squeezed Oakes for a lot of bread some years back for an abortion. There was talk that he had to go out of town to raise the cash so that it didn't show in his bank account. But he's still screwing her so she must be good at it.'

'What's her attitude to him?'

'I'd guess it was a money relationship. There's at least two other guys screwing her regularly. One's an out-of-town salesman, the other's a junior partner in a law firm in New Haven.'

'I'd like to meet her this evening, if you could fix it.'

'OK. There's a new bar called Pinto's Place two blocks down from me. Soft lights and a piano sort of dump. Say seven?'

'OK. But you leave when you've had a drink. I don't want any witnesses.'

'OK, pal. But watch it, she's not dumb. What are you, for the introductions?'

'IRS.'

Haig agreed on the telephone to see him at four but probed about the purpose of his visit. Nolan told him that he was from the Justice Department looking into a union problem.

Nolan was shown straight into Haig's office where Haig himself stood waiting. He waved Nolan to a chair after shaking hands, and retreated behind his massive desk.

'What can I do for you, Mr Nolan?'

'I'd like to go back to a strike you had here about six or seven years ago. The strike that Logan Powell settled.'

Haig tapped a metal letter-opener on his blotter, waiting for the first question. Nolan sensed that he was already suspicious.

'Can you give me the name of the union official who represented your work force?'

'Not off-hand, I couldn't.'

'But it'll be in your records?'

'I should think so.'

'Were you satisfied that the arbitration was properly done?'

Haig shrugged. 'I've no idea whether it was properly done or not. The company were satisfied with the outcome.'

'From the press reports I gather that Powell received no fee for his work?'

'That's true.'

'But you gave a substantial sum to his campaign fund? Was that you personally or the company?'

Haig's face was grim. He thrust down the letter-opener and, with his elbows on the desk, he leaned forwards towards Nolan.

'What's that got to do with a union investigation, Mr Nolan?'

'There's no trace of the union chipping into the campaign fund a similar amount.'

'So what?'

'So I'd be grateful for an answer to my question. Was the contribution yours or the company's?'

'Mine.'

'Was it registered?'

'I've no idea. I assume it was.'

Nolan shifted in his chair as if he were making himself comfortable.

'I'd be glad if you could check the union man's name and number, Mr Haig.'

Haig put his hand on a single sheet of paper and slid it across the desk. It said 'SIWECKI TADEUSZ 770431/1 Electrical workers 95'.

Nolan picked up the paper and stood up.

'Thanks for your help, Mr Haig.'

Haig looked surprised.

'Is that all?'

Nolan gave him a long, hard look.

'Unless there's anything else you'd care to tell me.'

Haig shook his head slowly.

'No, Mr Nolan. There's nothing else.'

Pinto's Place was about what he expected. The electricity bill wasn't going to be high because of the lighting. It was pink-shaded everywhere, and faces were only recognizable close-to. An ideal set-up, he thought, for those meetings after office hours before the tired businessman faces the rigours of his home. Gary Baker was sitting with a girl in one of the curved booths that were built up on a dais so that the occupants were almost out of the line of sight.

The young man introduced Nolan, finished his drink, and left Nolan to take his place opposite the girl.

As Gary Baker had said, she was gorgeous. Big brown eyes, a neat nose and a wide mouth with healthy teeth. The tight-fitting dress had a V-neck that revealed a lot of bosom but, somehow, the effect was not of deliberate provocation but more an indifference or acceptance of the fact that men would look at the lush mounds anyway. The amused smile as his eyes went back to her face was more of an invitation than the cleavage.

'Gary says you're interested in some of our local brass?'

'One or two. Tell me about you.'

The big brown eyes looked at him shrewdly. 'Whatever it is you want you don't have to go through that jazz.'

'What jazz is that?'

'My life story, and what a nice girl like me is doing in a dump like this.'

Nolan smiled, waved over the waiter and ordered drinks for them both.

'I was genuinely interested, Miss Angelo. I'm sorry if I sounded impertinent.'

'What were you interested in?'

'Well, you're very beautiful, very lively, very . . .' He hesitated for a word and she said, 'Sexy?'

'No,' he said. 'Well, yes . . . but the word I would have used was vital.'

She was smiling and it was a genuine smile.

'My Momma came from Laredo and my Daddy was from Acapulco. He was a lawyer. A very handsome man, and Momma was very pretty. When they were married they moved to New York. Daddy was crazy about girls and they fought like tigers. He couldn't help it, it was all that inbred Mexican machismo. Finally Momma had had enough and she threw him out. *He* lived happy ever after, collecting

69

teenage blondes, and Momma was desperately unhappy for twenty years. She died two years ago.'

'And your father?'

'Still happy. He's raised the age limit to twenty, now.'

'You sound as if you like him.'

'I liked them both. I understood them both. He didn't want to marry them. He thought he was happily married. He would visit Momma long after they were divorced. Big white smile, bunches of roses, invitations to dinner. He never understood.' She looked at him smiling. 'So that mixture is me. Brown skin, white smile and unmarried because I'm still not sure who was right.'

He looked at the lovely face and found her strangely, exotically attractive. It was like the fascination of reaching out to touch two bare electric wires.

'Would you stay for a meal?'

For a moment she hesitated, then she nodded. 'Thanks. That would be nice.'

When the waitress had brought the main course he looked over at her.

'D'you mind if we talk business while we eat?'

'No. Go ahead. It's Oakes, isn't it?'

'Yes. Tell me about him.'

The big brown eyes looked at his face.

'You're not IRS are you?'

He hesitated only for a moment. 'No. What made you doubt it?'

She shrugged. 'For one, I see plenty of IRS guys and you don't fit. For two, there was an IRS senior man down here a month ago just before the election, sniffing around Oakes. Some Democrat had put the pressure on Washington to check out the possible new Senator. Both parties do it, it's routine. For three, I'd guess you'd never catch Jim Oakes on tax. It's his speciality, and he's good at it. For four, I rather like you, and that means you couldn't possibly be IRS.'

Nolan smiled slowly. 'Sounds a pretty shrewd list.'

'So what are you?'

'If it's the only way you would help me I'll tell you, but I'd rather not.'

She waited while he poured her a coffee.

'What is it you want to know about Jim Oakes?'

'I don't know. Just tell me about him.'

'He's just short of fifty. Married. Senior partner in a respected law firm that's not as financially successful as he gives out. Owns 40 per cent of a real-estate development by the river. Leading political figure for years. Was Chairman of Connecticut Republican Party before the election. Newly elected Junior Senator.'

She smiled as she finished, and Nolan nodded.

'That's the image. What's behind it?'

'He was desperately short of money until this real-estate deal came up. Now he's got plenty. He's a man with money. And he's a randy bastard.'

'Where did he raise the money for the real-estate deal?'

'A New York outfit called Gramercy Realtors. The guy he writes to is named de Jong. He also gets separate payments from an outfit called the Halpern Trust.'

'What amounts are we talking about?'

'He's got two New York accounts, both at least a hundred grand. And the payment from Halpern Trust is a thousand a month.'

'What account is that paid into?'

'At First National here in Hartford.'

'How d'you know this, Maria?'

She looked at him calmly. 'You know how I know. I'm sure Gary told you that Oakes screws me.'

He looked down to avoid her eyes and stirred his coffee. Then he looked back at her face.

'D'you know a guy named Siwecki?'

'Yeah. I know the family.'

'Tell me about the union one.'

'That's the father—Tad Siwecki. He was union organizer at Haig Electronics. There was a strike and a few months afterwards he left to run the AFL-CIO local. He retired about a couple of years ago. He lives in one of the houses on Oakes's development.'

'Must have a pretty good pension.'

'He gets a monthly payment from Oakes.'

'How much?'

'Last time I heard it was five hundred a month.'

'What's the payment for?'

'I'm not sure. It's some sort of deal with a guy named Dempsey. The one who's alongside Powell.'

'Tell me about Dempsey.'

She smiled. 'Real dishy, heir to a few millions, something to do with art in New York. Not married, but not for lack of opportunity, I'd guess. Only got mixed up in politics when Powell first ran for Governor. Nice guy.'

'Is Oakes out of town very often?'

'Not much. He generally takes a family holiday in Miami, and apart from that it's mainly New York.'

'How often does he go there?'

'Once a week generally.'

'Where does he stay?'

'At the Waldorf Astoria unless I've been with him, then we stay at an apartment on 38th. It belongs to some friend of his.'

'Are you fond of him?'

'Not the slightest, or I wouldn't be talking to you.'

He looked at her intently. 'Why the relationship, then?'

She shrugged. 'Way back I was impressed that he was interested in me. Now I guess it's habit and money. I guess I'm like my Daddy, too. I like what he does.'

'Can I give you a lift home?'

'Sure.'

He pulled up on the forecourt of the block of flats where she lived, and her eyes caught the lights from the foyer as she turned to look at him.

'Where are you going to now?'

'To see Siwecki.'

'And afterwards?'

'Back to my place.'

'Where's that?'

'Just out of town.'

Her face was lifted to his and she said softly, 'Come back and see me after Siwecki.'

And instinctively, unbelievably, his mouth was on hers. The soft lips responding, and the soft warmth of her breasts against his arm. He pulled away gently.

'I'm sorry.'

'Don't be silly. I wanted you to. Say you'll come back later.'

'I'm married to a gal like your momma, Maria.'

'You want me, don't you?'

'Of course I do, you're beautiful.'

She took his hand and slid it up to her breast, and as they kissed again his fingers squeezed the firm mound and she pulled her mouth away from his.

'Have me now. Quickly.'

'That's crazy, Maria. People would see us, for God's sake.'

'So come back later and have me. You don't have to stay, or say you love me. Just do it to me.'

'We'll see, honey. We'll see.'

As she opened the car door she leaned back to kiss him.

'I'll wait,' she whispered.

He turned the car at the hotel entrance and joined the traffic heading out of the city centre, and two cars waited in line behind him. When he turned off the main road towards the river the second car was a long way behind.

There were lights on in Siwecki's house as he walked up the drive and there was the sound of music inside as he reached up to ring the bell. A woman answered the door. She was black-haired and handsome in a gipsyish sort of way. Her eyes were suspicious, but he guessed that they always were.

'I'd like to talk to Mr Siwecki.'

She turned away and shouted in Polish, and a man's voice shouted back. The woman looked back at him.

'He say who are you an' what you want?'

'My name is Nolan, I'm from Washington.'

She shouted again, and a few seconds later a man appeared at an inner door, a newspaper in his hand.

'Come in,' he called. And he held the door open for Nolan to go through.

There was a three-seater sofa in front of the TV set. And John Wayne was giving one of his closing sermons to a small boy who was holding the hand of a beautiful but unlikely mother. Siwecki leaned over and switched off the set.

He waved the paper at the sofa. 'Sit down, mister.'

He waited while Nolan took off his coat.

'The old lady say you from Washington. I don't believe that.'

Nolan smiled. 'I am, Mr Siwecki, and I need your help.'

The big man snorted his disbelief but said nothing. A legacy from years of hard bargaining.

'I'd like to go back to when you were at Haig Electronics and you had a strike.'

The Pole's eyes half-closed. 'What about it?'

Nolan looked at him calmly. 'Who fixed that strike, Mr Siwecki?'

'You mean who was the arbitrator?'

'No. I know that was Mr Powell. I mean who arranged the strike?'

'Nobody arranged it, mister. It happened.'

'Why do you live here, Mr Siwecki?'

Siwecki looked surprised. 'Why not? Why does anybody live anywhere?'

'I mean why do you live in this particular house?'

'Because I like. Is nice house for me.'

'You never earned enough money at Haig's to buy this house.'

Siwecki shifted uneasily then smiled. 'I win money on horses. I save it up for when I retire.'

'Why do you get money from Mr Oakes?'

Siwecki growled. 'Who are you, mister?' And he stood up, his face contorted with anger, his big hands closing and opening.

'I've told you, Mr Siwecki. I'm from Washington. Please sit down.'

Siwecki clenched a massive fist and held it aggressively. Nolan didn't move.

'Mr Siwecki, it looks to me as if you are likely to be charged with a number of serious offences. I suggest you don't make things worse for yourself.'

'I told you. I told you they'd bring us to trouble.'

Neither of them had noticed the woman come into the room and her voice surprised them both. Siwecki turned aggressively towards her. He spoke angrily in Polish, and the woman spat back at him, her eyes flashing. She slammed the door as she went. Siwecki turned back to look at Nolan.

'What is it you want, mister?'

'Who paid you to fix the strike?'

Siwecki's face looked as it must have looked a hundred times as he negotiated with some recalcitrant employer.

'Who are you from, mister?'

'I told you. I'm from Washington.'

'Is many people in Washington. Who are you?'

'My name is Nolan, Mr Siwecki. I already told you. I am investigating the strike at Haig Electronics. You were the union negotiator.'

'So what is that you investigate? It happened. It is finished years ago.'

'I believe that it is possible that the strike was contrived in order to influence the election of a State Governor. And as you know, Mr Siwecki, that is a very serious offence. If you were a party to this you could be charged on many counts, including the 1925 Corrupt Practises Act.'

Siwecki looked at Nolan's face speculatively. Then he said in a whisper, 'How you know about this thing?'

'It's my job, Mr Siwecki. I'm an investigator.'

'So you ask I give you information to incriminate myself?'

'If you testified, Mr Siwecki, you would be protected.'

'And if I not tell you?'

'Then sooner or later you'll go to jail, Mr Siwecki, if you are guilty.'

Siwecki looked at him, as if he might read some solution in Nolan's face.

'Maybe they kill you first, Mr Nolan.'

'Who might do that?'

The dark eyes looked at him shrewdly. 'If you know these things then you know which peoples I mean.'

'You'd better tell me, Mr Siwecki. If any more crimes were committed in connection with this business you would be an accessory to those crimes, too.'

The old man put his head in his hands, rocking from side to side, moaning softly. Nolan knew that Siwecki was really frightened now.

'I will arrange for you and your family to be protected, Mr Siwecki.'

The old man looked up at him. 'You want a name, or what?'

'Who gave you the orders?'

'Andy Dempsey.'

'And who paid you?'

'He did.'

'How much?'

'Twenty grand for the union, and five for me.'

'Did he say why it had to be done?'

Siwecki looked at him with a twisted smile. 'They didn't need to tell me, comrade. It was put up for Powell.'

'D'you think Powell knew?'

'I don't think he did at the beginning. He didn't talk like he did. But in the end I think he knew, but he didn't say anything.'

'Was Dempsey the top man?'

Siwecki looked towards the door as if he feared another intrusion. Then he looked back at Nolan.

'Are you FBI?'

'No. D'you want to talk?'

'Not to a mystery man.'

Nolan pulled out his CIA ID card and showed it to Siwecki who leaned forward and read it carefully, scrutinizing the words and the photograph. He looked up at Nolan.

'Can you give me a deal if I tell you more?'

'Are you a Party member, Siwecki?'

'Yeah.'

'Is Dempsey?'

'Yeah.'

'Oakes?'

'No, but they got something on him. He fixes things they want, for money.'

'Will you testify to this?'

'Jesus. They'd kill me.'

'You'll get protection from the FBI and my people.'

'Mister. They got people everywhere. I'd wanna go somewhere else outside this country.'

'We'll see what we can do, but you'll testify, yes?'

'OK.'

'Will you swear a deposition tonight?'

Siwecki shrugged. 'If you want.'

Nolan walked into the hallway and opened the telephone directory to look up Gary Baker's number. With his finger against Baker's name he dialled. There was no answer. He hesitated and then checked the number against Angelo M. He dialled and a soft voice answered immediately.

'Yes.'

'Are you alone, Maria?'

'Sure I'm alone.'

'It's Nolan. I'm trying to contact Gary urgently. There's no answer from his home number. Have you any idea where he'll be?'

There was silence at the other end. Then she said, 'He could be at the office but he wouldn't answer the phone.'

'Thanks, Maria. See you.'

'Tonight?'

'Maybe. We'll see. I'm still working.'

He hung up and went back to Siwecki who was talking to his wife.

'Mr Siwecki. I'm going downtown to the DA's office and one of his men will come back here to take your statement. He'll identify himself properly. You stay here quietly with your wife and wait for him. He'll be here within the hour. When he's finished I shall come back for you both and take you to a guarded house just outside of town, OK?'

Siwecki shrugged helplessly. 'OK, mister.'

The swing doors crashed behind Nolan as he hurried up the corridor. There was a light on in the last office in the DA's section and Nolan walked in.

Gary Baker was dictating to a middle-aged woman and he turned, still speaking, to see who had come in.

'. . . and police officer Hagerty confirms that the accused was dead . . . Nolan. What's going on?'

'Gary, I need you to take a deposition from a guy named Siwecki. It's more than just important, and it's more than urgent.'

'Is he outside?'

'No. It'll have to be done at his home.'

'Why not here?'

'I don't want a defence to be that he was harassed or pressured late at night in circumstances that could frighten him or influence him.'

Baker stood up and lifted his jacket from the back of the chair.

'Miss O'Toole, I'll fix a car from the pool to take you home. Pete, what's this guy's address?'

Nolan reached for a pad and wrote out the address and handed it to Baker.

'Could I ask Miss O'Toole to do something for me, Gary?'

'Sure. Miss O'Toole, this is Pete Nolan, he's in the business.' And he flung himself through the open door.

'Miss O'Toole, is there a flower shop open at this time of night?'

'There's one at the Mayfair Hotel, sir.'

Nolan peeled off three ten-dollar bills.

'I want some flowers to go to Miss Maria Angelo and pay them extra so they get there tonight, please.'

'Of course, Mr Nolan. Any particular flowers for Maria?'

He opened his mouth, hesitated and then grinned. 'Yes. Make it red roses, if they've got them.'

'Yes, they'll have those because of corsages for the ladies. Do you need a car?'

'No, thanks. Mine's outside. Goodnight, and thanks for seeing to the flowers.'

Siwecki answered the door. As he peered out from the dimly lit hallway at the two men he opened his mouth to speak. One of them pushed the door aside as the other shoved him back against the wall.

He saw the pistol in the man's hand and, trembling, he walked into the sitting-room as they pushed him ahead of them.

His wife was watching the TV news-bulletin showing a pile-up on Highway 84. Without turning her head she said in Polish, 'Close the door, Tad.' And when there was no answer she turned, the look of irritation melting from her face as she saw her husband and the two men. And the gun. She reached forward to switch off the TV, the gun made a noise like a tyre blow-out and her eyes grew big with fear as her hand touched her chest. She looked down to where her hand came away bright red with blood and opened her mouth to scream. The second slug smashed into her skull above the right eye, and slowly her body collapsed, hung for a moment, then slid from the sofa to the ground.

Siwecki stood as if frozen, and then, his eyes blazing as he cursed in Polish, he turned on the two men, his arms flailing wildly. When the hard edge of a hand crashed against his mouth he staggered against one of the chairs and as their hands shoved him backwards, he clutched for support as his legs buckled.

One of the men gripped the front of his shirt and pushed him into the chair. The man with the gun was pointing it at his head as the other man spoke in Polish with a heavy Russian accent.

'What did he want to know, Siwecki?'

'Nothing. I tell him nothing. I swear.'

The man's boot slammed at Siwecki's kneecap and he screamed. What did he want to know?'

'Oh Jesus. What is all this? He asked about the strike at Haig's.'

'And you told him?'

Siwecki spread his arms, his eyes pleading.

'We send first for doctor for my wife, yes?'

'She's dead, Siwecki. You know that. Just talk.'

'They ask about Powell. They investigate. I tell them very little.'

'You bastard.' And as the silencer jerked and spat, the man cursed in Russian when he saw that the slug had torn open the base of Siwecki's throat. He fired once more and then put the gun against Siwecki's head as he fired a final round.

They switched off the lights on the ground-floor before they left.

★ ★ ★

It seemed a long journey back to the house by the airfield and as he turned into the drive a 727 was coming in to land with its lights winking and its belly light pointing forward.

He signalled to the desk clerk to walk with him up the broad staircase to his room.

'Anything vitally important before I hit the sack?'

'Nothing that can't wait. A few reports from New York and some microfiche from Langley. I don't think it needs processing until tomorrow, sir.'

'Right. Wake me if you need to.'

Nolan undressed slowly and got into the small divan bed. For a few moments he thought of Maria Angelo and the excitement of her body. Maybe if he was down here for a time . . . and he slept. Not, perhaps, the sleep of the just but at least the sleep that sends you down a hundred feet into the darkness.

In what seemed like minutes, but was in reality two hours, the duty orderly was shaking Nolan awake.

'There's a message from Washington says for you to contact the DA's office—Mr Gary Baker. He's waiting for your call.'

Nolan dressed immediately and phoned Gary Baker.

'You'd better come down here, Pete. Quickly.'

'What's going on?'

'I can't discuss it right now. Just get here.'

When Nolan got to the DA's office there was a tall thin man, elegantly dressed, as if the hour were normal instead of four am. Baker made a limp gesture towards the man.

'Peter, this is Hank Henney—he's chief of police. He's got bad news, I'm afraid.'

Henney nodded to a table and he and Baker sat on one side, leaving Nolan alone on the other. Henney looked calm but grim.

'Mr Nolan, I understand from Gary that you work for a government department. He refused to tell me which department. You'd better identify yourself.'

'Can you tell me what it's about, chief?'

Henney looked hard at Nolan. 'Mr Nolan, there's something going on in this city that I don't know about. I've got the feeling you're part of it, and unless you identify yourself to my satisfaction I'm gonna order my men to arrest you while we do some checking.'

Nolan reached in his inside pocket and laid his card on the table. Henney looked at it and handed it back. He didn't look any the less serious.

'Mr Nolan, you visited last night with a Mr Siwecki and his wife. What time did you leave them?'

'About 9.30. I was in this office at about ten o'clock.'

'Why did you visit Siwecki?'

'To collect evidence.'

'Concerning what?'

'The strike at the Haig plant some years back.'

'Did you threaten him?'

'I indicated that he could be indicted on various offences but that his co-operation would be borne in mind.'

'How did he react to that?'

'He agreed eventually to co-operate and I came back here to arrange for Mr Baker to take a signed statement.'

'Where did you go when you left here?'

'Back to my temporary base just outside the city.'

'Where? What's the address?'

'At the moment that's classified information.'

Henney leaned forward across the table.

'Did you resort to physical violence during your interrogation of Siwecki?'

'No.'

'Do you carry a gun?'

'Yes. And I have a licence to carry.'

'Where is it?'

'Back at the house.'

'What make of weapon is it?'

'A .357 Snub Magnum.'

'I'd like that to be brought in, Mr Nolan.'

'You'd better tell me what it's all about, sir.'

'Mr Siwecki is dead. He was shot three times in the neck and head. Mrs Siwecki is dead, too. She had been shot twice and she died on the way to the hospital. The police doctor assesses the time of death as being during the time you were at the house.'

Henney sat looking at Nolan silently and intently. Then he stood up.

'I want you to come with me.'

'To police headquarters?'

'No. You're not being charged with anything at this stage. Let's get along. Baker, you'd better come too, as you seem to be involved with Mr Nolan.'

The police driver turned into the parking area of an apartment block and they were walking through the entrance before Nolan recognized where he was.

The three of them stood in silence as they waited for the elevator. It stopped at the 17th floor, and outside the elevator a police officer stopped them. Then recognizing the chief, he pulled aside a chair and let them through. They went into the next apartment on the right. A photographer was taking photographs as they walked in and he moved his gear when he saw the chief of police.

Maria Angelo lay on her back on the floor, one leg still caught in the bedcover. She was naked and dead, and there were burn marks shaped like the sole of an iron on her breasts, her flat belly, and her thighs. There was a pool of blood from the hole in her throat and a clammy mess above her left ear. A small travel-iron lay on the carpet and the smell of burnt flesh still sickened the air. There was a bunch of red roses still in their paper wrapping on the glass coffee table.

Henney watched Nolan's face as he looked at the dead girl.

'You also talked with Miss Angelo yesterday evening?'

Nolan turned slowly to look at Henney's grim face.

'We'd better talk together, Mr Henney.'

'There's an empty apartment at the end of the corridor. We can use that.'

When they were seated Nolan's hands clenched on the arms of his chair and his voice was harsh and dry as he spoke.

'Chief. Three killings in one evening is problem enough for any police force, but these particular killings mean that Washington have

82

to be informed immediately and I should appreciate your co-operation on this. After I've spoken to them I'll answer any questions you care to put to me.'

'I'll want Baker and myself to hear the conversation. Both ends.'

'That's OK.'

It had taken fifteen minutes to trace Harper, who had obviously been roused from sleep.

'Harper. What is it, Nolan?'

'Sir. I'm speaking on an open line, and the chief of police in Hartford and an official from the DA's office are listening to the conversation.'

'Is that necessary?'

'I'm afraid so.'

'OK. Go ahead.'

'I had a long talk with a Miss Maria Angelo who works in the DA's office here. She gave me information regarding the strike at the Haig plant here some years back. Her information led me to a Mr Siwecki, the union official concerned at the time of the strike. I interviewed him and he gave me information that provides strong evidence concerning my major investigation.'

'Conclusive?'

'Pretty well.'

'Go on.'

'I left Siwecki at his home and came back to the DA's office and requested Mr Gary Baker of that office to go immediately to Siwecki's home to take the statement and witness the signature.'

'That sounds fine.'

'Sir, Mr and Mrs Siwecki and Miss Angelo have all been murdered and the chief of police here, Mr Henney, is concerned that I may be involved.'

'Put him on.'

'He's on the extension.'

'Mr Henney?'

'Who is that?'

'Mr Henney, my name is Morton Harper, Director CIA. I suggest you go back to your office and ask your operator for CIA Headquarters,

Langley. Ask for me, and then you will be satisfied about my identity. Meantime I should appreciate your co-operation with Mr Nolan who is one of our senior officials.'

'I'll do that, Mr Harper.'

It was two hours before Harper got back to Henney and during that time reports had come in of Siwecki's neighbours seeing a car with New York plates parked in the driveway of a vacant house almost opposite the Siwecki house. It had been driven off at about 10.15, by a driver with two passengers.

Two unidentified men had been seen by residents and security men at Maria Angelo's apartment block just before eleven o'clock. One was wearing a utilities uniform thought to be the telephone company, and one had talked to a boy delivering flowers. He had walked to the elevator and appeared to accompany the boy. They had been described as big built, dark with sallow complexions. They could be Italian or Spanish.

The Hartford police were to proceed with their investigations and a two-man team from Langley was flying down to assist them. Nolan was instructed to fly back to New York immediately.

Nolan slept in the Cessna on its way to La Guardia, and half an hour after he had landed the CIA driver turned off Lexington and dropped him at the Barclay. There was a message at the desk; he was to go to a private suite.

Harper was waiting for him, a drink in his hand as he waved him towards a chair.

'I think we have to look at where we're going, Nolan. It's time I put my head on someone's shoulder and cried.'

'I think there's no doubt now, sir. If you take what I found in Hartford, what we found in Kleppe's apartment, and what MacKay has dug up in Amsterdam, that's almost enough. And if you add on these murders then it's too much.'

'Tell me what you got in Hartford.'

Nolan went carefully through the information he had gleaned from Maria Angelo and Siwecki. Harper fiddled with a cigar and a lighter.

'All this is down the drain now.'

'No, sir. We've still got Oakes to work on, and Dempsey. They have the same information.'

'But when you start stirring around at that level we're going to be in real trouble. They'll throw everything into the ring against us. You don't murder three people in cold blood to cover up a few tax evasions.'

'Maybe it's time to consult people outside the agency, sir.'

Harper put his head on one side, half-smiling as if he were listening to some new thought.

'Like who, Nolan?'

'The Vice-President-Elect?'

'Powell chose him. How do we know he's not in the game on their side?'

'The Chief Justice?'

'OK. Go on.'

'The Congressional leaders of both parties?'

'Not yet appointed.'

'The incumbent President?'

'Any more?'

'The Chairman of the Joint Chiefs?'

'They have no standing in this. It's political *and* constitutional. It's going to come down to picking men, not offices. And one thing is for sure.' And he looked pointedly at Nolan. 'There ain't gonna be no medals and promotions out of this. Everybody's going to hate our guts. The FBI won't want to know. The politicians won't want to know. Not even the Democrats. Whatever we do it will probably be the end of the CIA.'

Nolan was silent. Harper continued, 'I think you've almost got enough to justify pressing the button for a full-scale investigation, but before I do that I want to discuss it with the Chief Justice and the present Speaker. If they want to draw in a couple of others I'll consider it. But make no mistake—right at this moment it is possible that we are acting unconstitutionally—we are into a real Bay of Pigs situation with no chance of winning. And I stress that to you. Whatever happens we *cannot* win.' He thumped the table to emphasize each word. He sniffed irritably. 'We've got fifty-six days left according to our original reckoning, but we can forget that. When we get what we need, *if* we get it, people other than us are going to have to deal with it. The fewer people who know what we're doing, the easier it will be for those people to act. For that reason we shall go on, Nolan, as we are. It's far from ideal but already I'm dreading a call from the media that I can't turn away with a plausible denial. We can't afford to extend this beyond the people who already know.'

'I'm going to need FBI help, sir. They'll have stuff on file that would take me weeks to find out.'

'Officially you get no help from them but I've talked to O'Hara and they've given us a liaison man; he's senior enough to get you what you want. But if he says "no" it's "no" without argument. We're only getting this co-operation on condition that eventually we inform them of what's going on.'

'I'd better get back, sir. Can I keep the Cessna at Hartford?'

'OK. But keep me in touch, and for heaven's sake tread carefully. If things start going wrong I want to know immediately. I don't want to come in at the crash-landing when it's too late.'

Harper bent down and picked up a package that had wax security seals. He passed it to Nolan.

'The transcripts of the stuff you photographed in Kleppe's flat. Much moaning from the translation section. It's Armenian shorthand and badly written at that. A combined effort by a girl at Amherst and an old lady in the Bronx. It makes interesting reading. We've put it on microfiche but that package has the only hard copy.'

86

8

Kleppe had a strong feeling that there *had* been someone in his apartment but he could find no evidence. The security network was in operation, the nylon fibres around the door were in place, the plastic plugs in the two key-holes were untouched and the underfloor pressure meters were still at zero. He stood in the loft for half an hour, examining with a magnifying glass the slots in the brass screws that held the cover on the radio box. The micro-meters on the electricity supply were still at their settings. There was nothing.

He had been back two hours when he got the call from Washington. He carried out the standard procedure and walked to a public telephone on Second Avenue. He could sense the panic in the first few words. The KGB surveillance team at the UN were certain that his apartment was under permanent surveillance. They had recognized a CIA agent named Altieri. They had tailed him to a known CIA 'safe-house' near Central Park. He had left the safe-house with a senior CIA man identified as Peter Francis Nolan, and had driven him to Floyd Bennett Field. A civilian clerk, who was operated by the KGB's section at the Consulate General, had supplied the information that Nolan had been flown to the civil airport at Hartford. Two KGB men had been sent to Hartford to locate Nolan. And as of that minute, Kleppe's operation was under the control of the KGB team at the UN. Yuri Katin was in command. Kleppe's operation was top priority, but of equal priority was preventing its exposure. Kleppe could continue his operation but there would be no signals traffic to Moscow. All communication would be through Katin to Washington. They would rather abandon Kleppe's operation than have it discovered. That was the prime consideration now, until the situation was under control. Kleppe was given strict instructions to inform nobody, not even Dempsey, of the new situation. He would carry on, as normally as possible.

He phoned Yuri Katin and arranged to meet him at Grand Central in half an hour. They walked in driving snow to a bar on 42nd Street. Katin made clear that Kleppe was now acting under his orders.

'What's happening about the people watching my place, Yuri?'

'You just carry on as usual, comrade. Keep your operation going until you're told otherwise.'

'Have you found out anything about the CIA man, Nolan?'

'We've got a file on Nolan. I'll be dealing with him eventually. But first we want to see what he's doing. They know something. Maybe not much, but we'll deal with him. I've got a full team on the operation now.'

'Is there any indication of how they got on to us? Why they were watching my place?'

'No. It doesn't matter. They're trying to find out anything they can. If they knew anything they wouldn't be running around in New York and Hartford.'

'Are they watching Dempsey?'

'We've had no reports that indicate that. The Washington team are taking care of Dempsey.'

'Is it safe for me to carry on as usual?'

'We'll make it safe, comrade. You do your part. I will do mine.'

Kleppe returned to his apartment cold and dispirited. Katin and his men were the 'heavies', despised by most high-grade agents but attached to all legal outposts like consulates, embassies and trade missions. Expert at breaking and entering, kidnapping and murder. He wondered who had talked. He couldn't believe that it was Dempsey. He wondered if Dempsey had gone too far with Powell.

He reached for the telephone and dialled Jenny's number. It was several minutes before she answered. She was obviously not alone but she mentioned the name of a Washington hotel. He checked with the inquiries operator and got through to the hotel switchboard. They said that Mr Dempsey was not taking calls, and Kleppe left a brief code message for him to ring 'Department 31' in New York.

Dempsey called twenty minutes later from a public callbox.

'Why the code, Viktor?'

'Forget it.' His voice was sharp and tense.

'OK. What is it?'

'I need to see you urgently.'

'It's going to be difficult. Can you come here?'

'That's impossible.'

'I'll come up and see Jenny. About eleven tomorrow night.'

'OK. How are things?'

'Fine. You sound worried. What's the problem?'

'No problem. I'm just screwed out from travelling.'

'Good. See you.'

'OK.'

Kleppe walked to the girl's apartment on 38th. Dempsey was already there and Kleppe handed him the envelope from Moscow. He saw Dempsey hesitate for a moment and then slip it in his pocket.

Jenny poured them drinks and went to her room.

'How are things with Powell?'

Dempsey shrugged. 'He's beginning to get the message. He knows the score and I'm not pressing him. There's no need. He'll co-operate. I laid it on the line. It's made him uneasy with me but that'll wear off. He loves the whole damn thing like a kid in a toy shop. Spent two hours this afternoon reading IRS and FBI reports on friends and enemies. He's flying down to LA tomorrow in Air Force One.'

'What's he doing down there?'

Dempsey smiled knowingly. 'Putting in a pre-emptive word with the company chiefs who'll lose defence contracts. Handsome compensation and prefabricated housing contracts instead.'

'Moscow will give contracts for modular housing as soon as you say the word.'

'All in good time, Viktor. Let the dust settle first.'

'Who's he picking for the senior appointments?'

Dempsey went over the list and gave background details on all of them. Dempsey was not attempting to influence any appointments. In the short term they didn't matter and in the long term a lot could happen.

Dempsey poured more drinks and took off his jacket. As he leaned back comfortably in his chair he laughed.

'You know, if Powell co-operates on all these points he's going to have Moscow's ear direct. They won't need us.'

Kleppe shrugged. 'So what's the bad news?'

'The bad news is that we shall be the only people who know everything that's gone on. Powell will know that, and Moscow knows it, too.'

Kleppe's head came up slowly and he swirled his drink around before he looked at Dempsey.

'And?'

'And we shall not only be superfluous but an embarrassment.'

Kleppe had already worked out that equation months ago, and it disturbed him even more that Dempsey found it an obvious solution. Yuri Katin would enjoy solving that little problem. He reached forward and switched on the TV. The newsreader was covering a homicide on the Staten Island ferry and moved on to the Traffic Commissioner's warning about dangerous road conditions on all roads out of the city. Kleppe was just reaching forward to switch off when the newsreader's eyes went from the teleprinter to a note that had been slid along the desk. With his eyes down he read the item.

'We have just received reports of a double killing in Hartford, Connecticut, late last night. A retired union official and his wife, Mr and Mrs Siwecki, and a secretary who was employed in the District Attorney's office all died from gunshot wounds.' The announcer looked up to the camera. 'We have no further details at this moment. The weather tomorrow is expected to be the same mixture of snow and . . .'

'For Christ's sake, Viktor. What's going on?'

'I've no idea.'

'Siwecki was the union negotiator at the strike at the Haig plant way back.'

'Who's the girl?'

'How in hell should I know?'

'Maybe it's some union fight.'

'Don't shit me, Viktor.'

'I'm not, Andy. I've no idea what it's all about. Phone your contacts down there and check it out.'

'No way, my friend.' He looked intently at Kleppe's face. 'If this *is* you, Viktor, or your people, then they're crazy.'

'Why should I do that? Give me a reason.'

Dempsey sighed. 'I couldn't, but some of those goons of yours at the UN don't need reasons.'

After Kleppe had gone Dempsey took out the envelope and looked at it. It was ten minutes before he tore it open. He read it slowly.

There were two pages in that big, childish handwriting, with small circles instead of dots over the i's. And as always she wrote in French, the only language they had in common.

Cher Andy,

Your lovely letter came last month and I've read it a thousand times. I am back from Leningrad. They gave me an exhibition there in the annexe to L'Hermitage. One reviewer said they reminded him of Van Gogh. Three have been bought by the Minister herself. One of them is to be a birthday present to the Chinese Ambassador.

Little Alexandra is with me and she is doing well at school. We have a refrigerator now in the Moscow apartment and we live very well. Always I am thinking of you and your sacrifice for us. The man who came with your letter said he had seen you in New York and you were well. Sometimes at night I think of us in the rue Mouffetard and how you loved the chocolate cake from the *pâtisserie* across the road.

Some day, perhaps, there will be no more problems for us.
Je t'aime, chéri, jusqu'au dernier jour de ma vie.
Ta Halenka.

Tears were running down his face when the girl walked back into the room.

'Andy, what is it, my love?'

He shook his head, and wiped his eyes with the back of his hand. The girl saw the letter and the photograph.

She said softly and gently. 'Is it from Halenka?'

He nodded.

'Are they both all right?'

'Yes.' He shuddered from crying, as children do. She put her hand on his knee. 'Don't be unhappy, love. She loves you. You can be sure of that.'

He shook his head. 'It's not that, Jen. I miss her so terribly. One morning we got up not knowing it was going to be the last. Eight hours later we were both in jail, and apart from that terrible journey to the airport that was it. Finished. Over.'

'When were you married?'

'A few weeks ago. Viktor arranged it. We were married by proxy.' He looked up at the girl, his face still wet with tears. 'I've tried to be patient, Jenny . . . But it doesn't work. I miss her so.'

'She'll know how you feel, Andy. It's the same for her.'

He picked up the photograph. Halenka was smiling at the camera, her thick, dark hair in plaits, her arm curved gently round the waist of the pretty, solemn-eyed girl who was his daughter. He turned it over, but there was nothing on the back. He turned it back to look again. There was no background, nothing to identify where it was taken. Halenka looked just the same. He wondered if she ever protested.

In bed he clung to Jenny like a child in the night, and then lay silent and inert until he fell into uneasy sleep. Jenny slid out of bed and stood by the window, looking out as the false dawn spread across the city. One of Nolan's surveillance teams reported seeing an unidentifiable figure at the apartment window.

She turned silently to look at the figure on the bed. He was handsome in a rather juvenile fashion. Quick to smile and laugh, but few of his friends would see him as the constant lover. Physically he wasn't constant. He slept with many girls, and with as much affection as lust, but he was never involved. Not even with her. He recognized that she really cared for him, and her reward was to sometimes share his distress about the girl in Moscow.

9

MacKay walked from the Central Station and crossed the bridge over the canal and turned into Hendrik Kade. The warehouses and shops served the ships' crews from the Oosterdok, and number 147 was at the side of the chandlery.

The narrow stairs led steeply upwards from the open door and the doors on the first two landings carried business names on typed postcards as if to emphasize their temporary occupation. Right at the top was a solid oak door whose brass-work shone, catching the colour from geraniums in a large clay pot. A small printed card said 'M. van Aker—Painter'. He pressed the porcelain bell-push, and waited.

The girl who opened the door was unexpectedly pretty. She was wearing an oversize sweater and blue denims. She half-smiled as she looked at him, as if she were used to men being silenced by her looks. She spoke softly.

'Can I help you?'

'Miss van Aker?'

'Yes.'

'Could I talk to you for a few moments?'

She made to open the door wider, and then hesitated.

'What about?'

'You.'

She laughed softly and opened the door. The studio was large and bare, except for two easels and the paraphernalia of painting. There was a low divan with a wolfskin cover, and a dozen or so unframed paintings on the walls.

The girl stood, one hand on her hip, sipping coffee slowly as she looked at him over the cup.

'I don't expect you remember me?'

She shook her head, smiling, as if she had heard that opening gambit before. He went on.

'I was in Paris in '68. My girlfriend was Adèle de Velancourt.'

She put down the cup and folded her brown arms across her chest. A bad sign when you're asking questions.

'How is Adele? I saw a piece in *Figaro* about her. It seemed she was doing well.'

'Yes, she *is* doing well. Do you remember Andrew Dempsey?'

She laughed. 'Show me a girl who didn't remember him.'

She pointed to a wicker chair. 'Do sit down. What's your name?'

'James MacKay. I was taking French literature at the Sorbonne.'

She nodded but made no comment. She wasn't refusing to talk but she wasn't going to help him either. He looked at the questioning, hazel eyes and accepted the unspoken challenge.

'Can we talk about Viktor Kleppe?'

'I wondered what it was going to be. The answer's no. We can't.'

She stood up and brushed imaginary specks from her jeans. MacKay sat, and looked up at her face.

'It would be easier if we could talk here.'

'As an alternative to where?'

'The Central police station.'

'Don't bluff, mister.'

'I'm not bluffing. Perhaps you'd like to phone Inspector van Rijk at Elandsgracht?'

She walked briskly to the telephone and asked the operator to connect her to police headquarters and when a voice said 'Polizeizentraal' she hung up, swinging round to look at him.

'You weren't bluffing, were you?'

'No.'

'What's it all about?'

'Are you a member of the Party?'

She sat down, slowly and carefully.

'No. I'm not a member of the Party.'

'But you've got connections?'

'Maybe.'

'I want to know why you help Kleppe.'

'I don't *help* him. He just shacks up here when he comes on business to Amsterdam.'

'I mean the trips to the Hague for the diamonds.'

Her mouth opened to speak, the shock all too obvious on her face. She swallowed, and then spoke in a whisper.

'How did you find out?'

'Miss van Aker, I think it would be better if you just answered my questions.'

'And then you arrest me. I should see a lawyer.'

'You won't be allowed any outside contacts until the inquiry is complete.'

'What do you want to know?'

'Why you helped him?'

'Is this to be used in court?'

'If you co-operate fully it's unlikely to go to court.'

She sighed. 'I've known Viktor for years. Way back I was a member of the Party. They told me to leave. That I could help more outside. I just passed messages and collected the packages from the Hague.'

'You knew the man who gave you the stuff was KGB?'

'I guessed. They didn't tell me.'

'You knew that you were committing a serious crime under Dutch law?'

She sighed again. 'I suppose so.'

'Did you know Kleppe was KGB?'

It was a shot in the dark and he saw her look towards the window to collect her scattered thoughts. He waited, tense and silent. Her head turned back to look at him.

'You can't expect me to betray a friend.'

It was answer enough. Enough to let him extend the bluff.

'Where did the messages come from for Kleppe?'

'The embassy in the Hague.'

'What were they about?'

'Just dates for him to come over.'

'How did you pass them on?'

'I phoned him in New York.'

'Who paid you?'

'The Soviet Embassy.'

'How did they pay you? And how much?'

'They bought a painting every month. They paid six hundred guilders each time, in cash.'

'How did you meet Kleppe in the first place?'

'He had an apartment in Paris when I was there. I met him through the Party and eventually I moved into his place.'

'Are you fond of him?'

She shrugged. 'I was in those days. I guess it's just friendship now. He was very important too, in those days. He had a lot of influence.'

'What nationality did you think he was?'

'He had a United States passport.'

'That's not the same thing, is it?'

'I guess not. I suppose I assumed he was a Russian.'

'Why?'

'The people who came to the apartment were mostly Russians from the embassy in Paris. He always talked Russian with them. At least I assumed it was Russian. And he seemed relaxed with them. They joked and laughed a lot.'

'What did you think his job was?'

'He was a diamond dealer in New York. I think he was very successful.'

'Do you remember when he got Dempsey out of jail?'

'Yes. Andy came back from Le Bourget with Viktor. He was terribly upset. We sat up all night with him, and Viktor calmed him down. He flew back to the States the next morning with Viktor.'

'Have you seen Dempsey since then?'

'No. Never.'

'Has Kleppe talked about him?'

'Not that I can remember.'

'Is there anything else you think you should tell me?'

She shook her head. 'No. What will happen to me now?'

'I expect Inspector van Rijk will want to talk to you, but I don't think they will bring any charges provided you will sign a statement.'

She looked relieved.

'I hope this doesn't mean problems for Viktor.'

'He had the problems already, Miss van Aker.'

MacKay took a taxi to van Rijk's office and from there he tried to contact Nolan. When he failed he asked for Morton Harper and gave him details of his interview as guardedly as he could. He asked for Langley's help in expediting his travel to Oslo. The only civilian flight that day had already left. Harper told him to go straight to Schipol and he would be contacted there.

The airport manager was paging him on the Tannoy as he walked with his bag into the main terminal building. A Hawker Siddeley training Harrier had already landed from Brussels.

He walked out with the RAF Squadron Leader to the side-bay far from the civilian airliners. He sat in the rear seat of the cockpit, his head almost touching the canopy, as the pilot listened to the air-controller clearing a Sabena 747. Then they were cleared for the main runway and ten minutes later they were cleared for take off. He heard them cleared through to the military airfield at Stavanger.

The take off and the steep climb left him shocked, and even at 30,000 feet up the clouds had raced below the aggressive wings at a sickening speed. He held his breath as they tore through the sky; and for the first time in his life he realized what modern warfare was all about. He had seen all the NATO orders-of-battle and those of the Warsaw Pact, and those squadrons of supersonic planes and strategic nuclear weapons had just been numbers on computer printouts, but as the plane carved its trembling strength through the clouds the whole nightmare was suddenly real. The things he normally dealt with had their own element of lonely fear but in this plane, knifing its way across the North Sea he knew the difference between fear and terror. He couldn't imagine this metal dart ever reducing its speed again so that it could land. He felt like an elderly aunt on the Big Dipper.

They screamed in from the sea to the airstrip on the coast at Stavanger. When he scrambled clumsily out of the aircraft there was the stench of hot metal, burnt oil, and burning rubber.

The vice-consul, a fellow Scot, was waiting for him at the airfield and drove him to a small hotel in the centre of the town. When they were alone in MacKay's simple bedroom the vice-consul handed over the big brown envelope.

'That's not the original, of course. But the original is held in the Record Office here and can be made available for inspection.'

'Is it possible to get a copy notarized officially?'

'Certainly. The Registrar can do that himself.'

MacKay's head still rang from the flight. He waved to the whisky on the bamboo table.

'Would you pour while I read?'

'Of course.'

He tore open the envelope and looked at the large rectangle of photo paper. It was a birth certificate of Viktor Per Kleppe, born 18 May 1938. Father—Per Trygve Kleppe. Born 2 October 1891 at Egersund. Exporter of iodine and seaweed products. Mother—Kirstin Ragna Cappalen. Born 13 May 1917 at Flekkefjord. Housewife.

The second photostat was much smaller. It registered the death of Viktor Per Kleppe, born 18 May 1938. Died 12 January 1942. Cause of death, pneumonia. Medical Registrar, Andreas Vostervoll. Stavanger.

MacKay looked up at the vice-consul.

'Is there a grave? A tombstone?'

'Yes. I checked it personally, as Mr Magnusson required.'

'Are the parents still alive?'

'Afraid not. The father was killed by the Germans. The mother died in 1950.'

'Can I see the tombstone myself?'

St Clair looked at his watch then looked up with pursed lips.

'It's 10.30pm, old chap. It would mean me contacting the chief of police and the parson at the church.'

'I'm sorry to trouble you but I think we'll have to do that. Could I possibly have a photograph too?'

'I'll see what the police can do. You stay on here. I'll use the manager's office. Give you some peace.'

It was just after midnight when they stood outside the tall wrought-iron gates of the church. The parson opened them wide, and with his torch swinging ahead of them, led them through the churchyard like an usherette at a cinema.

The three graves were side by side under an elm tree. MacKay bent down and flashed the torch at the tombstones one after the other. As he straightened up he realized that some KGB man must have done that twenty years earlier, so that they could apply for a genuine Norwegian passport. It was all too easy. A passport application with a photostat of a genuine birth certificate of somebody who was dead. And who had died at an age that meant it was unlikely that a passport had ever been applied for. In no country did they take the simple precaution of relating a death certificate to its relevant birth certificate.

An understandably crotchety Registrar was roused from his bed at one am to notarize the photocopies of the birth and death certificates. His curiosity held under control only because of the pressure of the police chief, he waved the papers to speed the drying of the official black ink and handed both documents to MacKay. The vice-consul paid the fee in cash.

At police headquarters MacKay waited for his call to Nolan to come through. It was a public line and insecure, but his news was too urgent to wait for the more secure facilities which could only have been provided in Oslo. He finally got the connection on a line that crackled with static, and surged from loudness to almost complete inaudibility.

'Can you read me, Nolan?'

'Yes, but it's very faint.'

'Kleppe's not Norwegian by birth. The passport was applied for with false documents.'

'False what?'

'Documents.'

'Have you got proof?'

'Yes. Notarized documents.'

'Anything else?'

'He's almost certainly Russian.'

'Any proof?'

'Only circumstantial. Enough to build on.'

'When do you come back?'

'Depends on transport. And I need to sleep.'

'Need to what?'

'Sleep.'

'Who can I liaise with on transport?'

'British vice-consul, Mr St Clair.'

'OK. Hit the sack. I'll arrange the transport.'

'Cheers.'

'What?'

'Good-bye.'

'Bye.'

They let him sleep until noon, and St Clair drove him to the airfield. A venerable Trident awaited him, and his travel papers showed that they would land at Glasgow, and he would there transfer to the PanAm plane to New York.

They landed to re-fuel at Goose Bay and there was a message for him. A room had been booked for him at the Barclay where friends would be waiting for him. He stuffed the paper in his pocket, pulled the blanket over his head and went back to sleep.

At Kennedy, one of Nolan's men was waiting for him and took him straight through immigration without any formalities. The CIA agent was not the talkative type and MacKay sat hunched up in the back seat looking out of the car windows. It was mid-evening and the traffic was heavy as they crossed the bridge, and heavier still as they crawled up Lexington. The driver dropped him under cover at the Waldorf and he took his bag and crossed the road. There was a message from Nolan to go up to his suite.

When he knocked, Nolan answered the door, holding the telephone body in one hand and the receiver crooked on his shoulder. He was talking still, as he pushed the door to with his foot and nodded MacKay to a chair. When Nolan had finished he walked over to sit down opposite MacKay. Without speaking, MacKay handed over the envelope, and Nolan opened it carefully and studied the documents. He looked up at MacKay.

'This is the real nail, Jim. We can pull him any time on this. Excuse me a moment, I must phone immigration.'

Nolan gave the number and details of Kleppe's passport, and put a stop on its use at all ports and airports. He looked again at the documents as he came back and sat down.

'This is the first piece of evidence we have that would stand up in court. Magnificent.'

'What have *you* got?'

'Look. Harper wants you to make out your report before I fill you in. He thinks they will have more force if they are done independently. There's a secretary in the next room if you'd like to dictate it. Do it as it comes, and she'll do a draft, and then you can hack it around. Is that OK?'

'Sure.'

'Have you eaten?'

'Too much already. It's early morning down in my guts.'

Nolan laughed, and walked with him to the next room, introduced him to the secretary, and left him.

It was midnight New York time when MacKay signed his final version, the notarized documents stapled to the four typewritten sheets.

Nolan filled him in on the events of the past few days and when he had finished MacKay sat silently for several minutes. Then he leaned back.

'You've got Oakes and Haig as sources who could possibly confirm Siwecki's statement.'

'True, but Harper's put a block on any further action until he's taken advice.'

'From whom?'

'From Chief Justice Elliot and Speaker Bethel. You and I are flying to Washington tomorrow, and both of us are seeing Harper. Then all of us are meeting Elliot and Bethel.'

'Won't they raise hell at me being there?'

'Harper says he's not going to sweep anything under the carpet. If he did and it came out later, some crafty bastard could pull it apart as a ploy by London. Harper's view is that it's too serious to play games.'

'I think he's right, but when you want me off the lot you just say so.'

'Don't worry, friend. We will.' He walked over to the TV and turned it on. 'I think there's going to be some sort of statement from Powell.'

The picture came up, and slowly the colour built up.

There were at least forty reporters at the foot of the aircraft steps. TV crews, and the usual foliage of microphones. Powell stood there with his coat collar turned up and the wind tugging at his hair, smiling, as Newman, who was acting as Press Secretary, made one of the crews shift lights so that the handsome face would lose its gauntness. He looked even younger than Kennedy had looked. He was forty in two weeks' time.

It was a crisp, cold night, and there was a fan-heater working from a generator to ease the cold of Powell's feet. He craned forward to catch the first question.

'I'm sorry I can't hear you, Mr Francis.'

'Have you any comment to make on the statement issued today from Bonn regarding US troops in Europe?'

'Yes. I think that the Federal German Chancellor is saying to the American people—remember your commitments in Europe.'

'And what's your answer, sir?'

'Our commitments remain, but the form of our demonstration of that commitment will not necessarily, in future, be represented by American forces in Europe. They could be sent there when, and if, they are needed.'

There was a moment's silence, and then a clamour of voices. Powell nodded at a girl reporter in a white fur hat.

'There have been recent comments from the Pentagon indicating that without US troops in Europe, Soviet forces would be at the English Channel in a couple of days. Have you any comment?'

Powell smiled. 'Not unless they're all driving Ferraris. Europe's a big area, ma'am.'

'Could I have a serious answer, Mr Powell?'

'Yes, of course. My administration are already preparing an agenda for talks with the Soviet leaders. They are spending billions of roubles on missiles and weapons. We are spending billions of dollars doing the same. There comes a point when this madness has to stop.' He paused. 'So far as I am concerned it stops on January twenty.'

'Did you discuss the effect on Californian unemployment of a cut-back in the arms programme while you were in Los Angeles?'

'I certainly did, and I made clear that my administration will give the highest priority to providing alternative work to all those areas of the country affected by these changes.'

'What do you expect the Soviet reaction to be, sir?'

'I guess they'll start making more freezers and colour TVs.'

'There has been talk of a possible trade and peace pact with the Soviets. What would you say to that?'

'I like trade, Mr O'Dell, and I like peace. That's what I'd say.'

'But what would be your first action in response?'

Powell looked down at his feet and stamped them before he looked up. 'I guess my first action would be to break open a bottle of champagne.' He looked around. 'And now, ladies and gentlemen, I must go. I don't want to read in the headlines tomorrow that the President-Elect admits that he's got cold feet.'

There was a ripple of laughter and a barrage of flashes, and Powell turned to walk to the car.

Dempsey walked a few paces behind him. He never ceased to wonder how a man could go from being a diffident candidate for State Governor to an apparently confident President-Elect in the space of a few years. Maybe what they said was true; any man *could* be President of the United States. Powell reminded him of those old cartoon characters who walked off the edge of the cliff and didn't fall until they looked down. They just went on walking.

Nolan turned, grim-faced, to MacKay.

'Well, that's it. That's the start, and he's not even in the saddle yet. Thank God he's said it tonight. Elliot and Bethel ain't gonna miss the point of that little piece.'

'What do you think the press will make of it?'

'In tomorrow's headlines they'll be shit-scared. After they've phoned around the grass-roots tomorrow they'll report widespread popular support. And if Moscow makes a tiny gesture to support him he's home and dry.'

'They'll make a gesture, there's no doubt about that.'

Nolan nodded slowly. 'You know we could already be too late.'

'Why?'

'Just look at the scenario. Years of phoney *détente*. The new President makes the big peace gesture. The Soviets appear to respond. What happens next? Some militant group in CIA, us, say that the President is a traitor. For co-operating with the Soviets. Is that treason, for Christ's sake? And what if we do nail everything down and the President *is* impeached and gets thrown out? We go back to the cold war, for God's sake. Big deal. The public will love that. No wonder Harper wants to play this cool. Jesus, what a can of worms.'

MacKay looked across at the American. He realized that it must be traumatic for a man like Nolan to contemplate what had happened already, let alone what was still to happen.

The American's stocky body and his open face were made for certainties, and the almost old-fashioned crew-cut with its sprinkling of grey hairs represented experience in a familiar set of political and intelligence parameters, not with this European fantasy of deliberate deviousness. The Americans were used to punch and counter-punch, not this cobweb attack that used the very basis of democracy as the means of its enslavement.

He looked at Nolan as he spoke. 'Whatever happens, Pete, the Soviets have lost the ball-game.'

'I'm not so sure, Jimmy. If we have to go all the way and expose the bastard, it's going to have an effect like the Kennedy assassination and Watergate combined. In spades.' Nolan shook his head. 'I can't explain it, but this thing is different from anything the Soviets have ever tried. It's kind of sick, in a special sort of way. It makes the Constitution itself look childish and pathetic. The reaction against the Soviets will make Joe McCarthy look like Snow White. It won't be a cold war. It'll be a new ice age.'

There was a long silence and then MacKay said softly, 'There *is* an alternative.'

Nolan looked at him intently. 'Don't think I haven't thought of it, fella. I have.'

'And?'

'Jesus. Who gives the order? And what effect would another assassination have on the public?'

'There are more ways of killing a man than a .45 slug.'

Nolan stood up, shaking his head. Not in disagreement but as if to rid his mind of the problem.

'This is other people's problem, not ours. Thank God.'

The next day the *Washington Post* carried a lengthy piece about Powell's Cabinet-selection interviews, and speculated on the likely recipients of the main offices. It concluded with a quote from Powell himself.

'There will assuredly be substantial cuts in the Defence budget. For too long the United States has been expected to act as fireman for every bush-fire in the world. We have our own bush-fires of inflation and unemployment. There must be adjustments, a sharing of the burden by our friends in Europe, the Middle East, and elsewhere. Let us send abroad the products of our great technology, of our farms, and of our research, not our young men.'

When asked if this meant withdrawing troops from overseas bases the President-Elect had replied, 'All options are under consideration.'

The *Washington Post* editorialized uncertainly.

'All the signs in Washington indicate that the President-Elect intends carrying out many of the major features of his election platform without delay, and many commentators have noted that he will not need the support of the finely balanced Congress to implement these changes, as many of them do not require new legislation. Comment from Europe has been muted but there is little doubt that in London, Bonn and Paris the situation is being watched with intense interest.'

IO

Nolan and MacKay spent most of the morning reading the transcript of Kleppe's notebooks. They made a long list of names for investigation and a short list of prime targets. The flow of money from Kleppe exceeded what even the most successful diamond-selling operator could have supported, but Nolan put through an urgent request to IRS for copies of Kleppe's returns for the last six years.

They took the shuttle to Washington and met with Morton Harper in his office at eight o'clock in the evening. MacKay felt the tension of the other two men and was glad that he was almost a passenger, a neutral observer.

Morton Harper wore a dinner jacket, and his black bowtie was undone, the two ends trailing down the front of his white shirt as he leaned with one elbow on the top of a metal filing-cabinet.

'I've no idea how we shall be received by the Chief Justice or Mr Speaker. They have no inkling of what I shall be telling them. And I have no idea as to what their reaction will be. Elliot was a Republican appointment. There was almost no opposition from any quarter. Bethel is a Republican too. An entirely political animal whose natural habitat is Capitol Hill. He isn't going to like it. Neither of them can order us to stop the investigation, but by consulting them I have almost given them some sort of power of veto. I am convinced, now, that our suspicions are justified. And almost convinced that they are correct. We really had no choice but to pursue the facts, but I would not be happy to go further without advice. If you are asked questions you will answer without reservation no matter what their attitudes may be.'

He looked at his watch.

'My driver will take me in my car. You two travel together.'

* * *

Chief Justice Elliot lived just outside Aurora Heights in a house that he had bought when he was first married. Its white boards shone in the moonlight and it looked, with the orange lights from its windows, like an advertisement for gracious living. In fact it was primitive compared with most dignitaries' homes in Washington, and he would have been lucky to get $80,000 for it on the open market. But as he had paid only $11,000 he wouldn't have worried.

When they were shown in he was sitting at a big round table with Sam Bethel, the tubby, white-haired Speaker of the House. He waved them to the seats round the table.

'Help yourselves to drinks, gentlemen.'

Only Morton Harper went over to the sideboard, and he poured himself a generous neat whisky. He sighed audibly but unconsciously as he sat down at the table.

'Now, I understand you've got something you want to talk about with Sam and myself. You were a touch coy on the telephone, Morton, so we're expecting the worst.'

Morton looked up sharply, and Nolan saw his fist clench as it lay on the table.

'Well, I'm not going to disappoint you on that score, judge. And I know you'll believe me when I say that I find this the most difficult meeting that I have ever attended.' He looked at both men in turn. 'I have rehearsed a dozen times my approach to this problem. I have sought for the right sentence that would lead me into talking with you gentlemen. And there isn't such a sentence. At least there is no such sentence that I can bear to utter.' He thrust back his heavy frame in the chair until it creaked. 'Nevertheless, utter it I must. We seek advice, either formally or informally, on a grave matter. We have reason to believe that Logan Powell, the President-Elect is, deliberately or accidentally, a traitor, under the influence of the Soviet Union.'

Two lesser men would have given some display of emotion; disbelief, curiosity to hear more, even fear or anger. Both men remained impassive.

'May I go on, sir?'

Elliot nodded. 'Of course.'

Morton went carefully through all that had been uncovered, and when he had finished he sat silently awaiting a response. Elliot didn't even exchange a glance with the Speaker. He looked straight at Morton Harper.

'At least half of what you have told us, Mr Director, would not survive in any United States court. You realize that, I'm sure.'

'I was relying, to some extent, sir, on the definitions for impeachment established by the House Committee.'

Elliot nodded and closed his eyes, trying to recall the precise words. '"It is not controlling whether treason and bribery are criminal." Is that it?'

'Yes, sir.'

'What do you say, Sam?'

Bethel hunched his shoulders and looked at the two CIA men, with the look he usually gave to the more obstructive filibusterers.

'I'm wondering, Arthur, if these men are not guilty themselves of treason.'

His flushed, red, bull-dog face glanced at them in turn.

'Do you people realize what you have been doing? Do you, Harper? You and your underlings have been conducting an investigation of the next President of the United States. On your own account.' His hand slammed down on the table. 'With no permission from any part of the administration you take it upon yourselves to ferret about like goddamn journalists into the lives of important citizens. And you bring your scurrilous offerings here like dogs with a bone. You must be out of your minds.'

'Three people have been murdered sir, to prevent us bringing more concrete evidence.'

'That is *not* the point, Harper. If you had a table full of evidence, concrete evidence, that would still not be the point. Where does your authority lie to do this? Why did you not do your talking before you started? Why did you not talk to the Secretary of State, or me, or somebody, for God's sake?'

Morton spoke very quietly. 'There were two problems in the beginning, Mr Speaker. Our evidence then, in terms of a court of law, was non-existent, but our training, our instincts, told us that there was cause for doubt. When we considered who we should consult we were uncertain about who we could trust. We also hoped that a superficial check would prove our fears groundless.'

'Don't give me that crap, Harper. You and your people have obviously gone at this in your usual style. Heads down and to hell with realities. If you didn't trust Elliot and me *then*, why trust us now?'

Harper looked down at his plump white hands. 'There was a point, sir, beyond which I was not prepared to go. I have no doubt in my mind now, Mr Speaker, that what I merely suspected is unfortunately true. At this point we should have to investigate some of the principals involved. And that I was not prepared to do without hearing your and the Chief Justice's advice.'

'So now I'm trusted, eh?'

'No, sir. At this point I trust your office.'

'And if we instruct you to close this inquiry, what then?'

'I shall report to the incumbent President, sir.'

'Why now? Why not before?'

'Because when we started we had sixty-six days before the inauguration. Now we have roughly fifty days left. After January twenty, what is difficult now would be almost unthinkable then. As unthinkable as doing nothing.'

Elliot had listened without interruption, his eyes going from face to face as they spoke. Then he nodded to Harper.

'I suggest you gentlemen retire to my smoking-room. That's the door. We'll chat, Mr Speaker and I, and then we will all talk again.'

They sat for twenty minutes in the book-lined smoking-room before Elliot opened the door and stuck his head in to call them back.

They sat down in the same seats that they had sat in before, and waited until Elliot checked the words on a sheet of paper. He looked up briskly.

'Well, gentlemen, you came to us for advice, and Mr Speaker and I have discussed the information you put before us. Neither of us is inclined to approve the action taken to initiate this investigation. You chose the wrong office-holders if it was approval that you sought. However, we have borne in mind that you have revealed a state of affairs that many would consider to have justified your initiative. And we both have no doubt that with this information you could have approached others in the administration, or in the House, who would have been enthusiastic about your efforts. Nevertheless, you came to us and you must have known that we were not likely to feel that the end justified the means.

'I have already put telephone calls through to the Senate Chairmen of both parties. I have asked them to come here urgently but they have not been apprised of any of the subject matter.

'Subject to what they may say, this ad hoc committee will instruct you to take immediate steps to crystallize this matter forthwith, but staying short of both Powell and Dempsey.'

Morton Harper's face was quite impassive, there was no sign of relief or pleasure.

'Would you like us to wait outside, sir?'

Before Elliot could reply, and as if he had not heard the question, Sam Bethel leaned across the table towards Harper.

'Tell me, Harper, have your people done any evaluation of how the Soviets hoped to influence the new President?'

'No, sir, but the President-Elect's statement last night that hinted at withdrawing American troops from Europe is indication enough.'

'But he has to convince Congress and the Senate before he can do a damn thing.'

Harper shrugged. 'There would be people enough in both places who would go along with cutting the defence budget, *and* removing troops from NATO if that's what a cut meant. He's been hinting about trade pacts with the Soviets. There will be many who will see this as good sense. You will have seen the report on potential trade with the Soviets from the State Department.'

'You're going to get trouble from the Republican Chairman on this. He'll see this as entirely political.'

Harper folded his hands carefully as he looked at Bethel.

'I'm going to get trouble from everybody, Mr Speaker. I'm the bearer of bad news, and in Ancient Greece they killed the man who brought the bad news. Some of them are going to wish they could do that now.'

Elliot interrupted. 'Would it help you if I broached the subject, Morton, and you filled in the details?'

'Yes, sir. But that could be construed as indicating your approval of what we had done so far.'

'So be it.'

'It would help, sir, immensely. Then we could give more time to where we go from here, rather than kicking around the emotional aspects.'

Salvasan, the Republican Party Chairman, was a tall thin Texan from Austin, whose business success had been built on ancillary equipment for radio and TV stations and then a chain of motels. He had been a diligent committee man, and chairman of the Securities and Exchange Commission. He had done much to improve the party image after the débâcle of the late seventies and had led the party through the mine-fields of a Democratic administration that had had the country behind it. He was an ardent advocate of what had been christened 'the art of the possible'.

O'Connor was from Boston and had survived that battleground with honours, and had been rewarded with the Democratic chairmanship after holding together the Los Angeles convention when it was in dire danger of splitting three ways as it breathed deep of success. He was still red-haired and freckle-faced, and had got his limp in Korea.

They stood waiting for their drinks to be poured, and Harper wondered what instinct made them both stand at the other side of the table. They sat down at Elliot's suggestion. When they were settled the Chief Justice looked in turn at the two newcomers.

'Gentlemen, I have some bad news, shocking news. When I have finished, Morton Harper will give you the facts in detail. Mr Speaker and I have had time to absorb the shock, and I want to ask if you could assist us in our thinking. Time is of the essence, and there is much to be done.'

Elliot paused as if he awaited some response. When none was forthcoming he went on:

'Almost by accident the CIA discovered an indication that we may have a problem. Force of circumstances decreed that they pursued the matter, and their worst fears were virtually confirmed. Gentlemen, it looks as if the President-Elect is not his own man. There is evidence that for years, in fact ever since he entered politics, he was assisted by Communists and others in this country acting on instructions from Moscow.' He held up his hand as O'Connor opened his mouth to speak. 'Let Harper outline the facts first, gentlemen.' He nodded to Harper. 'The facts, Mr Director.'

Morton Harper had outlined the facts enough times to present them now coherently, with a summary that brought the salient points together.

Looking at the two party chairmen, Harper was expecting a tirade from Salvasan. The tall Texan sat with raised eyebrows, relaxed in his chair as he looked at Harper.

'Who ordered you to carry out this investigation in the first place?'

'Nobody, Mr Chairman. The initial facts were brought to my attention. I felt that least damage would be done if our concern was treated as unconfirmed and purely internal.'

Salvasan grinned cynically, 'You're shitting me, Harper. Who gave you the tip off?'

'It came from London through Mr MacKay.' He nodded in MacKay's direction, but the Texan was watching Harper's face.

'Is that a fact. Who else knows about all this?'

'Nobody outside this room.'

'And what do you want from O'Connor and me?'

Elliot leaned forward. 'Harper and his people need to go further. We felt you should know.'

O'Connor smiled, and shook his head. 'Not me, Elliot. I'm not pulling your chestnuts out of the fire for you.'

Elliot had on his Chief Justice's face, solemn and intent.

'Jimmy. This isn't politics. It's a constitutional issue. We are back in the impeachment game again. Just think what it's going to mean. The country is going to be in trauma for decades unless we handle this carefully.'

Salvasan sighed audibly and theatrically. 'Judge, I propose that we consider ourselves a committee to see this thing through. You will expect me to raise hell because you're investigating our man. For us, we learned our lessons the hard way in '75 and '76. We shall not go down that road again, I assure you. I have no authority to speak for the party, and there is obviously no question of me discussing this with my colleagues, for reasons of security. However, I pledge my support to the investigation being pursued. If it leaks, I shall use all my influence to keep the furore under control on my side of Capitol Hill.'

O'Connor's face showed his annoyance. 'But, Tex. This guy's the best thing that's ever come down the pike for your people. They'll go berserk.'

Salvasan shrugged and turned to look at O'Connor. 'And if he is involved with the Commies it's gonna come out sooner or later. It'll do the country, and the party, more damage if it's later.' He turned to Harper. 'How long are you gonna need, Harper?'

'Two, maybe three weeks.'

Salvasan looked at Elliot. 'Can you freshen up on the impeachment procedures in case it's necessary? We shall only have ten days or a week before the inauguration.'

Elliot looked grim. 'There's no need to refresh on that, Tex. There are a dozen experts from the Committee of '75 still in the House.'

O'Connor said, 'What do you want me to do?'

Elliot frowned. 'We want you to go along with us.'

'No way, Judge. A trouble shared is a trouble doubled in my book. It's all yours.' He stood up and said, 'I'll wait outside in the car, Tex. I'll need a lift back into town.'

Salvasan stood up. 'My position's clear, gentlemen. You pursue this matter with my agreement.'

Elliot looked with his sharp eyes at Salvasan.

'Tex, I want you to keep O'Connor under control. He'll see this as a divine miracle for his people.'

Salvasan smiled. 'I doubt it, Judge. They've got too many wounds to lick of their own. But I'll lean on him just to be sure.'

Harper looked at his watch in the light from the car's headlights.

'It's a quarter past one. I couldn't face another bloody office. Let's go to that dump on 9th Street. Gino's or whatever they're calling it this week.'

They all piled into one car and were silent with their thoughts until the car pulled up at the neon sign that still said 'Gino's'.

The pianist was playing 'September Song' as they settled at an alcove table and ordered drinks.

Morton Harper's face looked as drawn as a face with treble chins can look.

'Well, what did you think of that lot?'

Nolan answered. 'I was surprised that Elliot was prepared to put his head on the block with us.'

'What else surprised you?'

'Salvasan. I thought he'd raise real hell.'

'Yes, that surprised me, too. I've been trying to work out the catch but I haven't got it yet, if there is one. Elliot, of course, was first-class. In fact Sam Bethel wasn't bad once he'd got over the shock. What do you want to do now, Nolan?'

'I want to check out a few names from Kleppe's diary and I want to interview Oakes and maybe go back to Haig. After that I shall have to spend time on Dempsey.'

Harper nodded. 'And what do we do about our friend here?' He waved towards MacKay.

'I'd like him to stay with me, sir. He's got the smell of this now, and he's less suspect with that English accent. He could be useful to me here in Washington.'

'What sort of cover?'

'Journalist, magazine writer, if you could fix that with London.'

'I'll see what I can do. Any doubts about anything, and you check with me.'

Morton Harper's eyes were closed, and when MacKay and Nolan were silent he spoke without opening his eyes.

'You know this whole thing makes me sick.' He opened his eyes and looked at them both. 'The whole bloody nation is excited that they've got a new kind of man. Somebody who isn't a lifetime professional politician. The man who's going to lead them to the American dream. By now I should be used to it all, but this . . .' and he waved his hand, disgust on his face '. . . this is really obscene. I find this more disgusting every time my mind steps back from the details.

Those bastards in Moscow planning this abuse.' He wagged a podgy hand at Nolan. 'You remember that, Nolan. Even if we can stop it and Powell's impeached, those bastards have won. The American people won't ever be able to trust the system any more, not just the politicians but the whole bloody set-up.'

Nolan nodded but said nothing, and Harper creaked his big frame upright.

'Let's go.' He turned to Nolan, his face serious. 'Whatever you want, Nolan. Let me know. Anything.'

'Right, sir.'

11

Logan Powell sat on the edge of his hotel bed, his hand still resting on the telephone. He pulled his hand away slowly and reached for the glass of whisky. She was a bitch, and he wondered what he had seen in her that led him into marriage. He had been lecturing at Yale when they first met, and they had married a year later. She had been one of his father's students and was taking one of those hotchpotch humanities courses that lead to jobs in the United Nations in New York or Geneva.

She had cooled towards him when he gave up his university job and set up the business consultancy in Hartford. And the coolness became coldness from the moment when he was nominated for the State Governorship.

He sat thinking, his drink forgotten as his mind went back to the night when the committee had nominated him as the Republican candidate. He had used the telephone in the hotel foyer and he had pressed the buttons and waited as the telephone rang and rang.

It was just after ten o'clock so she wouldn't be in bed. Finally, there had been a response.

'Hello.'

'Hi, Laura. Everything OK?'

'Yes. Mother's gone to hospital for a check-up. Dad's up here with Sammy and me.'

'I've got great news, kid. Guess what?'

'I've no idea.'

'I've got the nomination. It'll be officially confirmed and announced tomorrow night.' He waited but there was no response from the other end.

'Aren't you pleased?'

'If that's what you want.'

'Honey, at least you'll be the Governor's wife.'

'Don't be so childish, Logan. I shall just be me.'

'You don't think it's an achievement?'

Her voice had been cold, almost venomous. 'You've gone a long way, Logan Powell—down. And now you'll be right where it's all at, and your new friends can get the road contracts, the building work, and the jobs they're all hanging on for.'

'You think that's all it is?'

'Why do you think it is? Your big brown eyes or your non-existent political experience? You're kidding yourself my friend. But you'll find out.'

'You know, you said I wouldn't make it when I started up the consultancy.'

'Wrong, my dear, wrong. I didn't say you wouldn't make it. I said you shouldn't try. You should have stayed at the university when you had the offer.'

'Why, for heaven's sake, why only that?'

'Because you had something to say. Like your father had something to say.'

'But the consultancy is successful.'

'Oh for Christ's sake, Logan, you're just a kind of business call-girl . . .'

'. . . that's not true, Laura, and you know it . . . the work I . . .'

There was a click as she hung up and he crashed down the receiver in anger. 'You lousy bitch,' he had said through clenched teeth. And as he turned he had seen Dempsey at the door. He knew that he must have heard the last few minutes.

Dempsey had looked at Powell's grim face.

'No joy back at the ranch-house?'

'I guess she'll come round in time.'

Dempsey had nodded and looked away.

'Come back to my place and bed down in the spare bedroom and we'll have a drink.'

'OK.'

And he stayed at Dempsey's apartment through the week-end.

Dempsey had invited a girl down from New York and she was there when he and Dempsey had got back from the nomination meeting. He *was now the official Republican candidate, and only death or disaster could prevent him from being State Governor in a few months' time. Although he hadn't known it, that had been the beginning of the end so far as he and Laura were concerned. It didn't seem all that long ago. Jenny was younger than Laura and very beautiful, but that wasn't all the story. She could always put the Band-aid on his bruised ego, and with her he felt safe. From what, he wasn't sure.*

Like her name, Jenny Larsen was a Swedish-type blonde. A Hitchcock girl, but warm; and she had seemed either unaware or indifferent to the fact that her cleavage, as she leaned forward while they all talked, revealed most of the soft mounds of her breasts. And what had been almost as pleasurable, she was clearly impressed with his nomination and his plans.

By midnight they'd had enough whisky for him to feel warm and pleased with life. And Dempsey had said to the girl, 'Is Paula down here for the week-end?'

She had nodded. 'She said she would be. Shall I phone?'

'I'll check.' He stood up and walked to the study and closed the door.

Powell had looked through a slight haze at the big blue eyes and the soft mouth.

'Are you Andy's girl?'

She had laughed. 'No. We've seen one another a few times in New York, that's all.'

Involuntarily his eyes had gone to her breasts and when he had looked back at her face she had been smiling. She looked up as Dempsey came back into the room. He was smiling.

'Yes, she's here. I'm going over to fetch her.' He picked up his suede jacket. 'Give him a drink, Jenny, till I get back, then we'll all celebrate.'

Powell had been looking at the girl as the door clicked behind Dempsey and she had laughed softly as he moved over to sit beside her on the settee. Her mouth had responded as he kissed her and she had made no protest as his hand slid inside her cleavage to cup a full breast and lift it free of her dress. His fingers had kneaded the big mound as they kissed and only when his hand had slid back her skirt did she hold his wrist. She had looked at his face and said softly, 'Is this how you want to celebrate?' She was smiling as he nodded, and she had said, 'Let's go in the bedroom.'

'What about Andy and the other girl?'

Her hand touched his cheek. 'They'll understand. They're probably doing the same at her place.'

And this time she made no move to stop him as his hand went between her legs. For long moments she watched his face as his hand explored her and then she kissed him gently, 'Come on, let's go.'

He had scarcely noticed the bedroom in his awareness of her undressing, and then it was just a fevered vision of breasts and thighs, smooth, youthful, girl-flesh, and the sensations of being in her body.

The room had been dark when he awoke and he had reached out, moving his hand slowly to find a light. The pink light cast a glow on the white walls and across the face of the girl. He looked at his watch; it was 4.30. He looked back at the girl's face. She really was beautiful, her full lips barely meeting as she breathed deeply and regularly. For a moment he had a vision of Laura asleep in their bed at home, but it had gone as his hand reached for the sheet and gently rolled it down. Her head was on one side, the long blonde hair fanned out on the white pillow. He looked at her body. She lay on her back and the full breasts rose and fell with her steady breathing, their pale pink tips soft and innocent. Her belly was softly curved and muscled and he could see the blonde bush that covered the mound of her sex. When his hand moved on her, her eyes fluttered open and she said sleepily, 'Love me. Love me some more.' And she had lazily opened her long legs and folded her arms round him as he lay on her.

He turned and put down his glass on the bedside table and reached again for the telephone. His hand hovered over the instrument uncertainly. She could be here in three hours, and he wanted her. But he knew that Dempsey was right. An out-of-town girl, a New York girl, would be spotted in no time. And the press were watching his every move. They wouldn't print anything. He'd get his hundred days but they would start putting two and two together about him and Laura, and that would be considered legitimate news. He'd get Andy to fix the little dark girl again. She was only 18 but she was enthusiastic.

He reached for the file of 'possibles' for the London and Moscow embassies, and wondered why he still felt lonely despite all the people around him.

12

It was a bumpy flight in the Cessna and at La Guardia they were stacked for fifteen minutes while the long distance planes, short of fuel, occupied the glide path. Snow came down, a thick white curtain that was wrenched aside continuously by the gale force winds. Steiner was waiting for him at the terminal entrance.

'How'd you know I was coming up, Joe?'

'I contacted Hartford. They gave me your ETA.'

'You got a car here?'

'Sure. But let's grab a cup of coffee first.'

Nolan stood still, the snowflakes melting on his face as he stared at Steiner.

'What's going on?'

'Let's talk in the coffee-shop, chief.'

Nolan moved off, slapping the wet snow from his canvas travel bag. Until the coffee came he sat without speaking, but when the waitress left he looked at Steiner.

'OK. What is it?'

'We had to knock off one of the Russians.'

'Go on.'

'He pulled a gun on O'Hara. We checked it afterwards. The safety catch was off and there was one up the spout. O'Hara shot in self-defence.'

'Where was this?'

'In the yard at the back of Kleppe's block in Sutton Place.'

'When?'

'Just after seven this evening.'

'Which morgue is he in?'

Steiner took a deep breath. 'He's not in a morgue, Mr Nolan. I wasn't sure you would want that.'

Nolan watched the cream turning in slow circles on his coffee as he slowly stirred it.

'Where is he?'

'In the boot of my car.'

'Jesus God. Where is it?'

'Here. In the car park.'

'Have you gone over him?'

'Yes. His name is Pankov. Leonid Pankov. Based in the Soviet Consulate-General. Big fellow. Typical KGB hit man.'

'What was the weapon?'

'A standard Luger and special silencer. KGB pattern. We've been trying to get a bug on Kleppe's windows. O'Hara was checking. This guy came out of a garbage can.'

'What were you proposing to do with him?'

'Dump him.'

'Did you pay for the coffee?'

'Yes.'

'Let's go.'

Nolan was silent as they walked to the car park and as Steiner reached to turn on the ignition Nolan grabbed his hand.

'You did what was best, Joe. Is there any chance of a witness?'

'I'm pretty sure not, chief.'

'OK. Dump him. And dump him good. I don't wanna know anything about it.'

'Right, chief.'

'Take me to the Central Park safe-house.'

Nolan stopped the car at the Chase Gallery and walked the rest of the way.

He called for the evaluation file on the KGB teams at the Consulate-General, and stood reading it as he absent-mindedly eased off his wet coat. Still reading, his hand searched behind him for the chair, and he pulled it forward and sat down slowly.

He was still there when the false dawn broke over the Park.

13

When Nolan got back to the house at Hartford there was a message from Harper, instructing him to avoid any direct contact with Dempsey. As President-Elect's putative Chief-of-Staff, Harper felt that Dempsey was too important to risk any reaction from the White House at this stage. Kleppe also should not be contacted directly until further information was available from the FBI and IRS records.

Nolan telephoned police chief Henney at his headquarters but, apart from more detailed descriptions of the two suspects, there was little further information. They were checking Siwecki's tax returns for the past five years and there were several sets of fingerprints but none identifiable. Local fingerprint records and New York records had already proved negative. It looked like Oakes and Haig were Nolan's only hope for a fishing expedition.

He phoned Haig, who was obviously reluctant to see him again but when he insisted Haig agreed to see him at seven that evening, at his office.

The security guard at the factory gate phoned through to Haig's office and then he was escorted across the yard past the stores to the main office block. There was frost sparkling in the lights from the big workshop windows, and a general air of busyness. Haig Electronics were obviously doing well.

Haig called out for him to come in when the security man knocked at the door, and Nolan noticed that Haig's desk was clear of all papers as he lifted himself grudgingly from his chair to take Nolan's outstretched hand.

'What can I do for you this time, Mr Nolan?'

'Well, much the same as before, Mr Haig. I want to talk about that strike.'

Haig looked across at Nolan.

'Are you some stooge from the Democrats?'

'Why should I be that, Mr Haig?'

'You obviously want to find out something to the President's disadvantage.'

'The President-Elect, Mr Haig.'

'OK. The President-Elect.'

'I'm not a Democrat, Mr Haig. I'm not political. And all I want are the facts. And maybe we should widen this chat a little.'

'By all means.'

'Mr Haig. I know that the strike was phoney. I know that it was contrived to help Powell's bid for nomination as Governor of this State. That doesn't necessarily mean that you were part of this set-up.'

'You say you know. D'you mean you guess?'

'Not at all. One of the principal parties to the affair has told me. Told me also what he was paid to go along with it. And told me also who paid him. We are checking on bank records and tax returns right now.'

'Why don't you go ahead with whatever you intend on that evidence, Mr Nolan?'

'I think you know why I can't do that, Mr Haig. Or you can have a damn good guess.'

'Siwecki being killed, you mean?'

'Yes.'

Haig pushed his chair back so that he was parallel to his desk, still looking at Nolan.

'I swear I didn't know at the time, Nolan. It was two weeks before I knew.'

'How did you find out?'

'I got a confidential phone call from the vice-president of production at one of our car customers. They were one of the complainants about our sub-assemblies and Powell had called down one of their inspectors. He had reported back to his management.'

'What did he tell them?'

'That the circuit boards had been deliberately damaged before they left here by scoring them with a sharp instrument.'

'What did you do?'

'I got Siwecki in and talked to him about it.'

'What did he say?'

'He denied it, and when I pursued it he threatened another strike.'

'And you concluded that Powell had contrived the strike?'

'No, I didn't. I don't think Powell knew any more about it than I did. He may have uncovered it when he was arbitrating, but even then he may have decided it was better to get the strike over. And he may have been right at that.'

'Who do you think could have contrived it?'

'It beats me, Nolan. I've thought about it a hundred times but it doesn't make sense. Take Siwecki. He's a Commie so he'd have no interest in helping Powell—a Republican. It couldn't possibly be Powell, he couldn't have influenced our work force in a thousand years. But let's say he did. He couldn't possibly have known we and the union would ask him to arbitrate. It was just chance that he was chosen.'

'How *did* he get chosen?'

'The board and I were thinking of going to a New York consultancy and we also considered using somebody from the Department of Labour. Then on the same day two people suggested Powell. The first was Siwecki and the second was Jim Oakes, who was the company's legal adviser. He's the new Senator.'

'And that's how Powell was chosen?'

'Yes. Pure coincidence.'

'Which of your customers tipped you off?'

'General Motors.'

'That's where the inspector came from who was called in by Powell?'

'Yep.'

'As I understand it your people went on strike because they lost substantial bonuses because of sub-assemblies manufactured here that were rejected by your Detroit customers.'

'That's it.'

'And in fact, the sub-assemblies had been deliberately damaged before they left these premises.'

'Correct.'

'And Powell was made aware of this during his investigation and arbitration because one of your customers showed him a sabotaged sub-assembly.'

'Yes.'

'So Powell knew, and so did Siwecki.'

'I don't know that Siwecki knew.'

'I'm telling you, Mr Haig. He told me he knew. The sabotage was deliberate. The strike was contrived so that Powell could be made into the local hero by settling it.'

'Why should Siwecki, a union man, help a Republican?'

'Money, orders, who knows, Haig.'

Haig looked uneasy.

'Are you suggesting that I gave such orders?'

'I'm suggesting that at some stage you knew what was going on or had gone on. The very least you did was to cover up a criminal conspiracy.'

'Why should I go along with something that damaged my company?'

'You sold a substantial holding of your shares the week before the strike, Mr Haig. And more after the strike was over. Why was that?'

'I needed the money for other purposes.'

Haig's eyes looked down at his desk to avoid Nolan's stare.

'Your bank account shows a pretty healthy balance over that period, Mr Haig.'

The older man's head came up quickly and for the first time since they had talked Haig looked scared.

'You must have had a Federal warrant to get that information, Mr Nolan.'

'I have.'

Haig shifted in his chair to face Nolan.

'What the hell are you after? What is it you want to know?'

'Everything.'

'Are you charging me with some offence?'

'Not yet.'

'Right. So get the hell out of my plant.'

Nolan stood up. Haig was frightened now and one more small pressure would be enough to make him crack. But there was no point in giving any clue as to what they were investigating. The first arrests would have to be the top people.

Back at the house Nolan read through the radio reports from New York. Kleppe had only left his apartment for local shopping but they had noted two public phone boxes that he seemed to use regularly. Arrangements had been made to bug them during the night.

There were reports of three men who also could be watching the apartment. Photographs had been taken and sent to Central Records for possible identification. If they were watching it was considered that they might be professionals, as they were doing it so well.

Attempts were being made to use a window bug on Kleppe's apartment but so far they had been unsuccessful. Was Nolan prepared to authorize an application for a full-scale tapping at the telephone exchange? He initialled the sheet with a negative.

MacKay came in as he signed the last sheet. Nolan spoke while he manoeuvred a refill into his ball-point.

'Get out a pad, James, and let's have a look at what we've got.'

They took a break for a meal but it was three hours later when the list was complete.

Operation 66
Established material at 1 December. Items asterisked considered strong enough for court.

Kleppe
* 1. Entered US on false documents.
* 2. Speaks Russian.
* 3. Has influence with Russians in Paris.
* 4. Illegal diamond transactions.

* 5. Has latest KGB transceiver.
* 6. Almost certainly Soviet citizen and KGB operator.
* 7. Has lent or given large sums of money to wide group of influential people at all levels.
* 8. Known associate of Dempsey.
* 9. Known associate of girl at 38th Street apartment.
* 10. Has visited Moscow in last two years.
* 11. Has connections with Oakes.
* 12. Used Soviet influence to release Dempsey and girl from Paris jail.

Dempsey
* 1. Was member of CP in 1968.
* 2. Had Soviet girlfriend, also Party member.
* 3. Known associate of girl at 38th St.
* 4. Paid Siwecki for strike.
* 5. Gave orders to Siwecki who was CP member.
* 6. Known associate of Kleppe.
* 7. Has received large sums of money over long period from Kleppe. Possibly for onward distribution.
* 8. Obligated to Kleppe for release from jail.

Powell
* 1. Known associate of Dempsey.
* 2. Knew strike was 'fixed'.
* 3. Was least likely nominee as Republican candidate for governorship of Connecticut.
* 4. Has indicated policies, since election, favourable to Soviets.

Nolan looked unhappy as he read down the final list.

'You know what's wrong with this, James?'

'Tell me.'

'We could arrest Kleppe right now. And have him deported. We could prove that Dempsey fixed the strike at the Haig plant and that that helped Powell. And we could prove that he is an associate of Kleppe. But that's all. And throwing out Kleppe wouldn't do a damn thing. They would have been warned and Kleppe's replacement would have to be more careful. That's all we could do.'

'All we need is to link Dempsey with Kleppe. His link with Powell is public.'

'That wouldn't prove that Powell knew what they were doing.'

'But it could invalidate the election if it was proved that the result was achieved by criminal conspiracy.'

'Maybe. I'm not sure what the ground rules are. But that would be a last resort.'

'Let's try and establish what the ideal solution would be.'

'You mean assuming that Powell is part of some conspiracy?'

'Yes. Let us assume that we can prove Dempsey and Kleppe were working under Soviet orders to get Powell in the White House. What would we want to happen?'

'It depends on whether Powell was part of the conspiracy. Did he know, or was he in total ignorance of what was going on?'

'Let us assume that it is neither extreme. He wasn't in total ignorance but Dempsey and his backers had never told him what was going on.'

'He'd have to be out of his mind not to notice that something was odd.'

'Or maybe just blinded by ambition?'

Nolan looked towards the window as he absorbed the facts. Finally he looked back at MacKay.

'We'll have to assume that he wasn't fully in the picture but he was aware that something was going on. And that's too indefinite a condition for us to prove. A court or a committee could easily come to that conclusion after hearing all the evidence, but that's all.'

'So they hit Kleppe and Dempsey, but Powell carries on.'

'Congress would turn their backs on him. He would be a cypher, and the whole country would be in turmoil for four years. God knows what the rest of the world would think. It would be an impossible situation.'

'So we've got to do two separate things. We've got to prove that there's a Soviet plot that got Powell into the White House and that it was organized by Kleppe and Dempsey. And when we've proved that, Powell has to be pressured out on fear of exposure.'

Nolan groaned. 'That's it, friend. It sounds so short and simple, but it ain't.'

'May I make a suggestion?'

Nolan grinned. 'Sure.'

'How about I look into Powell's background while you're dealing with Dempsey?'

'OK, but just desk research, no personal contacts.'

14

The house facing Gramercy Park had been built in 1846 to the design of Alexander Jackson Davis and only the ornate railings and balconies could be accused of being Gothic. But it was not its outward appearance that impressed Jim Oakes. It was the cool, calm interior, and the man who seemed to have all the time in the world before he got down to why he had called him there. He was a handsome man, sun-tanned, with a large head and features that could have graced a Roman coin. White hair, almost crew-cut, and eyes that looked as if they could extract the truth without effort. His shirt was a dazzling white and although he was noticeably still, when he moved his hands Oakes noticed the sparkle of diamonds in the gold cuff-links. And when he spoke, the questions were short, but so precise that they admitted no answer but the truth.

This was Oakes's seventh visit in the last ten months, and he was flattered at the courtesy he was always shown. Pieter de Jong's family had been around when New York was New Amsterdam and he wore his role as Republican Party Vice-Chairman with an air of it honouring the party more than the man.

De Jong poured the drinks himself, and when he sat back in the white garden chair he raised his glass.

'Your good health, Mr Oakes.'

'And yours, Mr de Jong.'

'And how is our friend finding Washington?'

'I haven't seen him since the election but I hear that he's working hard with his take-over teams.'

'Seems to be charming the press and the public.'

'I guess that's not too difficult at this stage.'

De Jong laughed softly.

'Have you had any contact with Markham?'

'We've met a couple of times. I guess Vice-Presidents-Elect are not so hard pressed as their masters.'

De Jong leaned forward and put down his glass. He reached over and pressed a bell on the wall.

'You'll lunch with me?'

Oakes recognized immediately that it was a command rather than a question.

A manservant served the simple but superb meal, and de Jong talked about the New York party organization and the set-up in Washington. It was when they were sitting with their coffees that Oakes sensed that the mealtime talk had been time-filling and that they were now back to business.

'And what are they saying, Mr Oakes? Now they've heard his plans?'

'Difficult to assess, Mr de Jong. There's no doubt that the public like it, but on the Hill there's discontent.'

'From whom?'

'From our side mainly. They don't like the defence cuts. They don't like the playing footsie with Moscow bit.'

'So why don't they say so?'

Oakes shrugged. 'Who is going to talk against billions of dollars of trade, or bringing American boys back home? You might just as well talk bad about mothers. The polls show ridiculous figures like 75 per cent for Powell.'

'Have you had any more dealings with Dempsey?'

'A couple of phone calls. Just routine stuff.'

'And Kleppe?'

Oakes shook his head. 'No. Since you gave me the loan to pay off my indebtedness he's not been in touch.'

'And how's business?'

'Very good, Mr de Jong. I've brought a cheque with me.'

'I think I could help you there. I'll talk to you about an arrangement, a new arrangement, in about two weeks' time.'

'It's not a problem now.'

'I'm glad to hear that. But you just hold your horses, my friend. Has there been any development on the murder investigation?'

'Henney tells me that they're working in the dark. Seems like the Treasury is involved some way. He says it was definitely a professional job.'

'You mean a Mafia job?'

'No. I got the impression he meant foreigners.'

'Who's the Treasury man on this job?'

'Henney wouldn't say. He's been warned off about talking.'

'You know that old man Haig had a man visit him? Said he was investigating a union problem.'

'No, he didn't mention it to me.'

'A fellow named Nolan. Said he was from Washington. I've got a feeling he might contact you.'

Oakes looked surprised. 'Why me?'

'Who knows? But if he does, I suggest you hold him off until you've had a word with me.'

'I'll do that. But why me?'

'You're a stockholder in Haig Electronics.'

'So?'

De Jong shifted in his chair and half-smiled.

'Maybe about the strike they had way back.'

Oakes's watery eyes noted the smile.

'You knew about that?'

'Not at the time. But I know now.'

'It's covered in every possible way. They'd never break it open.'

'It only wants one man to talk, Mr Oakes.'

'Well, I can assure you it won't be me.'

De Jong smiled, stood up carefully and held out his hand.

'Keep in touch, Mr Oakes. Keep in touch.'

Kleppe's tongue explored his lower lip slowly and reflectively as Dempsey waited for his comment. Finally Kleppe spoke.

'I think it's best you don't tell him right now.'

'I've done everything except say the words.'

'And he still doesn't see you as part of the control group?'

'No. I'm just a go-between. A fixer. The guy who waves the magic wand. The carrier of messages.'

'Maybe it's better that way.'

'I don't think so, Viktor. Or I'll have to argue every point to the bitter end.'

'What do you think his reaction will be when he really gets the point?'

'I'm not sure he'll be able to bring himself to believe it. He's really beginning to think he made it on his own. A bit of assistance here and there. It's understandable in a way. He's had the support of people that even I wouldn't have expected to pitch in for him.'

'Like who?'

'Hard line Republicans like Pardoe in LA, de Jong in New York, the Lowry gang in Chicago. I'd have thought they would hate everything he proposes to do. They want the old system, where everybody delivers votes and gets their rewards in the usual way.'

'Moscow's analysis was that those boys would go along with a nice mix of isolationism and an extended market in the East.'

'Sure they will, but they still want the building contracts, the Federal hand-outs and the rest of the Washington fruit-salad. In the beginning they were trying to put the skids under him and suddenly they find he's the guy in the white hat.'

'Why do you think it's so urgent to establish the situation with Powell right now?'

'He's sorting out new appointments, and a couple of weeks from now I'm going to be one of a crowd. I'll have direct access but I shall not get much of his time.'

Kleppe nodded. 'You're right, but I think we don't have a confrontation. He's doing what we want, and that's what matters. If you have to wrestle him a bit, then do it.'

Kleppe's red telephone rang half an hour after Dempsey had left.

'Yes.'

'Shoot if you must this old grey head.'

The voice paused, and Kleppe replied slowly.

'But spare your country's flag instead.'

'There's somebody followed your friend since he left you.'

'Where'd they start?'

133

'Right at your place.'

'Why didn't you phone before?'

'Because I don't know who he is, and your friend's only just stopped moving.'

'Where are you now?'

'In a public box near the girl's place on 38th.'

'Where's the tail?'

'Walking up and down. I think he's got a radio.'

'I'll phone my friend, you just follow the tail and get an identification.'

'OK.'

Kleppe dialled the girl's number and she answered.

'Is Andy there?'

'Who's that speaking?'

'K.'

'Just a moment.'

There was a clatter at the other end, then Dempsey's voice.

'Andy.'

'There's a guy tailing you. Leave that place, go to the Waldorf, nice and slowly, have a drink in the downstairs bar, talk to someone, anyone, and then leave. Go to the cinema or somewhere public. Get rid of the tail and then phone me.'

'Who is he?'

'I don't know but I'm gonna find out.'

Steiner watched Dempsey talking to two men at the Carousel Bar at the Waldorf but he was sure they were not contacts. He saw Dempsey walk out of the doors on Park Avenue, stand hesitating for a few moments, then turn left and walk down to 42nd Street and through to Times Square. Steiner watched as Dempsey stood looking across at the cinema posters. He watched him cross and enter the foyer of the cinema and followed after Dempsey, who bought a ticket and walked through the swing doors. Steiner bought a ticket and as he went through the doors Dempsey came back through the other set of doors and walked briskly across the street and along to a cluster of phone booths by Bryant Park. He telephoned Kleppe and then took a cab to the garage to pick up his car. Neither Steiner nor Dempsey noticed the man who had followed them both.

Kleppe's man phoned him just before midnight and gave him the name and room number of Steiner's hotel. He was registered as Josef Steiner and the room had been booked for two weeks by the CIA office in Washington with an address on Pennsylvania Avenue a couple of blocks from the White House.

Nolan got up early and by six o'clock he had trotted in his blue track-suit round the lawns in front of the house, breakfasted, and was sitting at his trestle table reading through Steiner's reports. He telephoned Harper's Secretariat for the IRS information on Kleppe, and New York for further information on the apartment block on 38th. His man carrying out surveillance at Dempsey's Hartford apartment radioed in that Dempsey had arrived back from New York at 3am and had gone straight to his apartment. Oakes had agreed to see Nolan at his office at noon.

Looking down the list of company names on the board in the reception area, Nolan saw that there was still a panel saying 'Logan Powell & Associates, Business Consultants'. The address was the floor below Oakes's law firm.

Nolan sat in the lawyer's reception room. It was pleasantly old-fashioned, and on the wall was the original artwork of a Norman Rockwell *Saturday Evening Post* front cover in a plain white frame. Nolan recognized Powell and Dempsey in a group photograph showing Oakes receiving some sort of certificate.

In a cluster of black frames were photographs of Oakes on a tennis court partnering a blonde woman, Oakes in a USAAF officer's uniform, and Oakes in the company of various important-looking men whom Nolan could not identify.

A middle-aged secretary came out of the far door and invited him to enter, with a smile and a lift of her eyebrows.

Oakes stood behind his desk and waved Nolan to a chair. He was in his late fifties, a lightly-built man with a ruddy complexion and

135

very pale-blue eyes. The tweed suit he wore fitted his body loosely, and he hitched up his trousers as he sat down.

'What can I do for you, Mr Nolting?'

There was something in Oakes's look that made Nolan certain that his name had been deliberately mispronounced. He wondered why Oakes should be playing games before he knew what it was all about.

'I thought you might be able to help me, Mr Oakes. I'm making some inquiries about the strike a few years back at Haig Electronics.'

Oakes fiddled with a pipe and an old-fashioned tobacco pouch. Without looking up he said, 'In what way can I help you?'

'You were Haig's legal adviser at the time.'

'Still am.'

'I've had a chat with Mr Haig himself. He didn't mention that to you?'

'No.' Oakes looked up and the washed-out eyes were alert, like a bird of prey's. 'Any reason why he should?'

Nolan was used to tougher adversaries than Oakes and he ignored the question and the challenge.

'Looking through the stockholder's register I noticed that you bought stock in the company yourself about a week before the strike. Why was that?'

Oakes smiled. 'It sometimes pays to show faith in important clients' enterprises.'

'But why at that particular time?'

Oakes shrugged. 'Why not?'

'Because you had been their legal adviser for eleven years without holding any stock. Why was it suddenly so important?'

'There was no particular reason. I had some cash to invest. I chose to invest it in Haig Electronics.'

'Not true, Mr Oakes. Your bank statements at that period show that you had an overdraft facility of twenty thousand dollars fully utilized. Your tax return for that period showed a net income for that year of fourteen thousand dollars gross. You bought seventy-five-thousand dollars worth of stock. Where did the money come from?'

'Let's say it was from gambling, Mr Nolan?'

Nolan raised his eyebrows. 'You want that to go on the record, Mr Oakes?'

'What record would that be?'

Nolan sat silently for a few moments and then spoke quite softly. 'The record of a conspiracy to distort the due process of an election.'

'And what election would that be?'

'The election for State Governor of Connecticut when Logan Powell became Governor.'

Oakes leaned back in his chair, no longer smiling.

'Maybe I should inform you, Mr Nolan, that I have been elected Senator for this State, and as such . . .'

His eyes were angry as Nolan cut off his flow.

'I am aware of the election results, Mr Oakes, but you will remember, I am sure, Article 20 Section i. You are not Senator for this State until the third of January.'

Oakes's fist came down on the desk-top and the telephone tinkled from the vibration. Saliva bubbled on his thin lips as he shouted, 'Are you threatening me, Mr Nolan?'

'In no way. I am asking for your help as an individual, as a lawyer, and someone deeply concerned with the Constitution, to make a report on what seems to be a serious matter.'

With the bluff of his anger called, Oakes leaned forward. His face was relaxed, and his mouth was attempting a smile.

'You tell me you are investigating a strike that *might*, and I repeat *might*, have *influenced*, not decided, a comparatively unimportant election some years ago. Is this perhaps getting out of proportion, Mr Nolan?'

He leaned back as if he were in court. He was resting his case. His mouth twisted in the near grimace of victory.

'It got out of proportion when three people were murdered for what they knew about it.'

Oakes's mouth fell open, his surprise and shock obviously genuine. 'Who has been murdered?'

'Mr and Mrs Siwecki and Maria Angelo.'

'But surely they were nothing to do with this.'

137

'Siwecki was the union negotiator and Maria Angelo had background information. That is why they were killed.'

'But who in God's name would *do* that?'

'You have no idea yourself, Mr Oakes?'

He shook his head in bewilderment.

'A union quarrel. That's what I put it down to.'

'And the girl? Miss Angelo?'

Oakes looked disturbed and shifty.

'I thought perhaps that was a crime of passion.'

'Why did you think that?'

'I gathered there were some flowers sent. A bunch of roses.'

'I sent her the roses, Mr Oakes.'

'Oh. I see. I didn't mean . . . er . . .'

'To say "thank you" for helping me with my inquiry.'

Oakes was silent, his face turned towards the window, his hands fiddling with the pipe and the tobacco pouch. Nolan sat quietly, watching him. He knew from experience that Oakes was very near to talking and he prayed that nobody would disturb them and that no call came on the telephone.

Finally, Oakes turned to face Nolan.

'I'd like to speak to a colleague of mine. I shan't be long. Maybe I *can* help you.'

He stumbled as he stood up, and his steps as he walked to the door were uncertain.

The secretary brought Nolan coffee and stayed talking. He guessed that it was to prevent him listening to the voice in the outer office. It was fifteen minutes before Oakes came back into the office. He looked uneasy but calmer. The secretary left as Oakes settled himself behind his desk. He put his hands palm down on the desk. People under interrogation often did that when they were going to confess. He looked up at Nolan.

'I've had a word with a colleague of mine in New York, Mr Nolan. I needed his agreement. Am I right in thinking that you want to establish if that strike was deliberately contrived to give Powell the nomination?'

'Yes. If that is the truth.'

'Are we just talking or does my statement become evidence?'

'That could be necessary. But your co-operation would be seen as mitigating.'

'You're asking me to face criminal proceedings, be debarred from practising law and to cease being Senator. That is asking a lot, Mr Nolan.'

Nolan sighed. 'Tell me what you know, Mr Oakes, off the record. If it is what I think it is, I shall eventually want a written statement—signed and witnessed. But before it would be used I should ask the Chief Justice to speak to you and give you certain assurances.'

Oakes looked amazed. 'You mean Elliot?'

'Yes.'

'My God.'

'Who gave you the money to buy Haig stock?'

'Andrew Dempsey. He was Powell's campaign manager.'

'Why was it necessary to buy stock?'

'So that I could pressure Haig to appoint Powell as arbitrator. In the event it wasn't necessary. He agreed straight away.'

'Did Dempsey say why he wanted Powell nominated or elected?'

Oakes shrugged. 'Just that they were old friends and he wanted Powell to win.'

'Did you know that Siwecki had been fixed, too?'

'Yes. Dempsey and I had a meeting with him. I paid the money to him and the union. And I paid him monthly until his death.'

'Why did you go along with this?'

'They promised me business and cash. I needed it badly at the time.'

'What about the payments to you from Gramercy Realtors and the Halpern Trust?'

Oakes's face went white, and his hand trembled as he put down his pipe.

'Those payments were nothing to do with the strike business. I assure you of that.'

Nolan sighed. 'I need to know, Mr Oakes. I need to eliminate that matter from my investigation.'

'And it won't be used?'

'Not if it isn't relative.'

'Have you heard of Mr de Jong?'

'I'm afraid not.'

'He's Vice-Chairman of the Republican Party.'

'National Vice-Chairman?'

'Yes.'

'Go on.'

'He owns those companies and the payments were made to me to keep him in the picture about Dempsey and Powell.'

'What kind of things do you report to him?'

'Anything and everything.'

'Was he a Powell supporter?'

'Not in the early days.'

'When did he become a supporter?'

'At the Convention.'

'Did you tell him about the strike business?'

'Yes.'

'What was his reaction?'

'That was when the payments started. But he's not a man who shows his reaction. Not to me, anyway.'

'Was it de Jong who you telephoned just now?'

'Yes.'

'You asked him if you should answer my questions?'

'Yes.'

'What did he say?'

'He said that I should co-operate with you.'

'Apart from the de Jong payments, will you make the statement and sign it?'

Oakes nodded. 'Yes.'

The secretary was brought in to take down Oakes's statement and when she had typed it she came back in to witness Oakes's signature. After she had gone Nolan folded the document and put it in his pocket.

'Are you married, Mr Oakes?'

'We don't live together, but we're still married.'

'Would you be prepared to take a holiday?'

Oakes looked surprised.

'I don't understand.'

'I could arrange for you to have a secure place in Florida. Otherwise I shall arrange police protection for you here and at your home. They'll be in plain clothes.'

'You mean somebody could . . .'

He couldn't bring himself to finish the sentence, and Nolan stepped in.

'It's possible.'

'I think I'd better stay.'

'Fine. May I use your telephone?'

'Of course.'

Nolan telephoned the house and arranged the guard detail, and then waited in Oakes's outer office until the first man came and took over.

Nolan was making notes in his office at the house when the call came through from New York. As he heard the garbled speech he pressed the scrambler button.

'Nolan.'

'Did you hear what I said, sir?'

'No. Is that Joe?'

'No, sir, it's Steve Langfeld. I've got bad news, sir.'

'Go on, then.' Nolan was aware of the hesitation in his own voice.

'Joe Steiner's dead, sir. He was shot in his hotel bedroom.'

'When?'

'About an hour ago.'

'Were the police called in?'

'No. Not so far. But the hotel manager is very jittery. I hoped you'd speak to him. I've put two men there.'

'Any indications?'

'The shell's 9mm, and a caller ten minutes earlier has been identified by the reception clerk. It was one of our friends.'

'Give me the manager's number. I'll phone him, and I'll leave straight away. I'll be at La Guardia in about seventy minutes. Send a car for me.'

The manager accepted Nolan's request without argument. The assurance that there would be no mention of the affair in the press tipped the balance.

Joe Steiner had one living relative, a brother. He lived in Paterson and was a sports goods dealer. Nolan drove through the night and arrived at three am. The local police had been asked to alert the brother. Minimum details to be given. He wanted, if possible, no publicity about Steiner's death.

A man in a red tartan shirt stood in the lighted doorway as Nolan crunched in the snow from the garden gate.

'Pete Steiner?'

'That's me.'

'Could I come in for a moment?'

The big man shrugged and walked into the hallway and through to the living-room as Nolan followed.

'Mr Steiner, I've got some bad news, I'm afraid.'

'About Joe, huh?'

'Yes. He's dead. He was shot.'

'So why tell me?'

'You're down on his papers as next of kin.'

'Joe and I ain't spoke a word together in ten years. We didn't get on.'

'I see. You know how he was employed?'

'Some gov'ment agency in Washington, he said.'

Nolan suddenly felt tired and cold. The man's indifference was unexpected. He had come out with his arguments carefully marshalled. But Joe Steiner's only living relative didn't care that he was dead. Nolan suddenly needed to leave, but he had to go through the routine.

'Have you any objection to Joe being buried in the cemetery at Arlington?'

'Don't make any difference to me, mister, where he's buried. Was there any effects?'

Nolan could feel the blood rush to his head, and he breathed deeply before he answered.

'A few, Mr Steiner. We'll send them to you in the next few days.'

The man folded his arms.

'Better leave it a coupla weeks. I'm going for a week's fishin' from Sunday.'

'Well do that, Mr Steiner. Goodnight.'

'OK. You wanna cawfee or sump'n?'

'No thanks. I'll get on my way.'

Nolan stopped the car a hundred yards from the house. He sat with his face in his hands and saw the hotel bedroom. Joe Steiner had gone to the door of his room wearing just trousers and shoes, his face half shaved, half lathered. The hole in his big white chest was neat and round and there had been no blood. Just a bruise round the small indentation. The blood had come from the hole in his throat where the flexible tube of his windpipe had been ripped open. His shoulder holster was draped over the cold tap, and his small two-way radio was on the bedside table. And the doctor had had to stitch Joe's eyelids to keep them closed.

As the winter wind howled round the car there was just the noise of the fan and Nolan's tears.

15

Nolan slept until ten at the safe-house. He stood at the window of his room and looked out at Central Park. The snow was thick on the sidewalks and there was a golden slush like brown sugar on the street. The sky was leaden, and the cars and trucks still had their lights on.

He breakfasted slowly, reading the night's reports and half listening to the radio news bulletin.

The Dow-Jones had gone up on a White House rumour that there would be a $6 billion public works programme. But in specific areas like aircraft and electronics share prices had fallen sharply in expectation of defence budget cuts. Some commentators were forecasting that the cuts would be more like wounds. A warehouse fire near Flatbush Avenue was not yet under control but it was reckoned that the American ski team on its way to Val d'Isère had never been stronger. The Vice-President-Elect was expected to make a trip to European capitals immediately after the inauguration.

When he had finished eating he called for the tapes of the tap on the girl's telephone and laced them up on the Revox. There was very little traffic except for the appointments made with her from a series of spurious calls by Nolan's men to ensure that there was no interruption in the operation.

At four o'clock he pressed the elevator button for the top floor of the apartment block on 38th, and a few seconds later he was outside the door of P4.

He pressed the bell and waited. The girl who opened the door was breathtakingly beautiful, even more beautiful than in the photographs taken by the surveillance team. She was wearing an emerald-green towelling bath-robe that clashed vibrantly with her startlingly blue eyes.

'Yes?'

'Miss Jennifer Larsen?'

'It's appointments only.' And the door swung to. Nolan's foot prevented it from closing.

'My name is Nolan, I'm from NYPD. I'd like to talk to you.'

He saw her hesitate, and he thrust forward an NYPD identity card and badge. She leaned forward to check the photograph and then looked up at his face.

'What do you want to talk about?'

'I think it would be better if you allowed me to come inside.'

Slowly she opened the door and stood aside as he walked in. He smiled.

'My apologies for the wet, but it's still snowing.'

She shrugged. 'Take your coat off. Hang it in the closet.'

When he walked back into the living-room the girl was sitting on a large settee, her legs curled under her, and a drink in her hand.

'Help yourself,' she said, and gestured with her glass to the whisky bottle and glasses.

'I'm hoping that you can help us, Miss Larsen.'

'Jenny. Just call me Jenny. What's it all about?'

'Do you know a Mr Dempsey? Andrew Dempsey?'

She reached for a pack of cigarettes, took one out and lit it with a match. When there was a cloud of smoke between them she spoke.

'No.'

'Do you know your rights, Jenny?'

'Jesus, am I supposed to know every guy who comes here?'

The blue eyes were angry and defiant.

'I'll have to ask you to get dressed, Jenny, and come with me.'

She watched the smoke curling up from her cigarette.

'Are you charging me?'

'No. Not yet, anyway. I just want you to answer a few questions.'

'What about?'

'Mr Dempsey.'

'What about him?'

'Why does he come here?'

145

She turned her head and closed one eye against the cigarette smoke as she looked at him reflectively.

'You know what I do, mister. That's why he comes here.'

'Nothing more than that?'

'Like what?'

'Why does Kleppe come here?'

'Kleppe's never . . . who's Kleppe?'

'He phoned you this morning, Jenny. He said he was sending a man round here with something for Dempsey.'

The big blue eyes looked shocked. 'Jesus, You're tapping my phone.'

'Tell me about Dempsey, Jenny. It's better for you if you do.'

She pushed a swatch of long blonde hair behind her shoulder and leaned forward to stub out her cigarette. The bath-robe slid from her shoulders so that she was naked to the waist. It was deliberate and effective, no man was going to be completely impervious to the two full mounds and their spiky pink tips. And when his eyes went back to her face she said softly, 'Are you a tit man, mister?'

He half smiled. 'I've never been sure, Jenny. I think I'm kind of an all-rounder. My name's Nolan, by the way, Pete Nolan.'

She nodded as she must have nodded to hundreds of men, he thought, as they tried to establish their shrunken egos. She lit another cigarette and as she blew the smoke aside she turned to look at him.

'I've got two hours, Pete. You could do a lot in two hours.'

'Why have you got two hours?'

'My first date gets here at 6.30.'

'Jenny, all your dates today are policemen. We didn't want to have problems in that area.'

She stood up and walked to the phone and then waited with the receiver to her ear, her fingers poised over the buttons. Then she put the receiver down slowly and turned to him, white-faced.

'The bastards. He said, "New York Police Department, can I help you."'

'Why don't you sit down, Jenny, and let's talk.'

She sprawled on the big settee, and closed her eyes as she spoke. 'OK. Talk.'

'How long have you known Dempsey?'

'About ten years.'

'How did you meet him?'

'I was sixteen when I met him. It was at a party at Kleppe's. Two guys got me smashed and took me in one of the bedrooms. They were taking turns to screw me, and Dempsey came in and chucked them out. I lived with him for about four months and he lent me five grand to set up in this place.'

'Why did he do that?'

She leaned up on one elbow to look at him.

'I wanted to make money, mister. He didn't mind. He understood. We liked each other but it was *like*, not love. He was too unhappy then to love anyone, and I was too young; and I knew that because of the way I'm built I could earn a fortune.'

'Why was he unhappy?'

'I don't really know.' When she saw his disbelief she went on. 'It was something that happened in Paris when he was painting there. I think that's where he met Kleppe. I think it was a love affair that made him unhappy.'

'Tell me about Dempsey and Kleppe.'

She sat up slowly, brushing the hair from her face so that she could look at him.

'Are you in New York often, Pete?'

'Quite often.'

'D'you think I'm attractive?'

'Sure. But you don't need me to tell you that.'

'How about a deal, Pete? I'll screw any time you want. And I'll tell you what I know about Kleppe. But we leave Andy out of it. Yes?'

'Why are you so protective about Dempsey?'

'You won't believe it, mister, but I love him. He wouldn't believe me either. But I'd do anything for him.'

'Did you ever pay back the five grand?'

'Not in money.'

'How?'

She shrugged. 'He sometimes wants me to screw with friends of his. Business people or buddies. He said he'd rather have it that way.'

'Does *he* sleep with you?'

'Oh, sure he does.'

'What's Dempsey's relationship with Kleppe?'

She shook her head slowly.

'No more about Andy. Let's go in my bedroom.'

'Tell me about Kleppe.'

'I don't know much. He's rich and tough. And he knows everybody. Not just in New York but all over. He's in jewellery. A loner.'

'D'you sleep with him?'

'No. I think he wanted to but Andy headed him off. He's got girls. I'm too old for him, he likes teenagers.'

'Does he live alone?'

'As far as I know.'

'What do they talk about, Jenny?'

The big, blue eyes looked at him, and she shook her head.

'You can do anything you want. Anything.'

He sighed. 'Jenny, you're very beautiful but I'm a policeman. You know I can't do deals like that.'

'There's at least ten from NYPD who come here for free. Lieutenants, captains, you name it.'

'Jenny. Andy Dempsey is already involved. There's no way you can protect him. He doesn't need to know that you told me. Stay out of it.'

There were tears in the big eyes and her lips trembled as she reached for a Kleenex.

'If I tell you . . .'

There was a ring on the door and the girl stopped speaking. She looked at Nolan.

'Is it somebody for you?'

'Are you expecting anyone?'

'No. It's phone appointments only.'

He stood up, walked to the door and looked round. There was a paperback on the table and he picked it up and slid it behind the far edge of the mirror on the wall. It tilted the mirror so that it reflected most of the door. He nodded to the girl and whispered, 'Don't check. Just open the door about a foot but keep on one side near me.'

She stood up and tied the belt of the emerald robe. She was

trembling as she stood beside him. He saw her hand close round the ornate brass knob and turn it slowly. Then his eyes went to the mirror. He saw the hand and the Walther and he slammed the door shut with his shoulder. He felt it crunch against flesh and bone and somebody screamed as the pistol clattered to the floor. He gripped the hand and flung open the door, and pulled in the man with one long movement. Still holding the man's wrist, he bent down and gathered the gun. There was a silencer, and the safety catch was off.

The man stood there, his top lip curled back in pain, his right hand hanging limp and useless. He was tall and thin, pale blue eyes in a sallow face, and one eyelid quivered as he looked at Nolan. The girl stood by the telephone, holding her robe with folded arms.

'What's your name?'

The man stood silently, the only movement was the quivering eye.

Nolan pulled back the slide of the pistol and a round flew out and rattled against the leg of the coffee table. Another round went in as he slowly released the slide. Without taking his eyes off the man he spoke to the girl.

'Go and get dressed, Jenny. Stay in your room and lock the door. Don't come out until I tell you.'

He saw her go, from the corner of his eye, and he turned to the man.

'Take off your coat.'

He watched as the man slid off the heavy overcoat. He reached out for it and threw it on the floor beside him.

'Now strip. Undress.'

He took a long time with only one hand and the injured wrist was puffing up tight and swollen, a livid mass whose colour was spreading to the back of the hand. When the man stopped he was down to his briefs. Nolan waved the gun.

'Take those off, too.'

When the man was naked Nolan told him to sit down, and pointed with the gun at the chair.

'What's your name?'

The man didn't answer and Nolan reached for the swollen hand.

It flapped loosely as the man tucked it between his knees. He was trembling violently as if he had an ague.

'What's your name?' Nolan said softly.

'They'll kill me. They'll kill me.'

'Who will kill you?'

The man gave a shuddering sigh. 'Katin's men.'

'Did Katin send you?'

The man nodded without speaking.

'What were your orders?'

'To kill.'

'Why should they kill the girl?'

The man's haggard face lifted, surprise in his eyes, his mouth open.

'Not the girl,' he said. 'You.'

Nolan's voice sounded thin and tense when he spoke.

'Who am I?'

'You're CIA. Peter Fleming Nolan.'

'What makes you think that's my name?'

'They showed me photographs of you. They told me who you were.'

'Where are you from?'

'Chicago?'

'Name?'

'Frankie Spadone.'

'How did they know I was here?'

'They've got a tail on you.'

'Why did they hire you? Why didn't they do it themselves?'

Spadone shrugged. 'There's too much heat on them. They wanted an outsider.'

'How much was the contract?'

'Five grand.'

'Who gave you the orders?'

'The old fella with the glass eye. Katin. Yuri Katin.'

Nolan lifted the phone and tucked the receiver under his chin while he pressed the buttons. When the voice answered he watched Spadone as he talked.

'Ziggy?'

'Yes, sir.'

'Send two cars. One for me and another for the girl. There's also one of their hit men, a local from Chicago named Spadone. Check the files on him. He needs medical attention. Bones and tendons. He's to be guarded full-time and I don't want him logged or booked.'

'You're at the apartment on 38th, Mr Nolan?'

'Right.'

'No more than ten minutes, sir.'

As Nolan put down the receiver he waved the gun at Spadone.

'OK. Get dressed.'

Nolan pressed down the silencer ratchet on the Walther and turned the cylinder so that it slid into his palm, and he pushed it into his jacket pocket. He knocked on the girl's bedroom door.

'Jenny. You can come out.'

She was dressed in a vivid-green jersey suit, a string of knotted pearls around her neck and a mink coat slung over her arm.

'Why the coat, Jenny?'

'I heard you on the phone.'

'You'll be safer with us for a day or so.'

He turned to look at Spadone who stood with his eyes closed in pain.

The door-bell rang, and Nolan walked over. The CIA driver and the two agents stood there, and he nodded to Spadone and the girl.

'Let's go. Lock up properly, Jenny.'

She pressed the spring on the lock and pulled the door shut.

'I'll take your keys.'

She hesitated for only a moment but that was enough, and he slid the keys into his pocket and nodded to the driver.

'Take them on. I'll be along later.'

The girl looked back at him, the big eyes apprehensive and pleading. When the others were in the elevator he took out the keys, walked back and let himself into the flat. He took off his coat and threw it across a chair. There was just the living-room, a bedroom, a kitchen and a bathroom. He walked across to the bedroom.

The dressing-table had a few bottles and packs. A bottle of 'Je

Reviens', an antiperspirant aerosol, eau-de-Cologne, three used lipsticks and a beautiful, silver hand-mirror. There were a few jars of creams, a box of cotton wool, tissues and a manicure-set in a leather case.

He pulled out the two small drawers and then the two full length drawers. There was nothing but underwear, briefs, suspender belts, and a collection of scarves and linen handkerchiefs.

In the small right-hand drawer was a kaleidoscope of necklaces, brooches and ear-rings. All things bright and beautiful, but nothing particularly expensive. There were a dozen or so postcards from holiday places around the world with brief messages on the lines of 'See you baby—Joe (Chattanooga)' and more pointed efforts like 'Sit on it until I get back next Wednesday—Charlie M'.

In the left-hand drawer was a red leather notebook with dates and initials. He put it on the window-sill. There were receipts in a spring clip, mainly hairdressing, doctors, and food and drink payments. There was a large, brown envelope and he tipped out the photographs. They were all of Jenny. A few glamour portraits and the rest were figure shots, erotic but not pornographic. In all of them she was naked, and the lighting so arranged that it emphasized and high-lighted her breasts and her crotch. He turned over one print and there was a negative number and a telephone number. He noted them both. There was a letter from an address in Pasadena that was obvi-ously from her mother, and another letter from a pilot on an aircraft-carrier, which described in vivid detail what he was going to do to her when he next got to New York.

He stood up, hands on hips and looked across the room. There was no expensive jewellery, no odd cash or valuables, yet there had been that scared look in her eyes when he took the keys.

In the wardrobe there were dozens of pairs of shoes, a squashed row of dresses and coats, and two flowered hats on a shelf. On the bedside table was a pink-shaded lamp, a small traveller's alarm clock in a leather fold-case, a Mars bar and an empty ashtray. In the drawer there was a box of condoms, a Kleenex pack and a copy of the current *Penthouse*.

He pushed the bed to one side and pulled back the carpet but the boards were clean and untouched. He moved on to the kitchen. There was nothing of interest on the shelves or in the cabinets. There was a combined freezer-refrigerator, an upright Westinghouse. The refrigerator was packed full of food, and cans of coke and beer. The freezer held four drawers marked 'Meat', 'Fruit', 'Packs', and 'Misc'. He was swinging the door to when he noticed that the pilot light was not working.

He pulled out the drawer marked 'Misc'. There were bundles of ten-dollar notes, still banded from a bank. About twenty thousand dollars. There were thick, brown envelopes crammed with used notes of all denominations. There were four bank pass-books with credits that totalled nearly a quarter of a million dollars and a safety deposit key.

In the drawer marked 'Meat' there were eight envelopes packed with photographs.

There were thirty or forty 10" × 8" prints in each envelope. They all showed the girl having sex with a man. The man in the third envelope was Powell. The photographs were explicit and comprehensive, with the action-stopping graininess of photo-journalism rather than the studio. The faces of the participants were clear and instantly identifiable, and in each envelope were a dozen strips of negatives in a transparent pack. He closed the freezer door, collected the envelopes and the black notebook, and left.

Nolan stood eating a chicken sandwich. The girl sat at the table, finishing her meal.

'I've fixed for you to go up to Albany. You'll be safer up there.'

'Am I in custody?'

'No way, Jenny. You can walk out of here right now if you want. But you wouldn't last a couple of hours.'

She put down her knife and fork and turned to look at him.

'You really think they would kill me?'

'I'm sure they would.'

'But why? I'm not part of anything.'

Nolan wiped his mouth with the back of his hand.

'I took the photographs, Jenny. And the little black book.'

'So what?'

'Those photographs link you with Powell. You are already linked with Dempsey. You and I know that you're linked with Kleppe, even if only indirectly. You're in the same position as Siwecki. He didn't know much but he was a piece in the jigsaw. They killed him and his wife and they killed Maria Angelo who knew even less. Why shouldn't they kill you?'

'Andy wouldn't let them.'

'My love, Dempsey wouldn't lift a finger. And if he would, he couldn't stop them.'

'Who's *them*? What's it all about?'

Nolan shook his head slowly.

'Just do as I say, Jenny, and maybe we'll be able to keep you out of it.'

She left a list of things she wanted from the flat and went off by road to the safe-house just outside Albany.

The CIA doctor eased across the three velcro straps on the splint. He lifted Spadone's forearm and started wrapping the bandage over the dressing and the splint. He looked up at Nolan.

'There's a simple fracture of the ulna and probably fractures in some of the smaller bones. I'll know better when I can X-ray the wrist area. He won't be able to use the hand for at least six months and I suspect one finger at least won't articulate again.'

Nolan looked at Spadone who was sitting alongside the small table. The doctor packed his case and left them alone. Nolan pulled out a chair and sat down.

'Where did you meet the Russian?'

'In the parking lot at the medical centre.'

'Which medical centre?'

'NYU.'

'How did you recognize him?'

'I'd seen a photo and he was carrying a copy of a magazine. We both had one.'

'What magazine?'

'*Popular Photography* of last June.'

'How much did you get?'

'Three and a half grand. The balance to come when it was done.'

'How did they originally contact you?'

'Kleppe arranged the deal with O'Reilly. I work for him.'

'A hood?'

'I guess you'd call him that. He's got a plumbing and air-conditioning business in Chicago, out by the race track in Cicero.'

'Are you ready to sign a statement?'

'If we can do a deal.'

'No way, Frankie. You'll be charged for possession of a firearm without a licence.'

Spadone's face was vacant, and then the penny dropped and he smiled.

'OK, Mr Nolan. I'll sign.'

President Grover had extended every courtesy to the President-Elect, and Logan Powell and Andy Dempsey sat together in the Presidential compartment of Air Force One for their journey to Los Angeles. When the meetings were over they left the evening sun behind as they flew out across the Texas panhandle, and two hours later the plane was under the cloud cover and they could see the lights of Charleston as the plane came under Washington control.

Powell sat back with his head against the soft, white pillow from his bed and Dempsey gazed out of the window, his face tense and pale. He turned to look at Powell.

'Just find an excuse to talk with Harper. He's a political appointee. You haven't said you'll let him stay at CIA. Let him know that he could be out in three weeks' time.'

Powell spoke with his eyes still closed.

'You don't know that they're doing anything, Andy. It would be the FBI if it were anyone at all. It's not CIA territory. They won't want to tangle with me so soon.'

'For Christ's sake, Logan. The people have been positively identified as CIA. They had to deal with Siwecki to head them off.'

'That's absolute crap, my friend. I'd put my silver dollar on Siwecki's murder being the usual union Mafia at work. By the way, what's the Vice-President-Elect doing today?'

'He's at the White House meeting the new Senators.'

'He's gonna be OK, you know. He's hard nosed but that ain't bad in a Vice-President. He's going to be a strong link with Congress and we're gonna need one.'

'Will you let *me* see Harper?'

Powell opened his eyes and slid the pillow from behind his head and put it alongside him on the seat. They could see the White House below and ahead, looking like a wedding cake in the glare of the floodlights. He looked back at Dempsey.

'Have you seen Laura lately?'

'Not for ten days.'

'What did she have to say when you saw her?'

'I told you. She won't make any trouble. She's agreed not to file for divorce until we're ready, but she wants the house made over to her.'

'That's OK. Get Jim Oakes's outfit to deal with it.'

'Aren't you worried at all, Logan? Don't kid me.'

Powell smiled and slid his arms into his jacket.

'In a few weeks' time, Andy, these people won't dare do a thing. And if they try anything then, they'll have their arses out in the snow.'

'You'd be out there with them, Logan. They mean business.'

Powell leaned forward to watch the landing and without turning he spoke as he shaded his eyes.

'Leave it to me, Andy. You've been over-impressed by these people. The CIA and FBI won't play games right now. The public and the media are agin 'em.'

16

Nolan sat in the unmarked van with the headphones on and the tape-recorder plugged in. He was listening intently, his hand half up to stop Langfeld from speaking.

Then he slid off the earphones and leaned back.

'That's it. Katin has called him to a meeting at the UN. Take the pick-up team and lift him, when he gets to Mitchell Place. Take him to King's Point and isolate him. I'll be there when we've gone through his apartment.'

'OK, Mr Nolan.'

He gave his team careful instructions. There was a man on the fire-escape already and the rest of the team were waiting for Kleppe to come out. They had monitored incoming and outgoing calls and the message from the UN building had been what they were waiting for.

Nolan wanted to go in the apartment before Kleppe was alerted and that was best done while he was out. If they tried to enter the apartment while he was there he could be phoning his influential friends.

At last Kleppe was at the entrance hall of the apartment block. They could see him talking with one of the security guards. He was laughing as he turned to come through the glass doors. He stood on the wide steps for a moment, looking up and down the street and then he turned left and walked slowly down Sutton Place towards the UN. Langfeld's men called the car and it turned round to follow Kleppe.

Nolan showed his card to the security men in the reception area of the apartment block and left one of his team with them. He guessed that they had been well greased by Kleppe and he warned them not to attempt to use the phone. Nolan's man would take all calls.

The search team piled into the lift with Nolan, their leather cases heaped in one corner. There was no hurry because Kleppe would not be coming back. He would be going straight to the safe-house.

The locksmith tested the two door locks for ten minutes before he turned to Nolan.

'I can't open the second one without breaking the alarm circuit. There's a whole loom of wires spread through the door.'

'OK. Break the circuit.'

There were no ringing bells or flashing lights but Nolan guessed that the signal was telling its story somewhere. He went to the telephone on the ornate desk and called his men in the foyer.

'We've had to break the alarm circuit. You'll be getting visitors soon. If they're from NYPD take their badge numbers and check their ID cards. Refer them to the downtown office. No explanations, just identify yourselves. If it's a captain refer him to the Commissioner. He knows about the search warrant. But no explanations. Understood?'

'OK, Mr Nolan.'

Nolan's team were already at work in pairs. One pair searched for electronics, a pair looked for documents and a pair checked the structure for cavities. One of each pair recorded comments into a portable cassette machine as they worked, and a photographer recorded the search. None of them had been told what they were looking for.

When the structure team came down from the attic they were shaking water from the three plastic bags and they had a small metal case. They laid them all on the long table. Nolan watched them unseal the plastic bags and shake out the shiny black notebooks. They opened one and after glancing at it briefly they passed it to Nolan.

'Looks like the Dead Sea Scrolls, chief.'

The radio team identified the contents of the metal case. They were spare circuit boards for the high-speed transmitter.

It was midnight before the search was complete and they took away radio equipment for evaluation, and piles of documents and correspondence. A reserve team re-checked the structure against the taped commentary with an electronic heat probe. They found nothing new.

Nolan went down to the lobby to check that the station wagon was there. It was. So was an irate police lieutenant and two sergeants. The lieutenant turned to look at Nolan.

'Are you Nolan?'

'Yes, lieutenant, I'm Nolan.'

'I'm taking you down to the precinct.'

At that point the first load of equipment and documents came down in the lift and the lieutenant verged on apoplexy.

'None of that goddamn stuff leaves these premises.'

His angry eyes searched Nolan's face for surrender, and not finding it, he called on his troops. Pointing to his two sergeants, he said, 'If they make one move to take away that stuff, book 'em and take 'em to Riker.' He looked back at Nolan in bristling challenge.

'What's your name, lieutenant?'

'Don't you back-answer a police officer in the course of his duty or you'll be down the precinct in two minutes flat.'

Nolan looked at him calmly. 'Maybe we'd better do that, lieutenant.' He reached for the warrant in his inside pocket and the lieutenant's hand flashed out. It stopped in mid-air as if it were set in concrete and as Nolan held it he said, 'I have a search-warrant including right of removal. My men have already told you that we are CIA. If you still want to play games there will be an official inquiry as to why you were prepared to ignore the documentation. And don't try to manhandle me again.'

The flushed face glanced at Nolan but the aggressive arm was lowered. 'Where's the warrant?'

Nolan removed it, folded, from his pocket and handed it to the lieutenant who unfolded it and read it slowly, his lips silently mouthing the words. When he was finished he held it in his hand as Nolan put out his hand for it. 'Not so quick, mister. I'll keep this. We'll check it out.'

Nolan turned to the driver of the car who was standing just outside the open main doors. 'Use the car radio, Finnegan, and call the Commissioner. Ask him to come down here right away.'

As the driver turned to the door the lieutenant shouted to his men. 'Stop him. Stop the bastard.'

'Hold it.'

Nolan's voice echoed in the tiled lobby and as the lieutenant turned he saw Nolan's hand and the gun. The two sergeants froze. Apart from the gun they would have taken a cut in pension rather than miss this scenario.

The lieutenant stood like some reconstructed cave-man, with red bulging eyes and prognathous jaw.

'By Jesus, you're gonna be right in the shit, mister. Obstructing an officer in the course of his duty. Threatening with a firearm, grand larceny, and God knows what.' His mouth was opening and closing silently, desperately searching for further offences.

Nolan kept his eyes on the lieutenant and said to the driver. 'Call the Commissioner.'

Neanderthal man had second thoughts.

'No need to involve the Commissioner, Nolan. He's a busy man. Just you and your men get your arses out of this building fast. We'll seal the apartment doors.'

'They're double-locked, lieutenant, but seal them if it makes you happy. I need the warrant.' And he held out his hand.

There was only a moment's hesitation before it was handed over. The lieutenant and his men watched as the station-wagon was loaded. They stood looking through the glass doors as the car pulled out into the traffic. Nolan wondered how much the lieutenant's rip-off had been. It must have been substantial for him to take those risks.

When the material had been unloaded at the safe-house at Central Park, Nolan walked back to the car. He was asleep before they reached the expressway and the driver shook him awake in the doorway of the house facing the sea. There was a glint of light on the sea from the false dawn, and he could see lights on some of the small craft moored in the bay. The week-end sailors who defied the winter weather.

He turned to look at the house. There were lights in every window and all the windows were barred. He walked slowly to the front door and the duty officer handed him a clutch of messages.

'Where's Kleppe?'

'In the basement, sir.'

'What was his reaction?'

'Your men are still here. They're in the canteen. I gather he put up a struggle at first but after that he's been tame enough. He won't talk.'

'I said he wasn't to be interrogated until I came.'

'I meant about food or coffee, sir. He's been left strictly alone.'

'Did he talk on the way here?'

'I understand not, sir.'

Nolan slid off his coat and slung it over a chair.

'Take me down to Kleppe.'

They walked down the stone steps to the basement. There were three rooms clad with steel plate and with heavy metal doors. Kleppe was in the last one and Nolan waited as the key was turned and the door opened. He slid the bleeper into his pocket and walked in.

There was a small table bolted to the cement floor and two light wooden chairs. Along the facing wall was a concrete slab with a folded sleeping bag. Kleppe sat at the table, hunched up and grim-faced, a lock of hair hanging over his forehead. Nolan sat down opposite him and looked at his face. It was a typical Slav face, dark skinned, high cheek-bones and a massive jaw. Kleppe's dark eyes looked back at him defiantly and uncurious.

There was no response of any kind. Nolan saw no point in playing formalities.

'We've been searching your apartment, Mr Kleppe. We've found the radio, and the papers are being sorted now, including the note-books from the cold-water tank. Do you want to talk about them now or later?'

Kleppe sat silent and unmoving.

'Kleppe, you can choose which way you want it. We can talk like this now or I'll get the medical orderly to give you a shot. You'll talk then.'

Kleppe spat, and the saliva was warm on Nolan's face. He wiped the saliva away slowly with his hand and then pressed the bleeper.

Nolan saw the small remote-control video camera mounted in the ceiling slowly scan the area of the table and then the walls of the room. A few seconds later the door opened and he walked out and on up to the entrance hall. He slowly mounted the wide staircase that led to the first floor. They had given him a temporary office facing the stairway and as he pulled up a chair to the desk he pressed the button in the panel beside the telephone. A young man came at the double.

'Sir?'

'Ask the medic to come and see me.'

'Yes, sir.'

'And I'd like a bowl of soup and a banana sandwich.'

There was a hesitant half-smile. 'What's a banana sandwich, sir?'

'You mash up a banana with sugar and make a sandwich.'

'Yes, sir.'

The medical officer wore a blue denim shirt and Levis. He looked as if he had just been woken up. He put his black bag at his feet.

'Fowler, Mr Nolan. You wanted me?'

'I want something to keep me awake for about three hours.'

'What are you going to be doing in that time?'

'Interrogating.'

'OK.'

'And I want the guy in the basement to keep talking—the truth.'

'Is he antagonistic?'

'Very.'

'We've got a choice; there's a pentothal variant that makes talking and response to questioning certain, but the subject can wander far away from what you're talking about and the guy can take hours to get back. It's a bit like unleashing a flood of words. They'll all be there but may be irrelevant. Or there's a new thing, TH 94. That gives a lower compulsion to talk. He'll talk but you've got to pull it out of his unconscious. The user reports we have had so far indicate high truth factors but slower commentary. You have to go a long way down.'

'Let's try the TH 94.'

'OK. I'll give you your shot first. I'll need a pulse count and a lung check.'

The young man put his fingers remarkably lightly on the artery at Nolan's wrist and closed his eyes. It was a high count and he did it again to make sure. He was used to abnormal counts. Adrenalin glands were generally working overtime when he was called in. He put the stethoscope probe up to his mouth and breathed on it. He went carefully over Nolan's chest and back. There were no lung problems, and he folded up the stethoscope and knelt down to his bag. He stood up and put two pills on the desk.

'Take those, without liquid, then they'll work faster.'

'Is it OK to eat afterwards?'

'Yes. It'll help. Where's the guy for the TH 94?'

'In the basement.'

'It will take half an hour to start working. Shall I go down now and give him his jab?'

'No, I want to be there. I'll give you a buzz when I'm ready.'

He pulled across the bundle of reports as he waited. There was a brief report on the electronics at Kleppe's place.

Prelim: *Electronics*.

Extensive anti-bugging frame covers all rooms and doors. Similar to MAJOR MK IX.

Miniaturized high-power transceiver. Modified SOVTORG model 30. Four crystal fixed frequencies. Component analysis indicates extensive use, approx. nineteen repeat nineteen hours.

Cameras Polaroid SX 70. Olympus OM2 with macro lens 55mm and copying device and Recordata back. Signed Harrap and Simon.

The soup and sandwich came, and he read the Moscow embassy report as he ate.

'Your 97016 stop subject Tcharkova, Halenka aged twenty-seven repeat twenty-seven with child (female) aged seven stop well-known painter acceptable to regime stop current address Minskaya Ulitsa 17 repeat 17 Moscow stop several successful exhibitions stop married stop photographs to follow message ends 147011.'

He pressed the red button and when the medical orderly came they walked down to the entrance hall and collected the duty guard.

Kleppe was still sitting at the table, as if he had never moved since Nolan had left him.

The young man checked Kleppe's pulse and then undid the cuff-links on Kleppe's right arm. He pushed back the arm of his jacket, and the shirt, swabbed the inside of his forearm and fetched up a vein with pressure from his thumb. The hypodermic looked more like a veterinary size to Nolan and he watched as the needle slid in. It took a long time for the plunger to empty the syringe. Kleppe watched the clear liquid empty into his arm. The puncture was swabbed and Nolan used the bleeper and he and the medical orderly walked back together. At Nolan's office door the young man looked at his watch.

'He'll be ready to go at five o'clock. You'll get four hours out of him.'

'Thanks.'

Nolan walked across the causeway at the end of the lane to the edge of the water. There was a watery sun now on the horizon, sending fingers of light to the edges of the dark clouds and across the choppy water. It reminded Nolan of a biblical engraving in his room when he was a child; in flowing script the title was 'Easter Morning'.

A 36-foot Hatteras was making its third attempt to tie-up at the jetty on the far side of the Bay. It came in sideways-on and an offshore wind held it too far away for a rope to be thrown. It came round again and the penny had dropped. It went in nose on and when the for'ard rope was fast the engines brought its stern round. A skein of geese flew overhead from the reed beds behind where he was sitting. And there were three tugs and a navy patrol boat coming under the Throgs Neck Bridge. On the bridge itself the commuters still had the lights on on their cars, and there was a long build-up for the toll booths.

Nolan, like most other senior operators in CIA, was well aware that he lived in a naughty world. It was that that justified much of what he did, or ordered to be done. Investigating committees frequently applied the word 'horrific' to some of their operations, but the CIA put that down to the luxury of a loftiness that only the CIA's work made possible. What the CIA did was generally all too routine, and the majority of their operations were counter-punching, resisting attacks rather than attacking. Nolan and the top echelons at Langley were used to their role, and the extravagant outrage of journalists and politicians. From time to time when depressions and storms rolled across from Capitol Hill there would be the pointed question asked of who would 'preserve, protect, and defend' if the CIA took the Boy Scout oath.

But this operation seemed as unreal to Nolan as other operations seemed outside the intelligence community. After they had proved that the President-Elect was a reed that bent to Soviet winds, what then? What happened? Every solution spelt disaster. Deep depression for millions of people, a hundred McCarthys, all the words of 1776 made nought, the checks and balances exposed as a dream, and an icy tension between the two most powerful nations in the world. And the final excuse for the buttons to be pressed to turn a grinding ache into a final amputation. It was like working diligently to prove you had cancer. Whatever happened was going to be bad for America.

They all knew that there was no easy solution. But he knew, and they would know, that there *was* an easy solution. It had lurked on the periphery of his mind for two weeks like a hungry animal at the edge of a wood.

He stood up, brushed the seat of his trousers and walked briskly back to the house to expunge the lurking thought.

Nolan looked at Kleppe's face as the door clanged to behind him. There was something wrong with Kleppe's left eye and that side of his face. It was like a man looked who had had a stroke. A kind of paralysis. He sat down facing Kleppe, and spoke calmly and quietly.

'You're Victor Kleppe. A Russian?'

The head shook vigorously and the mouth distorted with effort.

'Armenian. Not Russian.' The face contorted as he laughed.

'You're an officer in the KGB?'

The dark eyes flickered but he nodded as his mouth worked without making a sound.

'Andrew Dempsey is one of your men?'

''Merican, 'Merican.'

'He's an American?'

Kleppe nodded energetically.

'He's a Communist. He works for you?'

Kleppe put his hand to his lips as if to make them work. 'Yes.'

'He controls Powell?'

He nodded. 'Old friends, schooldays.'

'You get your instructions from Moscow?'

''Moskva and United Nations.'

'Moscow wanted Powell to be Governor and then President?'

'Money and influence. The networks.'

Nolan could just make out the words. He used the bleeper and when the door opened he called out. 'Get the medic down here.'

He sat silent until the young man came in. He looked up at him. 'There's something wrong. He can't talk properly.'

The young man bent down and looked at Kleppe's face. He touched the left side with his fingers then took a metal probe and touched the cheek. It drew blood but Kleppe didn't flinch or move. The doctor looked at Kleppe.

'Have you been taking penicillin?'

Kleppe nodded and touched his chest.

'You've had bronchitis, yes? Or influenza?'

'Yes.'

The young man straightened up.

'He's allergic to penicillin and this drug has geared it up. It's like when you get a dentist's injection, your mouth swells up and goes numb. And it's drying his mouth and his throat. I'll give him something to flatten it, but he'll be like this for two days.'

'You do that.' Nolan said, and bleeped for the guard and left.

It took them one hour to trace Harper. He was out of Washington.

'What's happening, Pete?'

'He's talking, but the drug's had side-effects, and I've got to leave him for a couple of days.'

'What's he said?'

'That he's an Armenian. An officer in the KGB. Dempsey is a Communist and works for him. They get their orders from Moscow and the UN and they used the networks to make Powell Governor and President.'

'Will he sign a statement?'

'I haven't asked him. I'd guess he will eventually.'

'Is it on tape?'

'Yes. But his speech is distorted and sometimes he nodded rather than spoke.'

'We can't wait two days, you know.'

'Why don't I pick up Dempsey?'

'Who do we get to sign the warrant?'

'Nobody. I just pick him up.'

'For God's sake. We can't just go on lifting people. He's been nominated as Powell's Chief of Staff.'

'We've got so much now. I don't feel it matters.'

'Pete, when we've got a cast-iron case, signed statements, the lot, we're still left with the problem of what to do. When Dempsey disappears Powell's going to raise hell all round. And who is going to interrogate Powell? There's going to be a point when it will be ripped out of our hands into the politicians' hands. We've got to see it gets into the right hands. If you picked up Dempsey then you'd have to work fast before it leaks out.'

Nolan noticed the 'if' and took it as quasi approval.

'Let me pick up Dempsey and give me two days. What day is it today?'

'My God, what a question. It's Tuesday, the nineteenth of December.'

'OK. Give me until Friday.'

There was a long silence and a sigh.

'OK.' And the phone was hung up.

Nolan phoned Langfeld and gave him careful instructions. He checked the paperwork and then slept. When he awoke at five o'clock there was a chit on his desk reporting that Dempsey had been picked up at 4.30pm. His ETA at Flushing Airport was 23.15.

They had taken Dempsey down to the basement. He was in the first interrogation room and, unlike Kleppe, when Nolan walked in Dempsey was eating from a tray. He looked up at Nolan and then got back to his eating. Nolan sat down and waited. Dempsey looked just like the photographs. His face unlined and youthful. They had taken his tie, and the plaid shirt was open at the neck. Finally he threw down the knife and fork with a clatter, reached for the linen napkin, and wiped his mouth as he leaned back in his chair and looked at Nolan.

Nolan had spent time carefully working out the order of his questions.

17

All that Nolan knew about Dempsey indicated that he was not a trained operator, but he was intelligent enough to have marshalled the nationwide resources that the Soviets had made available. He had that perpetually youthful air that successful actors have. Eyes that were blue and amused, and an alertness that was cloaked by a deceptive casualness.

'Have you had enough to eat, Mr Dempsey?'

Dempsey nodded, smiling. 'Give the cook my compliments. I'll recommend him to my friends.'

'Is there anything else you want?'

'Just to get the hell out of here.'

'Do you know why you're here?'

The lazy eyes smiled. 'No. But I guess you'll enjoy telling me.'

Nolan waited for a few seconds.

'Would you like to talk about Kleppe?'

'Not particularly.'

'How about we talk of Siwecki?'

'You talk. I'll listen.' Dempsey's eyes were suddenly hard and alert.

'You know he was murdered together with his wife?'

'I read it in the papers.'

'Did you regret the murder?'

Dempsey shrugged. 'I didn't consider it in those terms.'

'The sentence for an accessory to murder is quite severe, Mr Dempsey.'

Dempsey made no reply.

'There is evidence that you were an accessory to those murders, Mr Dempsey.'

'So charge me, Nolan. Stop bullshitting.'

'Are you a member of the Communist party, Mr Dempsey?'

Dempsey grinned. 'What do you want me to do, plead the Fifth?' Dempsey's face went pale with anger as he leaned forward. 'Let me quote *you* the Fifth, Nolan. "Nor shall any person be deprived of life, liberty, or property, without due process of law." When does due process start, Mr Nolan?'

'Not at the moment. But if you prefer the formality I'll start with holding you on a homicide charge.'

'What homicide?'

'The murder of Mr and Mrs Siwecki, Miss Angelo, and a CIA officer in New York named Steiner.'

'How did I murder them?'

'You were a prime accessory, you fixed it in conjunction with Kleppe.'

'For what motive?'

'To prevent them giving evidence against you.'

'Evidence of what?'

'Bribery, collusion, inciting a strike, illegal payments, blackmail. There's more, as you know, if you want it.'

'You know what position I hold in the new administration?'

'I know you were going to be Chief of Staff to Powell.'

'I still am.'

'No, Mr Dempsey. It's all over now.'

'Powell will have your guts, my friend.'

'Tell me about Halenka Tcharkova.'

Nolan saw Dempsey's breathing stop for a moment, and then go faster. For the first time his eyes held a doubt.

'I've never heard of her.'

'She will be in great danger now.'

'Why?'

'Because Kleppe and you have failed. They don't like failures, Mr Dempsey. They aren't going to like the international exposure they get from this little effort.'

Dempsey looked away, and Nolan pressed on.

'You knew that Kleppe was a KGB officer?'

'I don't give a shit what he is, or was.'

'And the girl in Moscow? What about her?'

'She's an established artist. They wouldn't dare touch her.'

'You don't believe that, Dempsey, do you?'

For a long time Dempsey was silent, and when he spoke Nolan heard the mixture of anger and fear in his voice.

'Isn't it time you read me your Miranda card, Nolan?'

'I'm not a policeman.'

'It applies to the FBI just as much.'

'I'm not FBI.'

Dempsey folded his hands on the table, the knuckles white as frost-bite.

'I demand to see my lawyer. I answer no more questions until he arrives.'

'Who is your lawyer?'

'Oakes in Hartford.'

'He couldn't act for you.'

'Why in hell not?'

'He has already signed a statement himself that incriminates you.'

'Of what?'

'Fixing the strike at Haig's Electronics, paying twenty thousand dollars to Siwecki's local, paying five thousand to Siwecki himself, and conspiring to illegally influence an election.'

'If you've got evidence why don't you charge me? Why this crap?'

'Because those are the least serious of the charges.'

'Look, Nolan, you may have forced some lying statement out of Oakes, but you won't do that with me.'

'Is Kleppe's statement a lying statement, too?'

'You've kidnapped him as well as me?'

Nolan didn't reply. He wanted to give Dempsey time to absorb what he had been told. Finally he stood up and pressed the bleeper. As he stood at the open door he said, 'Let me know when you want to talk.'

Dempsey didn't look up.

It was six o'clock when they roused Nolan from a deep sleep. Dempsey wanted to talk to him. He washed and shaved slowly, and dressed carefully before he went down to the basement.

Dempsey was stretched out on the concrete bed, on top of the sleeping bag. His face was pale and drawn, and the youthful look had gone.

Nolan dragged over a chair and sat alongside the bed. The blue eyes were paler as they looked at his face anxiously.

'I want to do a deal, Nolan.'

'Tell me.'

'I'll write out everything. Names, addresses, money, everything, but I won't sign it, and I won't give evidence, until you've done your part.'

'What's my part?'

'You get Halenka and the little girl over here permanently.'

'What if she doesn't want to come?'

'She will.'

'Will you dictate the main points as a précis right away?'

'If you want, but it depends on the deal.'

Nolan looked at the troubled blue eyes and spoke quite gently.

'You know the Soviets are unlikely to play ball.'

'She's my wife, Nolan. We were married by proxy. It's quite legal.'

'That won't make any difference.'

'It makes her an American citizen.'

'That won't make any difference either. There's no percentage in it for them.'

Dempsey looked at him, weighing up the odds before he spoke.

'They would trade her for Kleppe.'

'He's a prime witness.'

'There's very little he can cover that I can't cover.'

The bravado had suddenly gone. Dempsey was pleading now. The hostage he had given to fate all those years ago still controlled his thinking. It passed through Nolan's mind that if some diplomatic oaf had not alienated this man in 1968 neither of them would be standing in the steel-clad interrogation room now.

'He's their man, Dempsey. He must be their top man in the US. A court may not believe your evidence, and Moscow would dismiss it all as a ridiculous plot by the CIA.'

'I won't write a word, Nolan, until I know.'

'You'll only have my word. Nothing more.'

'I'll accept that.'

After Nolan spoke to Harper he did not go back to Dempsey. He walked down the driveway of the house and then to the shore of the bay.

It was bitterly cold as he stumbled over the shingle, and the snow still lay in hard icy lumps between the stones at the edge of the breakwaters. The sea looked heavy and solid under the black clouds, unfriendly and menacing as the incoming tide bit at the sandy shore. Nolan stood looking across the bay, his mind trying to follow the threads of what had to be done. It was like working out all the variations three moves ahead in a chess game. It was possible but unlikely. There were always responses that had not been evaluated.

There was already enough evidence to satisfy Elliot and Bethel when it was presented to them. But there would be others whose attitudes would depend on party politics, and some of them could be part of Kleppe's network. He had seen the names in the black books from Kleppe's water tank. Salvasan, the Republican National Chairman, had supported their investigation at the meeting with Harper, but from Oakes's statement it looked as if the party Vice-Chairman, de Jong, already had some knowledge of what had gone on at the time of the Haig strike.

Harper had not been satisfied that Dempsey's evidence would be enough. Enough to do what? It would depend on what the politicians decided to do. If it was a contested impeachment then Kleppe was not for sale, and if he were not for sale then there wouldn't be Dempsey's willing evidence. Which one was the key? Kleppe or Dempsey?

Nolan turned to walk back to the house and as the ice crackled under his feet on the marshy land he knew he had the answer in his head. He didn't know what the answer was, but he knew it was there somewhere.

He walked down with the guard to Dempsey's cell.

Dempsey was still lying stretched out on the sleeping bag, his eyes closed, but he was not asleep. As Nolan pulled up the chair alongside him Dempsey opened his eyes.

'Well?'

'I'm still talking with several people. The decision isn't entirely mine. There's one more question I need to ask, and I need the truth if I'm going to help you.'

'What is it?'

'Did Powell know what was going on?'

Dempsey swung his legs down so that he was sitting up. His hands massaged his face, his fingers rubbing his eyes. He looked up slowly at Nolan.

'He was never told in so many words, but he knew all right.'

'He knew the strike was fixed?'

'Yes, but he wasn't party to the fixing. He wasn't party to any of it. He just went along, turning a blind eye and reaping the benefits.'

'Since he was elected have you given him specific instructions?'

'Yes.'

'The defence cuts, withdrawing troops from NATO. Those were your instructions?'

'Yes.'

'He knew where they came from?'

'Sure he knew. I told him.'

'Did he protest?'

'Nolan, he was riding a tiger. He daren't get off or he'd have been eaten. And he knew it.'

'What was the Soviets' ultimate aim?'

Dempsey shrugged. 'God knows. I doubt if Kleppe knows.'

'Why did you go along with this?'

Dempsey looked up at Nolan's face.

'You won't ever understand, Nolan. I loved Halenka. I had enough money to give her anything she wanted. She didn't want anything. I joined the Party as a gesture to her—to show that I loved her. She didn't ask me to, she wasn't all that impressed when I did it. She was no more a Communist than I was. She was just a girl. Those French bastards beat us up and put us in jail. I wrote to our embassy and they left us to rot. Kleppe got us out. OK, they had an interest. I was in love with a Soviet girl. Some day I might be useful. It was years before they approached me. I'd almost forgotten about Kleppe. But I hadn't forgotten about Halenka. And I hadn't forgotten that some pig in our embassy had given us the thumbs down. Just a nod and the French would have released us. I was nineteen or twenty. Halenka was eighteen. What the hell danger were we to the United States?'

There were tears of anger and frustration in Dempsey's eyes as he looked at Nolan for an answer.

'It was stupid, Dempsey, I give you that.'

'No, my friend, it was more than that, it was deliberate, inhuman. She was pregnant, and she was my girl. And I was a US citizen born and bred. And because I scratched my name on a piece of paper they let us rot. The Soviets didn't let us rot, they got us out. Our embassy didn't make the rules. They carried out the rules that Washington laid down. I bought a *Washington Post* at Orly the day they let me out. D'you know what the main news item was? The President was defending his bribe-taking crony who he'd nominated as Chief Justice of the Supreme Court.'

Dempsey trembled with anger, and Nolan sensed that he was creating resistance by his questions.

'D'you want something to eat?'

Dempsey sighed and shook his head. And at that moment Nolan's radio bleeped and a message came through that there was an urgent phone call for him.

It was Harper speaking from Washington.

'I've had a call from Powell's secretary. He wants to see me. What's the position at your end?'

'I'm going to get a statement from Kleppe or an interview taped with a witness present. And then I shall do the deal with Dempsey.'

'How long do you need?'

'Twenty-four hours. Maybe a little longer.'

'Is there any chance that there were witnesses when your team picked up Dempsey?'

'None. He was driving his car. The street was empty. I've seen them do it. Even when you know what's gonna happen you don't absorb it.'

175

'If Powell raises any question about Dempsey I'll have to give a denial.'

'I don't think he will.'

'You've seen MacKay's report on Mrs P?'

'Yes. Interesting, but it doesn't help us.'

'When will you be ready for another meeting with Elliot and Bethel?'

'Sunday afternoon?'

'OK. Keep in touch.'

The CIA doctor had given Kleppe another shot and most of the paralysis seemed to have gone.

Kleppe tried to stand when Nolan went in, and he staggered and held on to the heavy table. Nolan shoved up the chair so that Kleppe could sit down. The remote tape-recorders were already on, and Nolan sat on the edge of the table.

'Just a few questions, Kleppe.'

'Da.'

Nolan hesitated, and re-framed his question in Russian.

'You gave the orders to Dempsey? Nobody else controlled him?'

'Just me. Only me.'

'How did you get your orders?'

'By radio. And the bag.'

'The diplomatic bag?'

'Yes.'

'Which one?'

'Both. The embassy and the United Nations.'

'Who controlled you in Moscow?'

'Directorate S.'

'Who?'

Kleppe seemed to have difficulty in breathing, and Nolan realized that Kleppe was fighting the drug. The words came out explosively when he finally spoke.

'Pelshe. Alexei Pelshe.'

'What is your real name?'

Kleppe shook his head slowly, and struggled to stand up. When he sank back on to the chair Nolan spoke quite softly.

'Tell me your name. Your real name?'

'Viktor Aleksandrovich Fomin.'

'Where were you born? What town?'

'Yerevan.'

It was enough. Nolan bleeped for the guard and went back upstairs to his office. He listened to the tape three or four times. It was clear enough for there to be no argument about the translation.

The FBI man stood with Harper outside the door marked 'President-Elect' until the green light came on. Then he knocked and opened the door for Harper to walk through.

Powell was speaking on the telephone but he waved Harper to a chair in front of his desk and carried on talking.

Harper looked at the man's face. He was good-looking in a thirties' musical style. Dark, wavy hair with no trace of grey, and heavy eyebrows. As he listened on the telephone, Powell's tongue explored his lower lip, and his free hand moved around a tray of pencils and pens. Finally he was done. He replaced the receiver and looked across at Harper. The brown eyes were soft and liquid, but their look was quizzical.

'I thought it was time we had a word, Harper. I read your current summary. Who prepares that?'

'My Secretariat prepares the first draft, sir. It is considered by the Director of Central Intelligence and, unless there are modifications, it is sent to the Secretary of State.'

'In future I want a separate copy straight to my office.'

'Yes, sir.'

'How long have you been Director of CIA?'

'Three years ten months.'

'Is your teaching job still open at Yale?'

'I've no idea.'

'Did you know my father when you were there?'

'Yes. I knew him well. I still do.'

'Do you know Mr Dempsey, the new White House Chief of Staff?'

'No. We've never met.'

Powell's eyes were concentrated on Harper's face. Then, as if he had made some sudden decision, Powell reached forward and pressed a button on the panel by the telephone and said, 'There may be some changes, Harper. I'll let you know shortly.'

'Right, sir.' Harper knew that the interview was over. He walked slowly to the door and stood aside as the FBI man ushered in Republican Chairman Salvasan.

Dempsey's basic statement had been typed in relays by four secretary-clerks. None of them had seen anything other than her own section.

Nolan sat reading it at his desk. There were forty-two pages of single-spaced typescript. There were startling names from broadcasting and journalism, others from state and federal politics that were merely surprising. Industrialists and union officials who had seemed to be mortal enemies rubbed shoulders co-operatively throughout the text. The amount of money involved was staggering, but probably less than the two major parties had jointly spent. Dedication and obligation were good substitutes for cash. The network covered the whole of the United States, and if anything was surprising it was that it was at grass-roots level. There *were* those startling names but there were not all that many. The influence they had was almost the traditional party influence of the big city.

He patted the pages together and pressed his button. When the duty officer came he said, 'The car to Flushing Airport in ten minutes. The chopper to La Guardia and the Cessna to Washington. Phone Mr Harper and tell him I'm on the way. I'm going down to Dempsey right now.'

Dempsey was beginning to look alive again. Nolan looked at him.

'I'll be back tomorrow. If you want to write to the girl let me have it when I get back and I'll get it over in the embassy bag. They'll get it to her. Just personal stuff. Understood?'

Dempsey nodded.

'Did your people agree the deal?'

'They've left it to me.'

'I was thinking.'

'What?'

'Won't they want to strangle the Soviets in public?'

'State could have done that years ago. That's not how we play this ball game, my friend. Half the world would cheer the bastards for trying. And the other half would try not to let us see them laughing.'

It had taken Yuri Katin and his team two days and thirty thousand dollars to trace where Kleppe had been taken and another day to plan their operation. They were waiting for Moscow's approval and meantime they had moved to the safe-house in Jackson Heights.

The cypher section at the Washington embassy had been working in shifts round the clock, answering questions and giving evaluations from His Excellency and his staff. The ambassador's advice had been to pull out everyone with even the vaguest connection with Kleppe's operation and leave the embassy to cope as best it could with the inevitable fireworks. Moscow's acid response had been a request for his suggestions as to how they should pull out Kleppe and Dempsey. His Excellency had suggested that they consult Katin on that point.

De Jong always disliked dealing with anything important away from his own house, and Washington hotels were not his idea of civilized living.

He sat uneasily in the brocaded chair, his attention wandering from the paperback of *Leaves of Grass*. He was trying to decide exactly how far to go but so much depended on the reporter's response. A nod may be as good as a wink to a blind horse but journalists had an occupational inclination to grind away for one more fact.

The knock at the door startled him for a moment and to recover his poise he carefully rearranged the glasses and bottles on the table before he walked slowly to the door.

Martin Schultz had interviewed de Jong dozens of times over the years. He found de Jong's mixture of right-wing capitalism and genuine culture an interesting mixture, but the big man seldom proved useful beyond non-attributable background material. But he was a useful part of the Washington jig-saw puzzle.

Schultz took the whisky that de Jong offered him and leaned back in his chair.

'How are things, Mr Schultz, in the nation's powerhouse?'

Schultz smiled. 'Disturbed is the word I would use, Mr de Jong. Or maybe agitated is nearer the truth.'

De Jong smiled back. 'You surprise me. The nation's capital disturbed or agitated at the prospect of peace and prosperity? Come now. There must be more than that.'

'We've had reports that Powell and his wife are in the process of divorce. Is that true?'

'My dear fellow, Presidents never get divorced. A woman who divorced a President would be a fool and a President who divorced his wife would be certifiable. I've heard gossip but not on that score.'

Schultz looked directly at de Jong.

'What gossip have you heard?'

De Jong moved around in his chair as if being comfortable was much more important than what he had to say. He refilled their glasses and leaned back.

'D'you know Harper?'

'Morton Harper, you mean?'

'Yes.'

'He's not my area but I meet him from time to time.'

'All our conversation is off the record, yes?'

'Whatever you say.'

He put down his notebook and took up his drink.

'I've got a feeling that he's playing footsie with the Democrats. Have you heard anything on these lines?'

'Not a thing. What's he doing?'

'A little bird tells me that he's having Dempsey investigated.'

'Andrew Dempsey?'

'Yes.'

'What's he after?'

'I'm not really sure, but there were some killings up in Hartford a few weeks back and I gather from my people there that there was talk of a strike some years back and Dempsey was involved in some way that might have involved Powell in election offences.' De Jong leaned forward, put down his glass, and wiped his hands on a linen handkerchief as if he had been soiled by both the glass and the rumours.

'Can I pursue this, Mr de Jong?'

'As long as my name is not brought into it, certainly. Mind you, it may be a wild goose chase. These things often are.'

Schultz smiled and stood up.

'I'll let you know what I find.'

'Yes. Do that, my friend. Do that.'

18

Morton Harper had insisted that the meeting should be held at Langley, and Chief Justice Elliot and Sam Bethel were ferried from Washington by Nolan, who escorted them through the security checks towards the Director's office.

Elliot held out his hand. 'My God, Morton, it's like a giant public washroom. This place would drive me crazy.'

'Welcome, sir. I guess I'd get dizzy sitting up on your bench a-listening to the mortals down below.'

'*Touché*,' said Elliot, and blew his nose violently as he looked around the office.

Nolan and MacKay were already at the big table in the corner of the room, and when the salutations were over Harper invited them to sit down. Nolan noticed that this time Harper was at the head of the table.

'Gentlemen, I've called this meeting because we now have the evidence that you asked us to obtain. My Secretariat have produced a four-page summary of our findings and there is supporting documentation in your folders. Can I ask you to read the summary before we talk? Take as long as you wish.'

Nolan watched the bent heads. The Chief Justice was underlining with a pencil as if he were reading a brief, and Sam Bethel was getting visibly more angry as he read on. He finished first and looked at Harper, shaking his head in obvious disgust. Then Elliot pushed his glasses back up his nose and leaned back.

'Well, Morton. A cast of thousands. You must be delighted.'

The eagle eyes watched the genuine surprise on Harper's face.

'That's not quite the word I would have chosen, Judge.'

'No, of course not. How foolish of me.' He looked across at Mr Speaker. 'What about you, Sam?'

Bethel leaned back. 'You know, I sometimes wonder if this damn country isn't going crazy.'

'Maybe you're right, Sam. But right now we've got to decide what to do about it.' Elliot couldn't hide his impatience.

Harper put his hands together and Nolan recognized the sign.

'There's a wide variety of action open to us. Would you like me to go over it?'

Elliot nodded. 'By all means.'

'In no particular order of importance, we can do these things. We can leak it to the press and let it go where it will. We can inform the out-going President. We can inform the Secretary of State. We can form an impeachment committee. We can confront Powell, who must be wondering by now where all his friends have gone. We can pass it all to the FBI whose province it really is. Or we can do nothing.'

There was silence round the table as each man wondered if there was yet another alternative. A nicer, simpler one. Nolan wondered if anyone else around the table had thought of eliminating Powell. On reflection he thought it unlikely. MacKay might, but not the others. It was Harper who broke the silence.

'What d'you think, Mr Speaker?'

'Well, we don't inform the press, that's for sure. And we should be causing maximum embarrassment beyond what we have already achieved if we told the present incumbent. There would be an inter-party dog-fight. The FBI won't pick up this hot potato, you can be sure of that. We can't even consider doing nothing. We'd deserve to be put up against a wall. The only thing possible is to confront Powell.'

Elliot raised his bushy white eyebrows.

'And what do we do if he tells us to jump in the lake, Sam?'

'You show him those bloody pictures of him screwing the girl.'

Elliot turned to Harper. 'Has he indicated anything to you about whether you'll be left at CIA?'

'He called me to a meeting yesterday. Implied that he hadn't made up his mind yet.'

'Was he suspicious, d'ye think?'

'I don't think so. He seemed very sure of himself.'

'Did he ask any policy questions?'

'No. He was telling *me* what it was all about.'

Nolan chipped in. 'Say we take it that some sort of confrontation is the only way. What's our objective? What do we want him to do? And what do we think his reactions will be?'

Sam Bethel belched softly. 'Pardon. His reactions are going to be unpredictable. When he confirmed my reappointment he wasn't the diffident new boy. He was enjoying the power. I even got a few words of advice on handling the House. I'd say his reaction's gonna be like a Doberman having two pounds of rump steak pulled out of its jaws. He ain't gonna go quietly. I'd put my silver dollar on that. He could have us all in the pen in hours.'

Elliot was not amused. 'Not me, Mr Speaker. Not me.'

'OK. You can send in the food parcels, Judge.'

Harper spoke softly. 'Who's going to be the one to approach him?'

'Mr Speaker,' said Elliot.

'The Chief Justice,' said Bethel.

Nolan caught Harper's eye. 'You want to say something, Mr Nolan?'

'Yes, sir.'

'Carry on, then.'

'It's quite clear from Dempsey's statement, and from the scuttle-butt in Hartford that Powell and his wife have been estranged for years. She was totally against him going into politics right from the start. In fact, she wouldn't have politicians in the house. Dempsey cashed in on this estrangement so that Powell would not have an alternative background. Nothing to fall back on. He was dependent in every way on Dempsey, whether he knew it or not.

'From what I've been able to find out it was a normal marriage up to the time Powell stood for the governorship. She met him when he was at Yale and his father still lectures there. It seems she had looked forward to sharing in an academic life. She tolerated him setting up as a business consultant but closed the shutters when he went into politics.

'She co-operated, but not very enthusiastically, during the Presidential election campaign but according to what I've gathered from White House security they haven't been together since the night of the election.'

Nolan paused and Sam Bethel said slowly, 'What's this got to do with the present situation, Nolan?'

'We want him out of politics, and so does she. She could be the one who confronts him.'

Elliot frowned. 'You mean tell her about all this, and leave it to her?'

'Not quite, sir. We could give her the pictures and suggest she could save his face. Tell him that if he doesn't opt out he'll be impeached or exposed. But we would let him off the hook if she could persuade him to bow out gracefully before inauguration.'

Bethel snorted. 'Oh, for Christ's sake, Nolan. The President-Elect announces to the country that because his wife doesn't like him being in politics he's decided to throw his hand in. Jesus.'

'Not exactly that, sir. But maybe the Physician to the President does a routine medical check and finds a serious heart condition and after deep reflection the President-Elect steps down for the sake of continuity and the country.'

Bethel sniffed loudly. 'And a few months later some press photographer takes a photograph of Powell playing tennis, or jogging or some damn thing.'

'Powell's own interest would be to play along with the scenario. He's gone along with Dempsey's film script, he'd go along with this.'

'What does he do after he resigns?' Elliot looked only mildly interested.

'He lives comfortably and quietly on his presidential pension. A hero and democrat to one and all.'

Bethel looked across at Elliot and said, 'What d'ye think?'

Elliot leaned back in his chair, thinking. It was several minutes before he spoke.

'The only alternative is to confront him. And Nolan's right. Powell's basically a weak man. He could panic and do something crazy if we put him with his back against the wall. If we leave a door open with the same pressures he might choose to accept the role and go quietly. If Mrs Powell refused to do this, or tried and failed, then we'd have to meet him head on and let the chips fall where they will.'

Bethel shrugged. 'So who tackles the Powell woman who loathes politicians?'

Nolan took a deep breath. 'I had in mind that MacKay might do it.'

Bethel frowned. 'MacKay? Who in hell's MacKay?'

Nolan flushed and nodded towards MacKay.

Bethel sighed heavily. 'My apologies, MacKay. My mind's getting bogged down with names.' He shook his head, looking at MacKay. 'With all due respect, Mr MacKay, I don't see you fitting into this role.'

Nolan interrupted. 'I haven't discussed this idea with Mr MacKay but he's the one person who has no axe to grind. He isn't even an American. And he's the man who exposed Dempsey. She'll like that. Any politician starts off with two strikes against him. And it could leave us so that, with Mr Powell included, only seven people will know what has been done.'

Elliot looked at Harper. 'How secure is Mr MacKay, Morton?'

'Totally, so far as I am concerned.'

Bethel looked at MacKay.

'No reflection on you, mister, but how secure *are* you?'

'In what way, sir?'

'From what Harper originally told us we may not have spotted this mess if it hadn't been for you. We're in your debt but, by God, you know too much. How do we know you won't talk?'

'What interest would I have in talking, Mr Speaker?'

'Now, Mr MacKay. You know as well as I do that you could make several millions out of this story.'

'I am officially seconded to the CIA from SIS. I have signed the Official Secrets Act form. Talking would get me in the Tower of London.'

Bethel looked at Harper.

'Is that the case, Morton?'

'Yes. Anyway, I think Mr MacKay could have made his millions without even coming over here. The media would have paid for the original tip-off.'

There was a brief silence and MacKay spoke softly to get their attention. He looked at Harper.

'May I make a suggestion, sir?'

Harper shrugged. 'By all means. Go ahead.'

'Mr Nolan will be arranging a deal to get Miss Tcharkova out. They've got a man of ours named Kowalski. I'd like him back as part of the deal, and that links me into the operation in an official capacity.'

Bethel was not impressed.

'OK. I won't pursue the point. By all means write your man into the deal.' He looked at Elliot. 'I've no objection to Mr MacKay talking to Mrs Powell but I'd like a contingency plan in case it doesn't work.'

Harper nodded. 'We'll plan it carefully, Mr Speaker.'

Elliot stood up. 'How many people outside this room know what's been going on, Morton?'

Harper raised questioning eyebrows at Nolan.

'Nobody outside this room knows that it goes beyond Kleppe and Dempsey.'

Elliot put his hand on Bethel's shoulder and winced as he stood up straight. He turned slowly to look at Nolan and MacKay.

'What makes you two think you can do a deal with Moscow? Why are you so sure?'

Nolan looked at Harper who nodded permission.

'There's three levels where we deal with the Russians. The public one of the media and public statements. The diplomatic one where professionals sort out what the statements really mean, and then there's an everyday working level where everybody faces the actual facts of life. The Soviets set great store by the first level. The statements, the treaties and the rest of it. Provided that doesn't get exposed, they work on our level on a routine basis. There's no problem.'

'But they have spent millions of dollars and years of effort to do this thing. They have now failed and you suggest that they send over a girl and her baby, and a British spy, and we all call it quits. Why should they agree?'

'Because they *have* failed. They don't want us to expose what they tried to do and they don't want us to expose that they failed.'

The old man looked down at the carpet absorbing the words, then he looked sideways at Harper.

'It's a funny world you and your people live in, Harper. What we have all been concerned with seems earth-shattering to me, but to you people it's like a couple of insurance companies settling a car accident on a knock for knock deal. Ah well. Keep at it.'

And he walked slowly and uncertainly to the door. He stood there for a moment, his mouth opened to speak. Then he changed his mind, waved his hand and walked out with Bethel.

Harper looked a little frosty, and as the door closed behind them he turned on Nolan.

'You were hinting before the meeting that you thought there was an alternative solution. Nolan. Why didn't you tell us what it was? Why play the Lone Ranger bit?'

'I thought you would not want me to mention my alternative in front of the others.'

Harper shifted in his seat. 'It didn't seem to inhibit you, all the same.'

'What was suggested wasn't the alternative I was thinking of.'

Harper's eyebrows went up. 'And what, pray, was the other solution?'

'That Powell should be killed.'

Harper's hand was squeezing a fold of his double chin. It stopped, and his eyes closed.

'How right you were, Mr Nolan. You were well advised to keep silent on that score.'

Nolan turned to MacKay.

'When do you want to go down to speak to Mrs Powell?'

'Not tonight. I want to sort out what I shall say.'

Harper nodded. 'It's all going to hang on the assessment of the lady; that she still gives a damn for him. If we are wrong on that, then she probably won't co-operate.'

'Can we arrange special transport and accommodation for her journey to Washington? I don't want anyone to see her and speculate.'

'Of course. I suggest you go with him, Nolan. Take the big Piper and put her up at a hotel or the house on Virginia Avenue. There are staff and facilities already there. Anything else you want, MacKay?'

'Just one thing, sir. If Powell is persuaded to resign on medical grounds that means he can't be seen to immediately start earning a living. What financial provision can we offer them?'

Harper leaned forward and shoved a pad across to MacKay.

'Write this down. First of all he would receive the usual presidential pension which will provide him and his family with a very high standard of living. He is likely to earn substantial sums from writing, teaching and lecturing when he has recovered from his medical problems.'

'If the state of his health made it sensible for him to live overseas would he still be entitled to the pension?'

'Certainly.'

'And finally, without giving a specific undertaking, can I take it that there would be no question of leaking details in the future about this operation?'

'It would be impossible, and unwise, to give any written guarantees but, so far as it is possible, a very supportive attitude would be taken by the administration. They would have no reason to behave otherwise.'

'That's all I need to know, sir.'

Harper smiled. 'You sound as if you have started thinking through your proposition to Mrs Powell already.'

'I have.'

'All I can do is wish you luck.'

Nolan and MacKay were at the door when Harper's telephone rang. He held up his hand.

'This might be for you, Nolan.'

Harper lifted the receiver and listened. He waved them back into the room and pointed to the chairs. He was listening intently and finally he said, 'Send it in to me right away.' He put the receiver back quietly and carefully before he looked up.

'There's a piece going in the *Post* tomorrow morning about the CIA investigating politicians in Hartford. They're bringing in the copy now. The *Post* have offered us an opportunity to comment.'

There was a knock on the door and a girl brought in a sheet of typed paper. When she had gone Harper read it aloud.

'The heading is "CIA investigation in Hartford" followed by an interrogation mark. I quote. "During routine inquiries related to the recent murder in Hartford of a retired trades-union official, his wife, and a secretary in the office of the city's District Attorney, it became clear that investigations have not been limited to the local police department.

"In the course of talking with various local citizens it seems that a Washington agency is also investigating the crimes. There are reports that the agency concerned is the CIA and the investigations cover local politicians of the Republican Party and the circumstances of a strike some years ago at the plant in East Hartford of Haig Electronics.

"So far, the chief of police, J. R. Henney, the president of Haig Electronics, Fred L. Haig, and officials of the District Attorney's office have refused to comment.

"With Hartford the power-base of the Powell election campaign, there is speculation that President-Elect Powell could be faced with the embarrassing task of deciding whether some of his local supporters have possibly allowed their enthusiasm to involve themselves with undesirable local elements.

"The acting White House press officer denied all knowledge of the investigation. A spokesman for the CIA said, brackets, leave blank for statement, brackets off.'"

Harper threw the sheet angrily on to his desk.

'Some bastard is leaking something somewhere. That's no bloody accident. It stinks of a leak. Any ideas, Nolan?'

'No. They could have found out about me being in the area easily enough. Somebody in the police department could have linked my investigation with the murders, but nobody except Oakes could possibly link me with Powell. And Oakes would lose his Senate seat, his business, and face criminal charges if this came out. I don't understand it. Who gains any advantage in doing this?'

Harper reached for the telephone.

'It could be that bastard, O'Connor. I can't believe he would, but there's only the Democrats that could gain.' He spoke to the operator. 'Find me Mr O'Connor, the Democratic Chairman.'

The call came back almost immediately.

'Mr O'Connor. That matter we discussed here a week or two back with Salvasan, Elliot and Bethel. You remember? . . . Yes . . . There's a small piece in the *Post* tomorrow that links our investigation with the Hartford killings and vaguely with Powell . . . no I don't think so, we can deal with it . . . yes. Who have you mentioned it to, may I ask? . . . you're quite sure of that? . . . agreed . . . agreed. If anybody pulls the plug on this there will be a lot of bodies go down the pike . . . I'm sure. I just wanted to hear it from you . . . of course. Well done . . . goodnight.'

He slammed down the phone and shook his head.

'No, it's not him. He doesn't want to know what's going on. He's too shrewd an operator to get involved. Nolan. See what you can find out from the *Post*. Use Fowler as a contact.' He turned to look at MacKay.

'Maybe you should go tonight?'

MacKay looked at his watch. It was seven o'clock.

'Right, sir. Can your people lay on transport for me?'

Harper reached for the phone.

'Drive him to Dulles, Nolan, and I'll see what they've got to get him to Hartford.'

There were only three men now at the safe-house in Hartford, and as MacKay stood at the window he could see the snow ploughs working to clear the runways at the airfield. Great curtains of snow curved up each side of the yellow machines and more was falling, slowly and quietly; building up into hillocks and valleys where the terminal buildings diverted the wind. It was the 23rd of December and it was going to be a white Christmas. But it wasn't much of a present that he was bringing for Laura Powell and her young son. Maybe she had had enough of Powell and wouldn't give a damn what happened to him.

He turned away from the window; the light was going now and there were things he had to do. He bathed and shaved and put on his blue suit and the black brogues. On the table he laid out Dempsey's report, and in a separate envelope the photographs of Powell and the girl. He hoped he wouldn't need to go that far. They could be counter-productive.

Nolan had gone off to the Powell house to ensure that there were no problems with the White House security men for MacKay's visit.

He radioed back to the safe-house that Laura Powell was not expected to leave the house that evening.

The snow was deep and crisp as Nolan's driver came on to the side-road but on the main road it had packed down from the flow of vehicles and the snow tyres got good purchase on the road surface.

The Powell house was on a small private development of ranch-style bungalows. There were other cars parked outside the house and half a dozen men stood near the white picket fence. MacKay could see at least two men at the side of the house. Somebody had swept a narrow pathway up to the front door. There were lights on in the house and MacKay could see the lights of a Christmas tree in the front room.

Nolan introduced him to the chief of the guard detail, who walked with him in single file to the door of the bungalow.

He rang the bell and they both waited, their breath misting in the cold air.

An elderly man answered the door. It was Laura Powell's father.

'Mr Bridger, this is Mr MacKay. He's been sent from Washington to see Mrs Powell. We've checked him. He's OK.'

The old man looked over his glasses at MacKay.

'You'd better come in, mister. She'll be down in a moment. She's just taken Sammy his medicine.'

MacKay shook his coat outside the door. 'Nothing serious, I hope.'

The old man showed him into the room with the Christmas tree.

'It's his chest. He's subject to bronchitis. He's much better today. I'll get her. Sit down.'

MacKay automatically looked around the room, but he absorbed very little. His mind was on his mission and suddenly it seemed all too possible that she could tell him to go to hell. Then the door swung open and she was there.

She was prettier than he had expected but the shadows under her eyes were not from make-up.

She was wearing a black wool-knit dress with pearls and looked more calm and capable than he had expected. And younger, too.

'I'm sorry, I didn't get your name.'

He stood up. 'MacKay, ma'am. James MacKay.' For a split second he wondered why he had said that American 'ma'am'. Too many films and Jimmy Stewart.

'Sit down, Mr MacKay. Would you like a drink?'

'I'd love a whisky if you have one.'

'Water, ice, soda-water?'

'Nothing, thank you. Just the whisky.'

She handed him the whisky and poured herself a coke. As she sat down she moved a cushion and then raised her glass, smiling.

'A happy Christmas, Mr MacKay.'

'And to you, ma'am.'

'I expect my husband sent you down. What can I do for you?'

He put down his drink and looked at her face.

'No. I was sent down to see you by Chief Justice Elliot and Sam Bethel.'

She frowned. 'I've already told Logan and Andrew Dempsey that I shall come up for the inauguration.'

'How well do you know Mr Dempsey, Mrs Powell?'

Her hand trembled as she put down her glass.

'Are you one of Dempsey's people?'

'No.' And he repeated his question. 'How well do you know Dempsey, Mrs Powell?'

She shrugged. 'I've known him for years. We all knew one another long before Logan and I got married.'

'What sort of man is he?'

'Handsome, rich, charming—a loner.'

'Did he have much influence over your husband?'

She looked down at her knees and flicked imaginary specks from her skirt. Then she looked up and as she spoke her voice trembled.

'More than I had, I'm afraid.'

'In what way?'

She looked at him. 'Hadn't you better tell me what this is all about?'

'There's a problem concerning the relationship between Mr Powell and Mr Dempsey and we need your help.'

'Who's we?'

'The Chief Justice sent me to ask your help.'

'Why didn't he contact me himself or send a note with you?'

'I think you will understand when I have told you the problem.'

'You'd better explain then, rather than ask me questions.'

'May I ask you just one more question?'

She shrugged. 'I guess so.'

'Would you help your husband if you could?'

She looked down at her empty glass and slowly put it on the low table between them.

'Probably. It depends.'

'It's almost certain that he will be impeached, Mrs Powell.'

Her hand went to her mouth. It covered her lips in a schoolgirl gesture. And when she spoke it was a whisper.

'I don't believe it. Who are you, Mr MacKay? This is some crazy game you're at.'

'I'm afraid not. I'm a CIA officer. Would you like to see my ID card?'

'Yes. I would.' There was a lift of the pretty chin, and a distinct air of hockey-sticks.

He took out his wallet and then the card. He leaned over and slid it across the table to her. She leaned forward to look at it. Ostentatiously not touching it, as if it might be contagious. She looked up at his face.

'What's it all about?'

As briefly as he could, he told her of Dempsey and Kleppe, and the Soviet network. Of Siwecki and Maria Angelo, and when he was finished she shook her head.

'I don't believe it, Mr MacKay. This is just political mud-slinging like Watergate. I don't believe it.'

MacKay bent and picked up the white envelope. He squeezed open the end and checked its contents. He held it out to her.

'That's Dempsey's statement. We picked him up a few days ago. I could arrange for you to speak to him, or Mr Speaker, or the Chief Justice.'

She unfolded the paper and started reading. MacKay sat silent and tense.

After the first two pages she read at random through to the end, turning the pages slowly as she read. Without looking at him she leaned forward and handed them back. She shook her head.

'I'm sorry, Mr MacKay, I don't believe it. It's too far-fetched, too . . .' she shrugged, '. . . too extravagant. It's politicians and I don't trust politicians—any of them.'

'A lot of it has been checked, Mrs Powell. His bank accounts and electoral contributions have been checked. It all tallies.'

'That can be forged or manipulated. That's what the CIA is for, isn't it?'

'Would you like to speak to Chief Justice Elliot?'

'No.'

'To Dempsey?'

'No.'

MacKay reached for the brown envelope and put it on his lap.

'You wouldn't save him from this disgrace?'

'Good God, why should he listen to me?'

He looked at the flushed face and said softly, 'Because you love him.'

She shivered as she stared back at him. But she shook her head.

'He wouldn't believe me. He would say what I say. That it's political mud-slinging.'

'There is other evidence that would be used.'

'Like what?'

He handed her the brown envelope.

'Like that. I'm sorry.'

She laid back the flap and took out the photographs. There were four, and she looked at each one a long time. Then she slid them back into the envelope, laid it on the table, and looked up at him.

'I guess those would be enough,' she said quietly.

MacKay sighed. 'I'm terribly sorry that you had to be shown those things.'

'By courtesy of the CIA?'

'No, ma'am. Courtesy of the KGB. Dempsey provided the girl, and arranged the photography.'

'And who's the lucky lady?'

'Dempsey's girlfriend. One of them anyway.'

There was a knock on the door and her father put his head in.

'Would you two young people like a coffee?'

'No. It's all right, Dad. We shan't be long.'

She turned back to look at MacKay as the door closed.

'What do you want me to do?'

'I want you to come back to Washington with me. See your husband. Show him Dempsey's statement, Kleppe's statement and the summary. Convince him that if he doesn't resign he's finished. Politically and privately. And that for the country it would be absolute disaster.'

'When?' She whispered.

'Tonight. We'll go by helicopter straight to Washington.'

She shook her head. 'It's incredible. It's like some terrible nightmare.' She sighed. 'I'll tell Dad that it's to do with the inauguration. He can look after Sammy.' She turned and rested her hand on his arm. 'It is all true, isn't it? It's not some terrible plot?'

'No. It's true, I'm afraid. Don't hurry.'

Half an hour later she was ready, with a small case and list of instructions for her father. MacKay took the list and wrote out a telephone number and handed it to the old man.

'If you need to contact Mrs Powell, sir, just get that number and ask for me. James MacKay. Don't hesitate to phone if you need to. It won't be more than a couple of days.'

She kissed the old man and turned to wave as they walked down the drive. The snow was thick and there was plenty more to come.

The car slid and lurched as they set off for the airport and MacKay prayed that nothing would happen to change her mind.

The snow-ploughs were working on the main runway and the chopper was nowhere in sight. A yellow truck came from the terminal building and turned in front of them and led them through caverns of snow to the far perimeter. The Cessna was there and its cabin lights were on. As MacKay pulled up a man stamped over and opened the door.

'Instructions from Langley, sir. You're to go in the Cessna to Floyd Bennett and the Navy will take you in one of their big choppers. It's a virtual blizzard.'

The Navy gave them coffee and sandwiches at Floyd Bennett and then they walked across to the big Navy helicopter.

Two ratings were holding the metal steps and one of the crew reached down for Laura Powell. The captain came back to speak to them both.

'It's gonna take us quite a time and I may have to land once or twice to check things out. That'll be at Trenton, Philly and maybe Baltimore. I'll keep you informed.' He looked at MacKay. 'We've got a radio net to Langley. I think they'd like to talk with you if you'd come forward, sir.'

The big curved door closed as MacKay went through, and the long shadows of the rotor blades flickered across the snow. The radio operator pointed to a metal seat and leaned forward to turn a dial. He took off the headset and passed it to MacKay.

'They're on. A guy named Harper.'

The voice was faint at the other end, the signal surging from loud to zero.

'MacKay. Can you hear me, MacKay?'

'Yes. I hear you.'

'What's happening?'

'Everything as arranged.'

'When do you arrive?'

'Nobody knows. It's the weather. It'll be five or six hours.'

'Anything you want me to do?'

'Yes, fix a bed for my passenger.'

'OK. I'll meet you at Dulles. Anything else?'

'Fix an appointment for the passenger for the evening.'

'I can't hear. Fix an appointment when?'

'For the evening.'

'OK. See you.'

MacKay went back to the cabin and fixed their seat belts, and saw an Aldis light flashing Morse from the control tower. Then the helicopter lifted and the airfield was way below them, lost in the swirling snow.

'Maybe by this time tomorrow it will be all over and you can be back home.'

'And you're sure there isn't some other way?'

'Only for him to be confronted by Elliot, Bethel and Harper.'

'What if Logan sends me away?'

'Then others will take over. And that will be the end for him.'

'He isn't a bad man, my husband, just weak. He was carried away by Andy Dempsey. He would have made a good lecturer. What do Elliot and Bethel think of him?'

'It sounds ridiculous but I don't think anybody has had time to think about him as a man.'

'And you?'

'I'm an outsider. And I've never met him.'

'If he hadn't been so American maybe it wouldn't have happened.'

'I don't understand.'

'There used to be old films, nice films, where an ordinary man becomes President because he's not a professional politician. It was generally Gary Cooper. And then there's the winning. Americans have to win. So it can get that it doesn't matter *how* you win. And all politicians are crooked.'

'What makes you think that?'

'They promise so much. And they know they can't deliver. Washington is just a thieves' kitchen.'

MacKay sat silently, hoping that his silence might calm her.

Then the pilot came back to them.

'We've been cleared through to Dulles. Let's go.'

At Dulles, after a turbulent flight, Nolan was waiting for them at the house. He told her that she had the whole day to rest and sleep as he had arranged for her to see her husband at seven o'clock that evening.

She slept until four in the afternoon and then she bathed slowly and dressed carefully. At five she ate with MacKay and to her surprise the rest and the food seemed to have given her back her confidence. As they drank their coffee she said, 'If Logan agrees to come back, to resign, what reason could he give that people would believe?'

'Medical grounds. We've checked his medical record. When he was young he had rheumatic fever. In some instances that can lead to heart trouble later in life. This will be one of those cases. We had already marked down a specialist from Johns Hopkins and a senior

Navy heart specialist who could provide the details. He does have high blood pressure anyway.'

'Does he know that?'

'I guess so. He had to pay a special supplement on his life insurances. Not much, because it wasn't serious. But enough for him to go along with the story if he wanted to.'

She looked at her watch. 'What time do we leave?'

'Now, if you're ready. Have you got the envelopes?'

'They're in my handbag.'

'I hope you don't need to use either of them.'

She turned to look at him. 'I think we both know that it *will* be necessary. Both of them.'

Nolan sat with them on the back seat of the black Lincoln and it had all the air of a funeral cortège.

Nolan saw her look at the lit Christmas tree on the lawn at the side of the White House as they drove by to Powell's hotel.

19

At the hotel, Laura Powell waited with Nolan until they were joined by an FBI man who took them both to a private suite.

Elliot, Bethel and Harper were already there. Elliot introduced her to the others and then turned awkwardly, his hand on Bethel's shoulder, to face her.

'I felt you should meet us all, my dear, so that you knew what you had been told came from us. And also to assure you that if you were able to persuade the President-Elect that what we are suggesting is the wisest course for him, then you have our assurance that our side of the bargain will be faithfully adhered to.'

'Could we talk about your side of this right now?'

'Of course, my dear, let us all sit down.'

They talked for ten minutes and she seemed to be satisfied.

Nolan said, 'I'm taking you to your husband's suite, Mrs Powell. I think we should be making our way there.'

Nolan and Laura Powell walked slowly down the wide corridor, right to the end, and were shown into a large waiting-room. As they sat waiting, she said, 'What did Logan say when he was told I wanted to see him?'

'There was no problem. No problem.'

Nolan's eyes avoided her face.

'What happens afterwards?'

'We've booked you a suite at the Hilton in my name.' He smiled. 'I'm afraid you're Mrs Nolan for tonight. My telephone number is on a card by the telephone in your sitting-room.'

A middle-aged secretary came through the door and smiled.

'He's free now, ma'am.' And Laura Powell followed her down

the thickly carpeted corridor. The secretary knocked at a door, opened it and then waved her in with a smile. Laura Powell had no doubt that their separate lives were well-known in Washington's inner circles.

The room was large and impressive. The furniture heavy and ornate. Powell was standing behind a desk, listening on the telephone. He smiled and pointed to a chair in front of the big desk.

'. . . it's an important committee, Eddie . . . of course. Well, call me tomorrow.'

He hung up and pressed a button on a white phone as he lifted it to his ear. 'No more calls, Molly . . . what? . . . until I tell you. Good.'

He sat down, smiling at her.

'A nice surprise, Laura. I couldn't believe it when they told me you'd called and were coming up. How on earth did you get through the snow?'

'Courtesy of the US Navy.'

'Good. I must say my "thank you's" to them.'

'How about you come out from behind the big desk, Logan Powell, and sit round here with the people?'

He laughed and walked round, pulling up the other chair to face her. She looked at him.

'How do you like it all, Logan?'

He leaned back, stretching his arms. 'You know, Laura, I haven't had much time to think about whether I like it or not.' He grinned. 'I guess I like it. Who wouldn't?'

'I'm the bringer of bad news.'

'What is it? Sammy?'

'No.'

'What then?'

She took a deep breath. 'Have you seen Andy in the last few days?'

'No. But he's had things to do. He's busy, too.'

'He's in custody, Logan.'

'Oh, Jesus. What's he done? I know, it's that bloody sports car. Speeding?'

'He's made a statement.'

'About what?'

'About how you got the nomination for Governor and got elected. And how you got the Presidential nomination and got elected.'

He shook his head. 'I don't understand, Laura. You're talking in riddles.'

'There's a committee already formed to impeach you.'

He stared at her, his eyes angry. 'You're crazy, Laura. This is jealousy taken too far.' He reached for the telephone. 'I'll arrange for transport home for you.'

'Don't touch the phone, Logan. Very few people know. It would be a disaster.' And something in her voice stayed his hand.

She opened her handbag and took out the white envelope. 'Read this. Don't bluff any more. I'm your wife, and I love you.'

He folded back the sheets of stiff paper and started reading. It was fifteen minutes before he had finished, and his face was white when he looked back at her. His voice shook as he spoke.

'You don't believe this, Laura? This is just the crap that people rake up as part of the political dog-fight.'

He tapped the papers with his finger. 'This is going to cut off a lot of heads. I'll see to that.'

'You must have known, Logan. You must have guessed that you couldn't have done all that on your own. The most experienced politician in the country could hardly have done it. Nobody could do it as an outsider.'

'Where is Dempsey?'

'I don't know.'

'Who gave you this stuff? Who told you about Dempsey?'

'A CIA officer.'

'What's his name?' His hand hovered over the telephone.

She reached inside her handbag and took out the brown envelope. She handed it to him.

'They also gave me that.'

He opened the flap and took out the photographs. She saw his eyes close. When he opened his eyes to look at her his voice was a whisper.

'What shits. After all this time.'

He pushed the photographs back in the envelope carefully and meticulously, and she knew that he was playing for time.

'Tell me about this committee.'

'All I know is that it exists, and that they are drafting an impeachment document to bring to the Senate in the next few days, if possible before Christmas.'

'Why did they tell you all this?'

'They wanted to know if I would see you and break the news. They'll let you resign. You could come back to us and we could just be a family again.'

'How many people know?'

'The Chief Justice, the Speaker, and some CIA people. Very few. They suggested that you resign on medical grounds. They have two heart specialists who could cover this.'

'They're very confident, the bastards.'

'They're not bastards, Logan. Your people were the bastards. Traitors.'

'I'm not the first Republican President to have support from the left. All the candidates court them. They always do.'

'They didn't give you support, Logan. They committed crimes, they *involved* you. Your old friend Dempsey fixed the girl and the photographs. They killed Siwecki and his wife to stop them giving evidence. They killed Maria whatever-her-name-was because she sent the CIA to Siwecki. They put in millions of dollars of Russian money to get you elected. That's not support, that's corruption.'

'That's what *they* did, not what I did.'

'Logan. Siwecki made a statement to the CIA before your people murdered him. That strike was contrived and you knew it. You knew it at the time and you went along with it.'

He looked at her. 'Old Elliot and that fat bastard Bethel must have enjoyed all this. You, too.'

'They could just have gone ahead and hit you with this in public.'

'They didn't not do that for my sake. They knew what it could mean to the country. Every bloody Congressman and Senator would have gone down with me and they know it. The public never liked politicians. They liked them even less after Watergate. This would bring the roof down on them all.'

'I don't care about the others, Logan. I only care about you. Please think of us all. You, me, and Sammy.'

'How is Sammy?'

'He's had bronchitis but he's getting better.'

'How's he making out?'

She shrugged. 'It's hard to say. He doesn't say anything but his grades are down and I was called to see Smithson. He said Sammy was defiant to the staff.'

There was a long silence before Powell spoke again.

'You know, it's odd. Up to a week ago I couldn't really believe I'd made it. And now I can't believe this.' He looked at her. 'I'll have to fight these bastards, you know, Laura.'

'You'd be lynched, Logan. Imagine the *Washington Post* when it was leaked. Imagine any paper in the country. Those photographs would be enough.'

'The media would know what it would do to the country. They might rally round for the country's sake.'

'Each one waiting for the other to break the story. The editorial boards sniggering at their copies of the photographs. And Congress and the Senate sending every Bill back automatically. They'd cut you into shreds with real venom *and* feel holy while they did it.'

'Even if I resign the thing will be leaked.'

'I don't think so. It would be a terrible responsibility if they did that after you'd resigned.'

'What the hell would I do?'

'You'd get the presidential pension. We could move to Europe on the grounds of your health.'

'And what about you?'

'What about me?'

'You'd spend a lifetime hating me.'

'My dear, I saw you and Andy Dempsey for the first time ten years ago tomorrow. Jimmy Rankin introduced me to you both. It was at a Christmas Eve dance held at the Women's College. You had a Ché Guevara moustache and it looked terrible, and you made two very witty cracks that impressed me. Even when I found out later that they were Dorothy Parker originals I was still impressed. I'm still impressed now. Andy Dempsey was a smooth character but you were straight off the front page of *Saturday Evening Post*. Good, honest American, reliable and all the jazz, and I guessed that one day you'd be a professor. Preferably at Hartford, come the worst at Yale. There was a touch of Scott Fitzgerald about you, and I loved it. And I loved you. And I love you now.'

'Why?'

'The same way I should still love Sammy if somebody conned him into doing something stupid. He'd still be my Sammy, and you're still my husband.'

'What about the photographs?'

She shrugged. 'You probably felt lonely. And you probably resented my non-co-operation. It doesn't matter.'

'I remember that night we met. You wore a white dress with big orange poppies all over it and an orchid in your hair.'

'Eight out of ten, it was an hibiscus.'

'Have you ever been to Switzerland?'

'No.'

For a moment his face was alight with hope and then it collapsed to the grim lines of tension again.

'It's phoney you know, Laura, all this crap they've scratched around for. You could do the same to any man in the Senate or Congress. They've all got skeletons in the cupboard. Women, booze, back-handers, conspiracies, the lot.'

He sat on the edge of the desk looking at her. Anxious for her agreement but guessing that it would not be forthcoming. And she sat without speaking, sickeningly aware of his indifference to the people who had been murdered, and those who were now in custody. His mind was still searching for a way to hold on to the prize. He stood up suddenly with manic energy, his fist pounding the desk top.

'I could have the FBI round them up. The whole damn bunch. For treason. God, I had that bastard Harper in here a few days ago. He never said a word. Just sat there in that same chair saying "Yes sir, no sir". And all the time he knew.'

His body slumped as he sat back on the desk.

'I could write, of course. Maybe a syndicated column on European politics. Switzerland's right in the middle of it all. There's quite an American community out there.'

'You need a rest first, Logan. A few months doing nothing.'

'Maybe you're right. Keep a low profile and let it blow over.'

He waved his hand at the files and papers on his desk.

'It'll take a few days to clear things up.'

'They won't give you that much time.'

He looked up sharply, unhealthy red spots of anger on his cheeks.

'It's not up to them, Laura. I haven't decided yet what I shall do. Are you staying somewhere?'

'I'm booked into the Hilton as Mrs Nolan.'

He stood up, gathering his tattered dignity around him.

'I'll arrange for one of my staff to take you.'

'What are you going to do?'

'I'll think about it tonight. I'll phone you in the morning.'

She reached for the two envelopes but his hand came down on them.

'Leave those with me, Laura. I want to study them again.'

'Don't do anything silly, Logan. They want to help you. They're bending over backwards to avoid unpleasantness.'

'The shits.'

He bent and kissed her brusquely, and phoned for a car.

He stood at the office door and watched as she walked with one of his drivers down the long corridor. At the far end she turned and waved. He wanted to wave back, but he couldn't.

For an hour Powell sat at his desk reading and re-reading parts of Dempsey's and Kleppe's statements. There were things that he was well aware of, and things of which he was completely ignorant, but with the vast majority he knew that he had ignored them deliberately. He had chosen not to notice, to turn a blind eye. But subconsciously he had known. He threw down the sheaf of paper, pulled out the photographs and felt a sudden wave of self-disgust as he realized that even in the middle of this nightmare the girl's body still aroused him. In a compulsive reflex he took out his pocket book and found a page at the back.

He pulled over the red phone and dialled the New York number. His heart leaped as the receiver was lifted at the other end. A man's voice answered.

'794106. Can I help you?'

'Who is that?'

'Roper, CIA, who is that?'

He slowly replaced the receiver. It was like some omen. A sign from the Fates. He hadn't believed that she really was in custody. Maybe the public already knew. Maybe they had leaked it and were leaving him to sweat. He reached for the radio and found the dial to the news station.

'. . . Vice-President-Elect Markham in New York today said that yesterday's statement by the Chairman of the Joint Chiefs of Staff was premature. President-Elect Powell had not yet discussed with the Joint Chiefs any details of his intended cuts in the defence budget. In questions afterwards the Vice-President-Elect made clear that General Macy's statement had not endeared him to the new administration. In Johannesburg fighting today reached the city centre and both the . . .' Powell switched off.

He picked up the envelopes, stood up slowly and walked to the door. The corridor was empty as he walked back to his private suite of rooms.

Nolan stood by the special switchboard that had been installed for Powell, to control and monitor Powell's calls, and now he dialled the special number at the Hilton. She sounded frightened.

'This is Nolan. Are you OK?'

'Yes, I'm out of breath. I've only just come in, and I heard the phone ringing.'

'How did it go?'

'He was angry and upset but I think he'll do it. He said he wanted to think about it overnight but I think he didn't want to have it look like he was a pushover. He talked about us all going to Switzerland and him having a writing career. Would that be possible?'

'I guess so.'

'They wouldn't leak it after he resigned, would they?'

'No way. You can rest assured. How about you? It must have been an ordeal.'

'Once we were talking it was OK. But I felt so sad for him. The shock was terrible for him. He looked like an animal that had been shot. Not knowing what had happened but knowing that it was dying. Even *you* would have been sorry for him, Mr Nolan.'

'We're all sorry, Mrs Powell. I voted for him.'

'Why?'

He gave a sharp laugh. 'I was sick of politicians.'

'Maybe it's best left to politicians, after all.'

'Is the guard there?'

'Yes, there's a gentleman outside and another in the hallway inside.'

'OK. Will you telephone me tomorrow when you hear from him?'

'Yes, I will.'

When he hung up Nolan pulled over a chair, and sat with the operator watching the lights on the switchboard. Powell's offices and living quarters had special red indicators, and none of them was alight.

Just before midnight Harper phoned.

'What's the situation, Nolan?'

'Nothing happened. He left his office not long after Mrs P had gone. He went to his own quarters.'

'Who has he phoned?'

'He tried to get the girl in New York.'

'But he must know she's in custody.'

'Yep. But he phoned. Mrs P says that he took it pretty badly. He's probably in shock. But she felt sure he was going along with it.'

'I've spoken to her. No other calls at all?'

'No. None.'

'I thought he might try Elliot or Bethel, and try to work on them.'

'Not so far, he hasn't.'

There was a long silence, and then Harper spoke again.

'Has he got any kind of radio in there, walkie-talkie maybe?'

'I don't know, sir.'

'God. We should have checked before. Find some excuse to go in there. Take him a telegram or a letter. He doesn't know you. See what you can see. The bastard might try some desperate throw like calling out the Army or something.'

'I doubt if they'd turn out for him after today's snub for Macy. I'll check sir, and I'll call you back.'

'OK. Meantime I'll see if the security signals people know anything.'

There were piles of mail for Powell tied in bundles with string, and a dozen telegrams. He ripped the telegrams open and read them. He picked out one that said 'Congratulations, give 'em hell. Orange County Republicans.'

He walked slowly down the corridor, and at Powell's door he hesitated with his hand raised to knock. It was better to pretend that he thought the suite was empty and walk in.

He turned the big brass handle slowly and tested it in case it was bolted. But the heavy door opened easily.

There was just the light from a reading lamp and a faint acrid smell of burning. And then he saw Powell. He was lying alongside a tapestry chair, his jacket hanging from the arm of the chair. There was a fat stubby bottle on its side on the carpet and a small metal container.

He rolled Powell on to his back, but as soon as he saw the blue around his lips and nose he knew that he was dead. He slid back an eyelid. The pupil was grossly dilated. He hurried back to the door and locked it.

He sniffed, and followed the smell to the bathroom. Papers had been burnt in the washbasin. The white porcelain was smudged with a sooty deposit and there was a wet black slush of charred paper at the waste-hole. To give himself time to clear his mind he slowly washed down the debris and cleared the bowl before walking back to the sitting-room.

The bottle was empty and it smelt of brandy which matched the label. The gummed label on the metal container said 'One tablet only, for sleep' and the maker's label said 'Modiren 2.5mg'. There was one yellow tablet on the carpet beside Powell's face.

Nolan picked up the bottle, the tablet, the metal container, its lid, and stuffed them in his pocket. At the door he looked back again at Powell's body as if it might be a mistake. Then he closed the door behind him and pocketed the key.

At the switchboard he lifted the scrambler telephone and nodded to the operator.

'Give me a line and then walk down the corridor that way.' He pointed towards the main stairs. 'And don't come back until I signal to you.'

He waited until the girl had walked off then dialled the number. Harper answered immediately.

'Harper.'

'Go over to the scrambler.'

Nolan heard the button go down.

'Done.'

'He's dead. Killed himself with brandy and pills.'

There was a long silence before Harper spoke.

'Christ. Are you sure?'

'Very, very sure.'

'Oh, God. Let me think.'

'I've already thought.'

'Go on, then.'

'The two doctors to confirm the heart attack. I've removed the evidence. Notify his wife. Let her believe the statement about a coronary. She'll guess, but she'll go along with it. Then get the Vice-President-Elect. Elliot can tell him the news. And get a team to deal with the press.'

There was silence at the other end.

'OK. Hold the fort until I get over there. Don't tell a soul.'

Nolan stood with the FBI man at the side entrance to the hotel, holding the portable radio to his ear. They were networking a concert from the Hollywood Bowl. The orchestra were well into the overture to *Die Meistersinger von Nurnberg* when the music was faded down and there was the crackle of paper near a microphone and a shocked voice began to read a bulletin.

'Ladies and gentlemen, we break off our scheduled programme to bring you a news flash from Washington.

'In an unconfirmed agency report we are told that the White House has just . . . a moment please . . . we can now read you the full statement that was issued from the White House at nine fifty-two this evening. I read verbatim.

'"At approximately eight-thirty this evening, the twenty-fourth of December, President-Elect Logan B. Powell collapsed and died at the Sheraton Hotel.

'"The two medical experts who were called in immediately, state that death was due to a massive coronary thrombosis." Message ends.

'There will be further bulletins from this station as more news becomes available. Stay tuned for further announcements. Our programmes will be modified during the period up to the early morning newscast when there will be special programmes covering the career of Logan Powell.'

Even before the news bulletin announced Powell's death, Oakes had been fetched from his bath to take a telephone call from New York. He stood naked and wet with a small towel draped round his middle.

'Oakes. Who in hell is that? I was taking a bath.'

'It's de Jong, Mr Oakes. Listen to the radio or the TV for the newscasts.'

'What is it?'

'Powell's dead.'

'My God. What happened?'

'They say it was a heart attack. That's what's going to be announced anyway.'

'What happens now?'

'The Vice-President-Elect becomes President-Elect.'

'Markham?'

'Yes.'

'Good God. But you hinted that there was a possibility of Powell being impeached.'

'There was. Maybe they went a bit too far when they gave him the news.'

'What about Dempsey?'

'I understand the CIA took him into custody a few days ago.'

'Did Markham know what was going on?'

'No way.' He chuckled. 'I wish I could see those bastards in Moscow when the news gets through.'

'How did you get the news so soon?'

De Jong laughed softly. 'We've been at this game a long, long time, my friend. And we're playing on our own home ground. It ain't just the Russkis who can play chess. Anyway, go and listen to the news.'

'OK. I will. Goodnight.'

'Goodnight, my friend. Happy Christmas.'

At two o'clock in the morning on the third day after Christmas there was very little traffic on the road from Brunswick to Helmstedt but the police had put barriers across the road half a mile before the check-point, and they were guarded by a platoon of the Black Watch and two Field Security officers.

Lights blazed on both sides of the check-point, and on the West German side the big black Mercedes stood with its engine running to keep the occupants warm. When a torch flashed twice on the far side of the striped poles Nolan got out of the car and walked slowly to the check-point. From the other side a man in a heavy coat and astrakhan hat walked forward so that they met each side of the barrier.

Nolan spoke first. '*Pa-Russki eta karta?*'

And the reply came. '*Nyet. Pa-Russki eta reka.*'

The red and white pole was lifted, and Nolan escorted the Russian to the car. He opened the door and the Russian bent to look inside at the passenger, his breath clouding in the cold night air. He closed the door and nodded to Nolan who walked with him across the check-point, past the second barrier to a Black Zil. The Russian opened the rear door.

She was prettier than he had expected but the big brown eyes looked apprehensive. The young girl in her silver fox furs was asleep in her mother's arms. Kowalski's face still showed the bruises and there was a suppurating scar from his eye to his ear. Nolan closed the door and straightened up.

In silence the two of them walked back to the guard-house and raised their arms.

Kleppe got out awkwardly and walked with his hands in his coat pockets towards the Russian, who grinned and shook his hand.

Kowalski was carrying the child, and Halenka Tcharkova walked solemnly beside him.

When they had crossed into their respective zones the barriers came down. The KGB man and Nolan shook hands and walked back to their cars.

Dempsey was waiting at the old-fashioned house off Husaren Strasse. He was standing with Anders at the open door, shivering with anxiety despite his warm clothes.

When he saw the girl they stood facing each other. Dempsey was speechless. He just stood looking at her until she put out her arms. He clung to her, his head on her shoulder until Nolan led them both inside.

It was three hours later when Nolan stood at his bedroom window unbuttoning his shirt. There was a British Army platoon guarding the house, and Nolan couldn't help contrasting the present heavy protection with the Paris embassy's indifference all those years ago. His tired brain tried to recall the words of a poem he had once heard.

> 'For the want of a nail a shoe was lost.
> For want of a shoe a horse was lost
> For want of a horse a battle was lost.
> For the loss of a battle a king was lost.'

He turned away from the window and lifted his jacket off the back of a chair. He wanted to get his mind off the whole damn thing. What he wanted was a girl. He fished out the small, brown leather book, and checked a number. He held it in his hand as he lifted the receiver. He had dialled two numbers when he stopped. He stood silently for a moment then said, 'Shit', jiggled the telephone to get the unit operator, and said 'Sergeant, get Mrs Sally Nolan, Washington 947210, person to person.'

He was asleep when the call came through, and it rang for four minutes before the operator gave up.

* * *

She was really rather young for MacKay, but she was so deliciously pretty. He had laid siege to her for ten days and that evening he had been crowned with success.

With a bottle of Mouton Cadet 1971 they watched a re-run of *Love Story* on TV. And after that poignant reminder that life is short and pleasures fleeting, she slid off her tight sweater and stepped out of her skirt, so that as he sat on the divan she stood in front of him naked, except for her tan coloured nylon stockings, and a small white suspender belt.

She smiled indulgently as he looked at the long slim legs, the neat black bush, the flat young belly, and she leaned forward as he looked at her full firm breasts. His eyes moved to her pretty face when the words distracted him on ITN's News at Ten.

'. . . do solemnly swear that I will faithfully execute . . .'

And only for a second or two did his eyes wander to the screen where a tall man in a dark suit stood with his hand on a Bible, in front of Chief Justice Elliot. But it was a second too long, and he heard her say, '*That* is the bloody limit.' And that, I am sorry to say, was that. It was Monday the twentieth of January.

TED ALLBEURY

The Dangerous Edge

The British Intelligence Services fear that a journalistic investigation into their collaboration with war criminals during and after World War Two will cause a political scandal. Mallory, one of their bright young men, is given the task of digging up the dirt before the press do.

What he uncovers in Holland and Germany is a web of deceit, betrayal and cold-blooded murder. But can he prove it to his bosses when the only person who has all the answers does not want to be found?

'The most consistently inventive of our novelists of espionage, the one that other thriller writers point to as the finest craftsman among them.'
The Guardian

MULHOLLAND
BOOKS
HODDER

TED ALLBEURY

Snowball

A long buried and shocking secret has been uncovered. In 1940, President Roosevelt and Canadian Prime Minister Mackenzie King secretly agreed to abandon the Allies and make peace with Hitler if the Nazis successfully invaded Britain. Decades later, Soviet agents are ready to use this information to shatter the NATO alliance and use the ensuing geopolitical chaos to strengthen their position in Europe.

Only one man stands in their way. Tadeusz Anders – half Polish, half English and totally professional – plunges into a series of cruel and violent manoeuvres to combat the cold-blooded operatives of the KGB.

'Skillful, bloody and chilling'
John D. MacDonald

MULHOLLAND
BOOKS
HODDER

You've turned the last page.

But it doesn't have to end there . . .

If you're looking for more first-class, action-packed, nail-biting suspense, join us at **Facebook.com/ MulhollandUncovered** for news, competitions, and behind-the-scenes access to Mulholland Books.

For regular updates about our books and authors as well as what's going on in the world of crime and thrillers, follow us on **Twitter@MulhollandUK**.

There are many more twists to come.

MULHOLLAND:
You never know what's
coming around the curve.

HODDER